DROP DEAD

By Mark Richard Zubro

The "Paul Turner" Mysteries

Sorry Now?
Political Poison
Another Dead Teenager
The Truth Can Get You Killed
Drop Dead

The "Tom and Scott" Mysteries

A Simple Suburban Murder
Why Isn't Becky Twitchell Dead?
The Only Good Priest
The Principal Cause of Death
An Echo of Death
Rust on the Razor
Are You Nuts?

DROP DEAD

A Paul Turner Mystery

•BY MARK RICHARD ZUBRO•

St. Martin's

Press

New York

Library of Congress Cataloging-in-Publication Data

Zubro, Mark Richard.
    Drop dead / Mark Richard Zubro. — 1st ed.
        p.   cm.
    ISBN 0-312-20532-5
    I. Title.
    PS3576.U225D76   1999
    813'.54—dc21   99-21852
                                                CIP

First Edition: June 1999

10 9 8 7 6 5 4 3 2 1

Dedication—

to Jamie Nabozny

You were right; you did it for all those who will come after,
but also for all of us who came before.

ACKNOWLEDGMENTS

Thanks to Barb D'Amato, Hugh Holton,
Kathy Pakieser-Reed, and Rick Paul

ONE

"Flat," Turner said.

"Flat and squishy," Fenwick said.

"I prefer just plain flat," Turner responded.

"You're probably right," Fenwick stated. "That squishy-jelly look might have a hard time becoming fashion law."

"I don't know," Turner said, "properly promoted . . ."

The medical examiner interrupted. "We talking doughnuts or dead bodies?"

"Either one," Fenwick said.

"Neither one," Turner said.

"Anybody seen his right eye?" the ME asked.

An assistant crime lab technician said, "I put it in the van with the other one."

"It was a he?" Fenwick asked.

"Definitely," the ME said. She glanced at the mess before them.

"Lot of dispersal. Must have hit something on the way down."

"I know I feel better because of that information," Fenwick said, "although I doubt if he does."

"Could he have been dead before he fell?" Turner asked.

The medical examiner looked thoughtful. "I can't prove that by what I see here. I can give you an opinion later."

Turner gazed up toward the top floors of the Archange Hotel. No hotel in Chicago was more exclusive or more expensive. It consisted of two thirty-story gothic towers on opposite sides of State Street, set back twenty-five feet from the street. Each edifice covered an entire city block, from Chestnut to Delaware.

Turner unbuttoned his overcoat. Since last week's record cold, the early January weather had been unusually mild. In the sun and out of the wind, the day was pleasant with an almost springlike warmth. Yesterday the mercury had crawled into the mid-forties.

The crime-scene van was parked halfway up on the curb near the east tower. The police had closed the entire block of State Street and pedestrians gawked from behind yellow crime-scene tape. Parts of the body were scattered from the point of impact near the east side of the street to the wall of the hotel and twenty feet in either direction north and south. Nearby cars had bits of blood, flesh, bone, and clothing on them. Two crime-scene photographers were carefully taking pictures of all the vehicles and each square foot of pavement.

"We have any kind of identification?" Turner asked. "Anybody in the crowd know him?"

A very pale, very young cop walked over. Turner noted his name: Domanici. "I found keys and a wallet next to"—the kid drew a deep breath—"a bone over there." He pointed between two parked Jaguars eight feet from the body.

Turner opened the wallet. He found an Illinois driver's license with the name Cullom Furyk. The name meant nothing to him.

Along with credit cards, he found slips with phone numbers, one hundred seventeen dollars, and two keys.

"We sure this is the dead guy's?" Turner asked.

"It was the only identification we found," Domanici said.

"Is there anybody who actually saw him fall?"

This part of State Street was a busy place even at midmorning. With a crime scene in a busy street it was easy for those who didn't want to be involved to simply walk away. It was also easy for the morbidly curious to trample over possible evidence.

"Some of them got splattered when the body hit," Domanici said. "A couple of them were pretty hysterical when I showed up. That group of people was closest." Domanici indicated a knot of men and women clustered on the pavement on the west side of the street. "Besides them we've got the crowd over there to talk to." A much larger group of people huddled near the north end of the hotel's west tower. "The hotel guests are still inside. One of the guys said they were getting pretty irritated. We're going to have trouble keeping them from leaving."

"Shoot one of them," Fenwick said. "The rest will be much more docile."

Domanici shrugged. "We've only got one guy who claims he saw the whole thing." He pointed him out. "Says he's a photographer." Domanici brought the witness over.

Clark Nemora was in his late teens or early twenties and wore glasses, a dark blue parka, blue jeans, and heavy work boots. Through the man's unzipped jacket, Turner could see a camera dangling on a leather strap.

The three of them sat in the detectives' unmarked car for the interview. The first thing Nemora said after getting settled was a whispered "I never imagined anything so horrible. Am I going to have nightmares about this?"

"What you saw was pretty tough for anybody to handle,"

Turner said. "It's a fresh memory. In time it will fade. For now, if you can, we'd like you to concentrate on giving us details about anything you can remember." Turner paused. Nemora's shoulders quivered and his hands trembled. Turner tried easing him into his statement. "What brought you down here this morning?"

Nemora leaned forward. "I'm an architecture student. I really love gothic structures. The Tribune Tower was the best example of that style in this area until the Archange was built. I was taking pictures of the Tribune earlier. I'm trying to catch each building from the same angle once each hour. I'm working on a project on the effects of shadow and light."

"Did you get a picture of the falling body?" Turner asked.

"No, I was still working on my camera setting and being sure I was at the same angle as I was before. It takes time to get a shot just right. It has to be perfect. This is for my senior project at school."

"Did you see him when he started falling?" Turner asked.

"Yeah." The kid swallowed hard.

"What did you see?" Turner asked.

"He was walking along the ledge on the top floor of the east tower."

"What happened?"

"I'm not sure. It was pretty high up, but I thought I saw some-one push him."

The detectives leaned forward.

"But you're not sure?" Turner asked.

"I don't know. Before he fell, the guy had his hands out—you know, like balancing on a high wire? Then he sort of twisted around like maybe he was trying to go forward and look behind at the same time. I thought an arm shot out and pushed him. He pinwheeled out and fell. I couldn't take my eyes off him. About halfway down, he hit one of those flagpoles. I remember thinking I should do something to help, but what could I do? I guess I could

4

have tried to catch him, but I just couldn't move. If I was really a professional photographer, I'd have gotten pictures, but he hit the ground before I could react. It all happened very fast."

"You wouldn't have been able to save him," Turner said. "Most likely you'd have been killed if he hit you when he landed."

A tremor shook Nemora's body.

"You're not sure about the hand pushing him?"

"I'm sorry, no. He was so high up, and I wasn't expecting anything to happen. I remember thinking he was nuts to be walking like that. Then I thought it might be one of those stunt guys, although I wondered where the cameras were to cover his feat. For a couple seconds I thought maybe he was, like, bungee jumping or something." Nemora gulped. "But there wasn't any wire to hold him. When I looked back up to the top, I thought I saw someone watching him fall. It was too far away to get a good look."

"Could the hand have been reaching to save him, not push him?" Turner asked.

Nemora paused a moment. "I hadn't considered that."

"Does the name Cullom Furyk mean anything to you?"

"Isn't he a fashion model? Involved in a lot of causes?"

"Did you know him?"

"I'm not famous."

They had one of the uniformed officers take him down to Area Ten headquarters to record his statement.

"I'm ready to vote for homicide," Fenwick said.

Turner said, "If somebody'd tried to catch him or stop him, I think we'd have an upset person down here saying he or she tried to save him."

Fenwick nodded.

They returned to the medical examiner. Fenwick asked, "Can we look at the body?"

"Yeah," the ME said. "But there is not much point to that

here. We'll reassemble everything as best we can at the morgue. We'll be able to give you a lot more then."

"We still have to look," Turner said. A fall from a great height was not Turner's favorite kind of crime scene to work. "We need a path to the most central point of impact."

The ME pointed and said, "Try approaching from the left front fender of that Rolls-Royce."

Turner and Fenwick followed her suggestion. Stepping carefully, Turner and Fenwick slowly approached the largest intact part. They stopped in a clear patch five feet away. After several moments Turner said, "Not much point in staring at it."

"Dead is dead, down is down, so to speak," Fenwick said. Turner watched Fenwick eyeing the bits and parts of the body strewn across the pavement.

"Don't say it," Turner said.

"I was just—"

"Don't."

Fenwick gave a martyr's sigh. "Okay," he said, "I see lots of blood, lots of gore, and absolutely nothing that's going to help in this investigation."

Turner looked up and swung his head from east to west to examine both towers. He held his hand up to block the sun from his eyes. After several moments, he turned his gaze back to the body. "We have two crime scenes."

"I hate that," Fenwick stated.

Turner continued, "Here and the point where he started from. I don't think down here is going to tell us much. I hope up there is better. We need to start working on the people in the hotel."

They walked over to Domanici. Turner asked, "Do we have somebody official from the hotel to talk to?"

"Yeah," Domanici said. "The manager, Bert Weeland. He's over there." He pointed to the revolving doors that led into the hotel on the east side of the street. Next to a liveried doorman, a tall, thin man in an Armani suit stood ramrod straight just inside the doors.

"You get anybody else who saw something significant, let us know right away," Turner said.

Domanici nodded.

Picking their way through the detritus, Fenwick and Turner ambled over to the hotel entrance. It felt good to locomote the streets without having to worry about patches of ice or inches of snow. Avoiding stray remnants of Cullom Furyk was another matter. The doorman swung the revolving door for them.

After the detectives introduced themselves, Turner said, "We need to talk to the people staying on the top floor of the east tower. We have reason to believe he fell from there."

"There was a brunch meeting in the penthouse catered by the hotel. We provided a gourmet meal for seventeen."

"Are they still up there?"

"I believe they are."

"We need to have several uniformed police officers seal off the penthouse immediately."

Weeland frowned. "I hate to have the guests disturbed. Are you sure the body fell from our hotel?"

Fenwick said, "We know the guy fell from a great height."

"You can prove that?" Weeland asked.

"Don't have to prove that which is obvious," Fenwick said.

"Both towers of your hotel qualify as great heights. Unless you're hiding another hotel on this block?"

Weeland paused and then asked, "Do you wish to go directly to the penthouse?"

"I'd like to get some general information first," Turner said.

"We can send several officers up for the moment."

Fenwick called a couple uniforms in from the street. "Make sure nobody leaves and nobody enters the penthouse," he told them. "Absolutely no one. Get them all into one area and keep them there. Ignore all complaints."

Weeland sent an attendant to escort them to the correct elevator with the proper key to send it to the penthouse.

After the uniformed officers left, Weeland asked, "Could we talk in my office, gentlemen? It offers more privacy."

With polished smoothness Weeland led them to his office. The lobby had the length, breadth, and width of a small gymnasium. The walls were twenty-two feet high. The ceiling was painted wood. The decor included deep red carpeting that was a pleasure to walk across. The walls were oyster-white hand-rubbed plaster. Deep overhangs shaded tall arched windows and large black-and-white abstract drawings adorned the walls at widely spaced intervals. In the center of the room four fifteen-foot black leather couches faced a small reflecting pool. The solid oak registration desk gleamed with an ocean of polish and wax. Turner wouldn't have been surprised to see Quasimodo swinging from the chandeliers.

Weeland's office continued the decorating scheme of deep red carpeting, abstract paintings, and black leather furniture.

Once they were seated Turner asked, "Only one elevator goes to the penthouse?"

"Yes. We issue as many keys as necessary for the guest or guests staying there."

"I like it," Fenwick said. "Cuts down on the number of people who could wander into a crime scene."

"We need to know if a Cullom Furyk was a guest here," Turner said.

Weeland picked up a sheaf of papers from his desk. "This is a list of everyone who is currently registered at the hotel." He handed the papers to Turner.

The detectives glanced at the list. "He's not on here," Turner said. He held out the keys Domanici had found. "Any of these for the penthouse or the elevator?"

"No, we use plastic cards. Do you realize Cullom Furyk is a very famous name? If this is the same man, he has stayed here before."

"I never heard of him until now," Fenwick said.

The manager gave no hint of approval or disapproval at this statement. He said, "Cullom Furyk is the most famous male fashion model in the world today as well as being involved in many charitable causes. He made millions for the international Save the Orphans campaign. He is the signature model for GUINEVERE, Incorporated. If this is he, his death would be great tragedy."

"What's a 'signature' model?" Fenwick asked.

"The person most identified with their products, their most prominent spokesperson. I know he has stayed in the hotel before. He was more than welcome to stay here again."

"He wasn't any problem?" Turner asked.

"As a guest he came and left without any incident of which I am aware." Weeland turned to the keyboard on his desk, tapped the keys for a moment, then examined the computer screen. "He always charged his rooms when he was doing the paying. There was never any trouble with the charge card."

"Who else would pay for his rooms?"

"His company."

"You mentioned them before," Fenwick said. "Who are they?"

"GUINEVERE, Incorporated is the name of one of the largest fashion houses in the country. They have their headquarters in Chicago."

"Are they renting rooms here now?"

"Yes, they have the entire penthouse on the east tower reserved."

Fenwick asked, "Don't guests have to register the names of all the people staying in the same room when they check in?"

"That would be normal procedure. We don't have very many people trying to sneak in a guest because they can't afford to pay the extra cost. The penthouses on both towers are available to one guest or many. They can accommodate up to ten people very comfortably."

"Who else is staying on that floor?"

"The list I gave you is alphabetical. I can get a printout of which of them are in the penthouse from the front desk."

"Thanks," Turner said. "We'll also need a schematic drawing of the penthouse. Probably numerous copies. I want to know the layout, especially which rooms had openings to the west balcony."

"That will take a few minutes to obtain. You know," Weeland added, "the guests in the penthouse aren't the only people connected with the fashion industry staying in the hotel. There are two large fashion shows in town this week. I am not aware of which other people in the industry in particular would be staying here. I just happen to know Mr. Furyk's name."

"You know him by sight?" Turner asked.

"I've never met him, but I've seen his picture."

"How long have you worked here?" Turner asked.

"Since the hotel was opened a year and a half ago."

"Any problems?"

"I don't know what you mean."

"In all that time was there anything unusual, out of the ordinary?"

"Certainly nothing criminal. The Archange Hotel attracts only the most exclusive guests."

"No obnoxious rock stars?" Fenwick asked.

"We discourage any element that might be disruptive."

Turner motioned to the printout Weeland had given them. "We need to speak with everyone who has a room facing State Street from both towers."

"I have been concerned about detaining them since your officer informed us of your intentions," Weeland said. "We are, of course, eager to cooperate with the authorities but I'm sure you understand my problem, gentlemen. These are very wealthy people with very special needs."

"I have even more special needs," Fenwick stated. "No matter how rich or poor, they're out of luck today. They will need to be interviewed."

"Some may have been planning to check out. They could conceivably have international plane connections to make or perhaps business meetings with important LaSalle Street bankers."

"I'm sorry if we inconvenience them," Turner said, "but they have to be interviewed. We'll take those who need to leave first, but whatever their time schedule, they will have to wait."

"Was it murder?" Weeland asked.

"All unexplained deaths are investigated as if they were homicides until it is proven otherwise," Turner explained.

Fenwick said, "We'll have uniformed officers start speaking with guests on all the floors below the penthouse. The two of us will start in the penthouse itself."

"Let me arrange with the staff to assemble whomever you need. At the same time I'll get you the maps and the printout of who is staying in the penthouse." He left the room.

Fenwick said, "I feel like pissing on the carpet."

"I'm not sure the class of people who stay at the Archange perform normal bodily functions."

"I could show them how."

"All that would happen is that some poor flunky in a minimum wage job would have to clean it."

"I wish I still smoked," Fenwick said. "I'd inhale a pack so I could drop a ton of ashes on the carpet."

"Aren't you being a little anal retentive?" Turner asked.

"Since when do you talk that shit?" Fenwick said. He looked pleased at his clever choice of words. "Besides, what you mean is anally fixated."

"It is?"

"Trust me. I took a mail-order abnormal psychology class last fall."

"News to me."

"Ha! I don't tell you everything. Madge insisted. She said I wasn't sensitive enough."

"And now you are?"

"More sensitive? To the rest of you, hell, no. To Madge, I have no choice."

The manager returned with more computer printouts in his hand. "I have a list of guests in the penthouse. I also ran off the names of all those who checked out of the hotel this morning, as well as those who need to leave, and those who are not yet scheduled to depart. It will take a few more minutes for us to get you copies of the schematic drawings of the penthouse." He held the sheets of paper out to the detectives. "Thank you for accommodating those who need to leave."

Turner thanked him for his help. They called in several of the beat cops to begin the canvass of the guests.

"Anything slightly suspicious," Fenwick said, "make them wait for us. I don't care how rich they are or how angry they get. Be sure to ask if they are connected to the fashion industry. Anybody who is automatically gets interviewed by us."

One cop asked, "What if they won't cooperate?"

1 3

"Throw another one off the balcony," Fenwick said, "and see if the rest aren't a little more forthcoming."

The beat cops looked at him blankly.

Fenwick shook his head. "Five, ten years ago that would have gotten a laugh or scared the piss out of some uniform. I've got to get better material."

"Maybe not everything's a joke," said a solemn-faced beat cop.

Fenwick scowled at him.

"Skip it," said Turner. "Let's get up to the penthouse. You five start the interviews down here."

Fenwick muttered as they waited for the elevator and on the swift trip to the top of the hotel. "It was funny. I know it was funny. Tell me my comment was funny."

"It was funny," Turner said.

"You're just saying that."

"I could sing it."

"Am I losing my touch?"

"As the world's worst cop humorist? Not a chance. I'd say your crack expressed who you are quite well."

"What does that mean?"

"That you weren't funny."

The elevator door opened.

T H R E E

They entered a crowded reception room with a uniformed cop standing guard. From leering granite gargoyles to rough-hewn stone walls, the decor shrieked of gothic.

At a Louis XVI table five feet from the elevators, two men and a woman were conferring. Ten feet behind them were a group of eleven or twelve people. Everyone turned to look at Turner and Fenwick. From the small group closest to them, a man with snow-white hair spoke to the detectives. "Now what?" he demanded.

"Let's shoot that one," Fenwick mumbled.

Turner and Fenwick strode forward, introduced themselves, and showed their identification.

The white-haired man said, "I'm Franklin Munsen, president of GUINEVERE, Incorporated. What's happened? Why are we being held? The police who are here won't tell us anything. One of us, Cullom Furyk, was here for brunch and is now missing. What has happened to Cullom Furyk?"

Turner said, "He's dead, Mr. Munsen."

Everyone fell silent. Several shook their heads. Someone gasped. Munsen whispered, "I don't believe it."

"We need to speak with all of you," Turner said.

Munsen pointed to the man standing next to him. "This is Evan Abarak, my assistant. He will be happy to set up appointments for you. All of us need to leave. This is the most important time of the year for us. We have vital engagements and meetings to attend."

Under his breath Fenwick said, "And miles to go before you sleep."

Turner ignored Fenwick. The few in the crowd who heard him gave Fenwick an odd look.

"We need to talk to all of you now," Turner said. "We believe that the dead person fell from this level."

"We all knew Cullom Furyk," Munsen said. "He was close to many of us. No one can believe he'd commit suicide."

Fenwick said, "We have reason to believe he was murdered."

A few of the people looked at each other. Some gaped. Nobody rushed up to confess.

"Is everyone else who was at the brunch still here?" Fenwick asked.

"Yes," Munsen replied. "I organized the brunch here today. Really, these people, including me, need to leave."

"We are all far too upset to be talking to the police," Abarak added.

Fenwick burst out laughing. "I don't know what silly soap opera you may have been watching, but witnesses and suspects don't get to declare when they are willing or able to talk to the police."

"There's no need to take that tone," Munsen said.

"Nor am I about to let you decide what tone I can or cannot take. This is a murder investigation."

"Why do you think it was murder?" Munsen asked.

Turner said, "We have a witness who says they saw him pushed from this floor."

"Impossible," Munsen said.

"Why is that impossible?" Fenwick asked.

"Well, it just is," Munsen said. "Nobody here is a killer."

"Certainly not," his assistant added. "Maybe what the witness saw was someone trying to save him."

Fenwick asked, "Has someone up here mentioned to anyone else that they were out on the balcony, saw him starting to fall, and tried to rescue him?"

All shook their heads no.

Fenwick said, "Then that person is incredibly shy, has remarkable self-control, or that person is the killer. Is an innocent person going to be able to keep that kind of experience to themselves? It's never happened in my years on the force."

"Maybe they're afraid they'd be accused of murder," Abarak said.

"We'll question everyone," Fenwick stated flatly.

"First we need to secure the area of the penthouse from which he fell," Turner said. "Then, Mr. Munsen, we might as well start with you. What would be the most convenient place for us to talk?"

Munsen made no further protests. Turner showed him the copy of the guest list they'd gotten from Weeland. Munsen confirmed its accuracy and completeness. He wrote down the names of the people who were at the brunch but not staying in the penthouse.

They turned to the uniformed officer stationed at the elevator. Turner said to her, "Get some more uniforms up here with the maps of the place. Check with Weeland, the manager. He said he'd get copies for us. Tell them to find out where everybody was or claims they were. Get their movements from the moment they entered the penthouse to the time we showed up. Write down which rooms they were in and at what times and make a sketch for each different person."

One of the cops on guard when they arrived gave them a brief tour so they could get a sense of the layout of the penthouse. Two wide and spacious corridors bisected the entire floor from north to south and east to west. Tall, severe statues of religious figures blessing the viewer stood in niches every twenty feet. Where the halls crossed in the center was a large oval room. From here, the inhabitants had a spectacular view. The dome in the center of the room rose two stories, culminating in a vast stained-glass window where thousands of tiny shards of glass formed an immense red rose surrounded by swirling waves of green and blue. It was in this room that the brunch had been held. The only remnants of the meal were two large coffee urns—one gold and the other silver—with trays of white porcelain cups next to each.

All four of the hallways ended in gothic towers. Walls of chiseled stone cut them off from the adjoining balconies. Each tower had a two-story panel of clear glass from which to view the scenery. Flanking these were stained-glass windows of brilliant ruby red and dark, saturated blue. For those who wished a more lofty perch, in each tower a black wrought-iron spiral staircase led up and outdoors to a farther balcony.

Leaving their guide behind, the two detectives climbed the black metallic staircase in the west-facing tower. A six-inch-thick wooden door led onto a twelve foot by twelve foot platform. The wind was cool, the sun was warm, the view was extravagant. The balcony they stood on had three pieces of white wrought-iron furniture—graveyard furniture.

As they gazed at the wintry sunshine glinting off the skyscrapers

Turner said, "Whatever else happens, never again quote poetry in front of possible witnesses or suspects."

"You don't like poetry?"

"I'm not opposed to it, but think about it, Buck. A poetry-quoting cop? Besides the fact that it is totally out of character for you, nobody would believe it about any cop anywhere."

"There's got to be poetry-reciting, even poetry-writing cops. Somewhere."

"Probably. That's not my main problem, though."

"What's your main problem?"

"The worst is, I might bust out laughing."

Fenwick grumbled, "I think I'm going to be miffed."

"Keep reciting poetry and you might end up miffing in action."

Fenwick glowered at his partner. "Comments like that are grounds for divorce."

"Do I get custody of the chocolate?"

"Just remember, I'm the one in this relationship that does the witty cop humor."

"I've been taking lessons from you. Besides, that wasn't humor. It was only a ghastly pun, which you walked right into."

Turner and Fenwick climbed back down and proceeded to the southwest side of the penthouse and entered the terrace. All the outside walls had immense sliding glass doors alternating with traceried rectangular panels. The tower walls of windowless stone made cold, blank, imposing barriers sixteen feet high. Each balcony made a right angle around the corner of the building. The parapets that formed the barriers between the terraces and space eternal were crenellated slabs of granite over six feet high. Two-foot gaps allowed those on the balcony to peer onto the passing scene below. In olden times, the defenders could shoot arrows, drop rocks, or pour boiling oil from these machicolations. The only decoration on the terrace was one piece of white wrought-iron furniture.

"How many entrances from how many rooms are there to this thing?" Fenwick asked.

They walked the length of the balcony. There were four sliding glass doors into four different rooms, two bedrooms—one of which looked occupied—and two studies, which looked unused. Two of the rooms faced south, two west.

Next the detectives examined the floor and the wall of the balcony.

After fifteen minutes of close inspection, Fenwick said, "Not a clue in sight." He peered at the pavement far below. "I always wanted to be the one dropping boiling oil on the attackers."

"A childhood fantasy?"

"Now would be perfectly okay. I can picture desperate criminals looking up and getting crushed by large jagged boulders. Or maybe judges and prosecuting attorneys running for their lives."

"You've been more irritable than usual since you got back from court today. You didn't get enough chocolate this morning?"

"Can you ever get enough chocolate?" Fenwick answered his own question. "I don't think so. No, I've got two words: Judge Cabestainey."

Turner nodded in sympathy. "I understand."

Judge Cabestainey was a bane to detectives in his courtroom. Turner figured the judge must have had a nasty run-in with cops somewhere in his life. Cabestainey had even been warned by the judicial commission about his hostility toward the police.

"That shit-face cost us the case," Fenwick said.

"That's more than two words, and I thought he'd been warned to behave."

"Can't prove it by me."

Before Fenwick could launch into a full tirade about the judicial system, Turner suggested questioning the assembled guests. One of the uniforms met them as they reentered the penthouse. He gave them a copy of a diagram of the top floor.

FOUR

They found Munsen, who led them to an opulent living room that faced south and east. Turner and Fenwick sat on a black horsehair couch with four-foot-high plaster statues of crouching lions at each end. Through the windows they could see the John Hancock Building and the tops of numerous other skyscrapers in the Loop. The balcony and wall they could see were exact duplicates of the one Furyk had been pushed from.

Munsen sat across from them on a chair whose back rose three feet over his head. The arms ended in carved lions' paws. It was more of a seat to hide in than sit on. Or perhaps a giant's throne borrowed from the prop room of a sixteenth-century costume drama.

Munsen wore a white-green cotton cricket sweater over a blue-white cotton T-shirt, madras-plaid cotton pants and sandals. Turner didn't see this as an outfit for the president of a fashion company. He glanced down at his well-worn sport coat and slacks and decided to keep his fashion comments to himself.

Munsen placed his right foot on his left knee and gazed from one to the other of them. He said, "I can't believe Cullom is dead."

"Was he staying here?"

"No. He'd arrived just before the brunch for a brief meeting with me."

"Who knew he was going to be here?"

"My staff, certainly. It wasn't a secret. A number of reporters probably knew."

"How well did you know him?" Turner asked.

Munsen's eyes misted over. "I was the one who discovered him. For a number of years he has been the spokesmodel for our line of men's clothes."

"When was it that you discovered him?"

"Ten years ago when we were just starting the company. He was sixteen then. He modeled for us. Teenage girls loved his look. When he was older, he branched out to many of our other products. When we launched our underwear line, his first ads nearly caused a stampede to the better department stores. He was good, extremely good, for sales."

"He's from the area?"

"Grew up in Evanston. I believe he still has some family up there, although he bought his parents a retirement home in Palm Beach several years ago. We had a huge talent search back then and it was one of our first big publicity gimmicks. It really helped set us up in Chicago. We got headlines in all the papers, and after that the gossip columns in town really followed us. Cullom was a tremendous discovery. He could convey an innocence and warmth and masculinity that was magical, natural."

"We understand he worked with the Save the Orphans campaign."

"That one and a number of others. He cared very much. Over time anyone with a cause called him, but he limited himself to a select few, mostly those having to do with children."

"Why were you having the brunch today?" Turner asked.

"There are two major fashion companies in Chicago. We started about the same time. Veleshki and Heyling is the other. As you've probably heard, we've been rivals for years."

"Never heard of either of you," Fenwick said.

Munsen's look mixed superiority with an ill-concealed sneer. "Each of us set out to rival the fashion houses in Paris, New York, London, and Milan. We both picked Chicago. I did because I was born here. I decided to use my inheritance to found a fashion company from scratch. It was not easy, and it cost a great deal of money. Each of our companies has succeeded to some extent. Today's meeting was to finalize our agreement to cooperate instead of compete. We wanted lots of pictures and publicity for our first cooperative efforts this week."

"Was this a formal merger?" Fenwick asked. "Was either of you buying the other out?"

"Despite vicious, unfounded rumors in the tabloids, this was definitely not a merger. No money was changing hands. The companies would most definitely be separate. It was an agreement to cooperate. It was my idea. For example, one year we had our runway shows on exactly the same day. It drove the press insane and ruined a lot of good publicity for both of us. Veleshki and Heyling are sensible. So am I. We worked it out. We had a very amicable meeting."

"Why was Cullom here?" Turner asked.

"We met about several new ad campaigns."

"How has he been lately? Any problems, concerns, enemies?"

"He'd just gotten back from a vacation in Greece. He seemed happy and content. As far as I know, he had no problems. Certainly no enemies that I am aware of."

"Precisely when did you see him last?" Turner asked.

"He excused himself from the table as the caterers were clearing the plates just before dessert was served. He never ate chocolate or sweets. He claimed it helped keep him in shape."

"That sounds criminal to me," Fenwick said.

"I beg your pardon," Munsen said.

"Excused himself?" Turner asked.

"He was always terribly polite, a very well brought up young man."

"And you didn't see him after that?" Turner asked.

"No."

"Did you go out on that balcony any time today?"

"No. I had no reason to."

"Did you notice anyone acting oddly before the police arrived?"

"No. I was too concerned about the brunch going well to notice. We've all been too upset since."

"Where were you while Cullom was out of the room?"

"I was in someone's presence the entire time. Are you sure he was murdered? That's quite high up for a casual observer to notice or to be certain of what he or she saw."

"For now, we have to go with what the witness told us," Fenwick said.

"Do you know where he was before he showed up here this morning?" Turner asked.

"He had a photo shoot at the Blue Diamond Athletic Club. He was to be modeling our new line of running shorts while doing a promotion for them."

"Did you see anyone go out on the balcony or follow Furyk out?"

"If I had, do you think I would have kept silent about it?"

"We don't know," Fenwick said. "Would you?"

"I'm not a killer."

"Nobody ever is," Fenwick stated.

They got no further information out of him.

F I V E

After Munsen left Fenwick said, "I don't like him."

"Name a witness you have liked in the past year."

"The woman from the opera who looked like a moose but who served us chocolate chip cookies."

"She wasn't a witness. She was the killer."

"I'll think of one. Give me time."

"I'm not sure eternity has that much time. Let's get on with this."

The next person called into the room was Dinah McBride. She wore a white fisherman's sweater and black jeans. She had a narrow face and high cheekbones that needed no makeup to emphasize. She had been the woman standing next to Munsen when they entered the penthouse. She placed her laptop computer on the floor next to a chair, then sat down. McBride folded her hands, placed her knees together at a slight angle to the left, crossed her ankles, and sat at the edge of the chair.

After introductions Fenwick asked, "Why were you at the brunch?"

"I'm the head of GUINEVERE's fashion design network."

"At what time did you see Cullom Furyk?"

"I didn't. He arrived before I did. Then I was out at the reception desk in the foyer by the elevators throughout the meal."

"Why was that?" Fenwick asked.

"I have a million things still to do for the fashion lines we're presenting. The last-minute details must be seen to. While Mr. Munsen sponsored the event today, I was the actual organizer and official greeter. Once the guests were past the foyer, my job was done. I can't stand these meetings where everyone is a hypocrite and professes eternal friendship. The owners don't like each other and it is not a secret that they are business rivals. But I don't concern myself with intercompany rivalries; I had phone calls to make and paperwork to do. I had them bring me a plate of food out there."

"After the guests arrived, no one else showed up?"

"Once all the guests were present, the foyer remained quiet. I got a great deal of work done until your police officers arrived."

Fenwick said, "You don't sound as if you like these people very much."

"I work for Mr. Munsen. I am very loyal, and I work very hard. My work has nothing to do with likes and dislikes."

"How well did you know Cullom Furyk?"

"I had very little to do with the models. I worked with the designers and production staff. From all I've heard and as far as I know, he was a perfectly nice man."

"You saw or heard nothing suspicious?"

"No. I stayed in the foyer."

"Alone?"

"Yes."

"The whole time?"

"Yes."

Unable to give any further information, she left.

"Kind of odd to be out front alone," Turner said.

"Based on who we've met so far in this crowd, that's where I would have been," Fenwick replied. "She is my favorite kind of suspect."

"How so?"

"No one to give her an alibi."

The next person to be questioned was Daniel Egremont. He had shoulder-length brown hair, narrow shoulders, a protruding nose, and hardly any chin. His black horn-rim glasses emphasized the dark circles under his eyes. He was cadaverously thin and over six feet six inches tall. He wore a pink-green short-sleeved cotton polo shirt under a summer blue-white gingham-cotton-seersucker shirt, plain-front chinos, and black work boots. Turner guessed he was in his late twenties.

Egremont carried a slender briefcase in with him. He sat in the outsized throne and said, "I'm the accountant for GUINEVERE, Incorporated."

"You been on the job long?" Fenwick asked.

"Five years."

"How's the company doing?" Fenwick asked.

"We went public last year with a stock offering. By our accounting, we are the second wealthiest fashion house in the United States."

"Who else's accounting would there be?" Fenwick asked.

"Wild rumors abound in the trade papers. I know we are richer than all but one other company."

"How do you know the financial status of other companies?" Turner asked.

"Former employees gossip. The strength of a stock offering. The size and scope of their shows and latest lines. Many things. Everyone knows Mr. Munsen started from scratch ten years ago. Even with all his private wealth, he has had to work extremely hard to make a success of this business. Starting a new fashion house is not simple. Without his private wealth, the company probably would have gone bankrupt in the first few years. Today GUINEVERE, Incorporated is immensely successful."

"What happened to the accountant before you?" Turner asked.

"He quit and joined one of the Parisian fashion houses. The companies can be intense rivals. It is a cutthroat world. The fights and feuds can be epic. Animosities can last for years."

"Was Furyk involved in any fights and feuds?"

"Not that I ever heard."

"You heard us say Cullom was murdered?" Turner asked.

"I could never believe he committed suicide, but murder is just terrible. No one would do such a thing."

"What kind of a guy was he?" Turner asked.

"Happy. Incredibly, deliciously happy."

"Why was he happy?" Fenwick asked.

"Most models aren't the brightest, but Cullom was at least smart enough to do what his agent told him to. He was great at a photo shoot, very cooperative. No attitude problem. He was happy because . . . well, because . . . let me show you." He opened the briefcase and searched for a moment. "Here. This is for a proposed ad campaign." He handed them a picture.

Turner looked at the picture of the man of whom they had seen only the smashed remnant. The photo was of Furyk with his shirt off. The light and shadow showed off his well-sculpted muscles to perfection. The top button of his carefully torn jeans was open, revealing a snippet of white brief. From his broad shoulders his torso sloped in a perfect V to a taut stomach and narrow waist. The puppy-dog eyes hinted at sensitivity and vulnerability, but a day's growth of blue beard, a swatch of unruly hair on his head, well-defined muscles, and a hint of black down on his chest said that here was a total stud. Turner thought the effect was altogether pleasing and desirable. If he were inclined to put up pictures of studly men, this might be one he would choose.

Fenwick looked up from the picture. "So?" he demanded.

"Have you ever seen that series of posters he did for the Save the Orphans campaign?"

The cops shook their heads. Egremont pulled out another photo, this one of Cullom Furyk sitting on a bench in a park with a kid about five years old snuggled in his arms, asleep.

Turner recognized it instantly. "These were on the buses a year or so ago."

"As a poster, this one sold five million copies around the world. He was as sexy as ever in the photo, but there was a tenderness that broke your heart. You wished he was your father. His death is a great tragedy." Egremont began to cry softly. Several minutes later, after he composed himself, Egremont said, "He was an extremely attractive man and a sweetheart. He could get whatever he wanted when he wanted it."

"I'm not sure what you mean," Turner said.

"I'm going to be very honest with you. I think that is important for me and for everyone. I think this whole thing was really a horrible accident. First, you must understand, the beautiful people of this world have it easier. It was a lesson I learned early in life. I was a clumsy, awkward, nerd teenager. I am now a clumsy, awkward, nerd adult. I wanted to be in the fashion industry. The only way I could get close to a runway was with my brains.

"Cullom could have anything he wanted. Anything. He was a gentle soul. Always willing to listen, which made him even more popular. He isn't smiling in either of those pictures, but when he smiled the effect was even more dazzling. He melted the hearts of men and women. He also had a bit of a wild streak." He pointed at the studio picture. "You can see a hint of it in his eyes. You'd fall in love with him, and you'd want to protect him, and yet you knew you could never have him permanently."

"How long were you in love with him?" Turner asked.

"I lusted after him since the day I first saw him in an ad. One of the reasons I applied for a job with this company was because he was the spokesperson."

"Did he reciprocate your interest?"

Egremont smiled. "For one glorious night four years ago."

"And then he rejected you?" Turner asked.

Egremont shook his head. "It didn't happen like that. I'm honest enough to realize that for him I was probably a mercy fuck, but it was enough for me. I knew what it was for what it was when it happened. I didn't care."

"Did he?"

"Cullom Furyk was a man apart. Very special. I will forever treasure the night we spent together, but I hold no resentment that it was only one night."

"Tell us about his wild streak."

"I know you said you think he was murdered, but I think it could have been something else. Earlier, before brunch, after he'd met with Mr. Munsen, Cullom and I were out on the balcony."

Turner and Fenwick barely concealed their keen interest.

"He was walking along the top of the wall as if it were some kind of tightrope. I'm afraid of heights so I didn't get near the edge. I urged him to come down. The more I urged him to get down, the more daring he became. When he got to one of the openings, he would jump over it. He would deliberately lean far out and then turn back to me and smile. His behavior made me very nervous. Maybe he was just doing it again after brunch and slipped. His fall could have been an unfortunate accident."

"Where were you after brunch?" Turner asked.

"I remained with Mr. Munsen to go over the final figures for the cooperation agreement."

"Money was involved?" Fenwick asked.

"Oh, yes."

"But the companies weren't merging," Fenwick said.

"Oh, no. We were cooperating on dates, shows, some advertising. I have a law degree as well and was advising on some legal points."

Turner said, "Your boss told us no money was changing hands."

"Technically he's right. We pooled a few hundred thousand for some ads. But money was not changing hands."

"Sounds like an awfully fine point to me," Fenwick said.

"It's not so fine a point when big egos are involved."

"Munsen has a big ego?" Fenwick asked.

"Everybody in this industry has a big ego. They thrive on minuscule distinctions alternating with huge, showy displays. It's a fast-paced, sometimes brutal world."

"Did you go out on the balcony after brunch?"

"No."

"Did you see anyone with Cullom or following him?"

"No."

They got no further useful information from Egremont. After he left Fenwick said, "Let's try somebody from the other company. These people were in love with him. I want nasty gossip."

"McBride wasn't in love," Turner said.

"Cool, professional, and distant, but those aren't actionable offenses."

Turner knew Fenwick spoke accurately. You were seldom likely to get vital information from friends and relatives of the deceased. Usually you had to go to someone who had a grudge or at least was at some distance from the victim. Looking at the guest list, Turner saw the names of Gerald Veleshki and Roger

Heyling. Turner pointed them out to Fenwick. "Aren't those the names of the rival company Munsen talked about?"

"Just the last names," Fenwick said.

"Let's try them next," Turner said.

Moments later the door opened and two men walked in. Both were slightly over six feet tall. Gerald Veleshki, the one with brush-cut hair, wore a long-sleeve indigo denim shirt with patch pockets and cotton-polyester indigo denim jeans with retro-style patch pockets. Roger Heyling, the one with the hair parted on the left, wore a bias plaid cotton-denim pea coat and cotton-polyester jacquard boot-cut jeans. Each wore black motorcycle boots. They were both handsome, clean shaven, and looked to be in their middle thirties.

Veleshki sat, while Heyling took several moments to pull over another chair from the wall. They both looked as if they'd just been forcefed extra helpings of the vegetables they hated most.

After introductions Veleshki said, "Let's get this over with. We're shocked at Cullom's death. Neither of us had anything to do with it."

Turner said, "You own the rival company to GUINEVERE, Incorporated."

"Yes. To be honest, and you'd find this out, if you haven't already, we don't like Franklin Munsen. He is one of the most hated men in the fashion industry."

"Why is that?" Turner asked.

"Besides being little more than a rag merchant, he's ruthless, unprincipled, and cruel. Vicious. Brutal. He keeps hired spies and saboteurs on his payroll. His employees hate him."

"None of them have said that," Fenwick said.

"Let me suggest a possible thought pattern," Veleshki said. "Say I'm an employee of GUINEVERE. Here are two strangers, police detectives. I could be implicated in a murder. I know the first thing I'm going to do is confide in them how much I hate the owner of the company. Does that sound likely to you?"

"Did Cullom Furyk hate him?" Turner asked.

"I have no idea."

"Did you hate him?"

"More than some. Less than others."

"But you were working with him," Fenwick said.

"We don't like his company or his business methods. We are working with him because it makes business sense. It was our idea."

Fenwick interjected, "He said it was his."

"Typical," Veleshki said. "Endless debates with that man on any subject are useless. We recognized a business decision that had to be made. Munsen started with a lot more money than we did. We've had to scrape to survive, but people liked our products more. This year, for the first time, we passed him in sales. The only thing that kept him in business was Cullom Furyk—he was the company's most valuable asset."

Fenwick said, "Their accountant just told us theirs was the second most profitable fashion house in the country."

Heyling snorted. Veleshki said, "That's nonsense. The companies in New York are far ahead of both of us. We're upstarts in Chicago. It will take us both years to catch up to the top echelon."

"Maybe your information is inaccurate," Turner said.

Heyling and Veleshki exchanged glances. "That is highly improbable," Veleshki said.

"Who is your source?"

"You can get thousands of little hints just keeping careful watch. For example, sometimes disgruntled employees leak sales figures."

"Spies?" Fenwick asked.

"We are hardly sophisticated or rich enough for that," Veleshki said.

"But you wish you were?" Fenwick asked.

"We know which subsidiaries he deals with. Information gathering can be based on something as simple as knowing how much fabric he orders. You don't always have to know someone specific, although that helps too."

"Did you know Cullom Furyk?" Turner asked.

"This next part is painful, but some vicious gossip would distort it in the telling. Roger and I have been lovers for many years."

"That's painful?" Fenwick asked.

Veleshki glared at him. "If I may be allowed to fully explain?" The detectives waited.

"It's better that it come from us. I had an affair with Cullom five years ago. It was a stupid, stupid thing to do. Roger forgave me, thank God." Heyling reached for his lover's hand and held it.

"How'd you happen to have an affair with him?" Turner asked.

"We met at a fund-raiser. Our liaison lasted all of a few weeks."

"Who broke it off?"

"I stopped calling him. He never called me in the first place. When I stopped calling, that was the end."

"Mr. Heyling," Turner asked, "did you harbor animosity toward Mr. Furyk for having an affair with your lover?"

Heyling shook his head. "No."

Veleshki said, "Over the years we saw him at numerous events. The three of us were cordial but distant. To be honest, I doubt if the affair had much effect on Cullom. He could have had sex with anyone he wanted."

"Did either of you go out on the balcony with Furyk before or after the brunch?"

"No," Veleshki said. "After the meal we had a private meeting with Munsen for a few minutes. The others from our company waited for us. Roger and I were in each other's presence the whole time."

"Nobody went to the john?" Fenwick asked.

"We were not out of each other's presence," Veleshki reiterated. After a few more minutes of questions that elicited nothing, the two of them left.

"Their relationship gives new meaning to the concept of silent partner," Turner commented.

"I don't like being double-teamed in a murder investigation," Fenwick said, "but then again, I say about as much when I go to a party with Madge's friends."

"They don't have an appreciation for your finely honed wit like I do."

"Maybe it was an accident."

"Your wit?"

Fenwick grumbled, "My wit can do without your comments, thank you. Maybe Clark Nemora was wrong. It is a hell of a long way up to see clearly."

The next six people they interviewed claimed to have eaten brunch, been in someone else's presence the whole time, and been preparing to leave when the police made them wait.

After the last one of this group left, Turner said, "Each person from GUINEVERE, except McBride, has claimed the guy was a charming sweetheart. And except for Veleshki and Heyling, the people from their company claim not to know him."

Fenwick said, "Sexual athlete, incredibly good-looking, immensely popular, totally sweet, and rich. What's not to like? I'm ready to puke."

The twelfth person they talked with was Eliot Norwyn.

Before he entered the room Turner said, "I know this guy, I think. Why do I know this guy?"

"He's the latest teenage heartthrob," Fenwick said. "He's on that new show set in Newton, Iowa. I think it's called *Farm Lust,* or *Farming First*. Every Saturday night my daughters are glued to the television for an hour to watch this guy. I've never figured out what the damn show is supposed to be about."

"*Teen Farm,*" Turner said.

"That's it," Fenwick said.

The short, slender, young actor entered the room. He wore a pure wool two-button charcoal-stripe suit and a polka-dot silk-crepe tie. His blond hair was swept straight back from the front of his head. The swirls of his hairdo seemed to have been gelled into place.

After introductions Turner asked, "Why were you at the party?"

"I came with a friend. People could bring guests."

"Are you connected with the fashion industry?" Turner asked.

"Both companies have approached me to do endorsements. I was willing to listen to both sides."

"I thought Furyk was the spokesperson for GUINEVERE," Fenwick said.

"Companies can have more than one spokesperson. Nike has more than just Michael Jordan."

"I knew that," Fenwick said.

"How well did you know Cullom Furyk?" Turner asked.

Norwyn shifted uneasily in his seat. He became teary-eyed. "I've got to be careful. I'm straight, you understand. That's important for my image, and it also happens to be true. There are all these rumors in Hollywood and on the set about me being sexually ambiguous, but I'm straight. People in the industry know I am, but letting fans think I'm bisexual or mysterious adds to my allure, or so my agent says."

"You don't agree?" Turner asked.

"I'm awful popular because of him. It's worked so far."

"It was a good idea at the time," Fenwick said.

"Pardon?"

"Nothing," Fenwick said.

Turner asked, "If being straight is important for your image, how does being mysteriously bisexual fit in with that?"

"People can think I might fool around with both sexes, but I only appear in public with women. Straight guys can identify with me, gay guys can have fantasies, and women can see me as sensitive *and* masculine."

"Puke," Fenwick muttered.

"What did you say?" Norwyn asked.

Fenwick gazed at him silently.

Turner stepped in. "You're telling us all this because . . ."

"It's best you hear this from me, so you won't think I'm lying or trying to hide anything. I had a brief fling with Cullom. The first year of my television show. I met him through some friends in Malibu. We spent the better part of a week partying at a friend's beach house. That's all it was, one week. We had separate lives. We never got together after that. I've never touched another guy."

"It just ended?" Turner asked. "You weren't angry about that?"

"It was a mutual ending, really. I had to get back to work. My agent gave me a big talking-to. He said Cullom was a big whore and just took advantage of everyone. I'm straight, but he was such a hot guy and really sweet."

"Where did you go after brunch today?"

"Cullom left just as they served dessert and didn't come back.

The others were discussing business so I left the room. I wandered around the penthouse." He sighed and shifted again. "I don't want to be involved in this. I'm straight."

"What happened?"

"I heard a fight going on out on the west terrace. Someone was arguing with Cullom. I could see Cullom, but not the person he was talking to. I couldn't hear the words, but Cullom was pointing with his finger and shaking his fist."

"Man or a woman?" Turner asked.

"I'm pretty sure it was a man."

"Could you tell anything at all about the other person?" Fenwick asked. "An outline, a shadow?"

"No. I didn't hang around. I don't like it when people argue. About five minutes later I heard one of the terrace doors thunk shut. I didn't pay much attention to it at the time. Thinking back, I guess it could have been Cullom or more likely his killer, because just a few minutes later I began to hear sirens."

"Did you go out on the terrace?" Turner asked.

"No. Never. Not for a minute."

"You didn't see who it was who came in?"

"No. Sorry."

He knew no more and left.

Fenwick said, "If Eliot Norwyn has had sex with only one guy, then I'm a drag queen."

"And more sensitive."

"A one-night stand, I understand," Fenwick said. "You shack up with somebody for a week, you've moved past a phase."

"Or an 'Oops, I was drunk.' "

"They must have had truth serum for brunch," Fenwick said. "All these people telling us things before anyone else can is kind of weird."

"Maybe they're scared," Turner suggested.

"They all lie," Fenwick said. He was repeating one of the great cop truisms about the people they dealt with—both the guilty and the not guilty.

Turner asked, "Did he get misty-eyed because Furyk is dead, or because we might think he was gay, or because he was worried about his career?"

"I'd vote for the last," Fenwick replied.

The next four people, including Evan Abarak, cleared interviewing easily. The second to the last was Sean Kindel.

After introductions Fenwick asked, "Why were you at the party?"

Kindel burst into tears.

The detectives glanced at each other.

"You were close to Mr. Furyk?" Turner asked.

Through his sobs Kindel said, "We were lovers." He took out a silk handkerchief and wept into it. He wore a gray-white microcheck shirt, a gray silk wave-striped tie, and patch-pocket cotton-denim painter's jeans. He was five feet eight, in his mid-to-late forties, and weighed maybe one hundred fifty.

When he finally controlled himself Turner asked, "How long have you known Mr. Furyk?"

"We've met at circuit parties off and on for a number of years. We'd been lovers only the past month. I was with him for part of the time on his vacation in Greece."

"What's a circuit party?" Fenwick asked.

"Parties around the country that the beautiful people in the gay world go to."

"Did he bring you as his guest to today's brunch?" Turner asked.

"No. I was here covering the event for the *Gay Tribune,* the city's gay and lesbian newspaper. I'm the gossip and fashion columnist."

"Did you know he was going to be here?" Turner asked.

"Of course."

"Why didn't you come together?" Turner asked.

"I had to go to work. He had a photo shoot."

"You were living together?" Turner asked.

"He stayed at my place sometimes."

"The impression we have is that he was fairly fickle in his relationships," Turner said. "He ever call you or did you just call him?"

"He called me. I have my pride."

"You loved each other," Turner said.

"Very, very much." He sniffed and dabbed at his eyes.

"Was he staying at your place during this visit?"

"Part of the time."

"Where was he the rest of the time?"

"Here, in the penthouse with the rest of the guests of the company. He really didn't have one place to stay. He had to be in so many cities for so many events. He traveled extensively for the company. He may not have modeled for the other fashion houses, but he was in great demand. The company wanted him to keep a high profile. He would wear their clothes in city after city at parties, events, fund-raisers, talk shows, any place their agent could get him even a few minutes' exposure to the public."

"How can you not have a place to live," Fenwick asked, "a place to put your stuff?"

"They can keep a lot of the clothes they model, but he gave a lot of them away to charities' benefit auctions. He was incredibly generous with his time for a good cause. One time, a pair of his briefs sold for over five thousand dollars."

"How could they prove he ever wore them?" Turner asked.

"The deal included watching him take them off."

"All this and heaven too," Fenwick said.

Turner said, "According to Mr. Munsen he was not staying here."

"I beg your pardon?"

Turner and Fenwick gazed at him.

"I . . . That's what he told me. Are you sure?"

"The people we talked to from GUINEVERE, Incorporated confirmed what Munsen told us. Where would he have been?"

"I don't know." Kindel looked forlorn and lost.

"What happened in the past month that made you lovers?" Turner asked.

"He told me he wanted to settle down. He wanted more of a normal life."

"Anybody else know you were lovers?"

"A few of my close friends. No one else."

"Did you and he talk at the brunch?"

"No."

"You're lovers and you didn't talk?"

"Our relationship was not common knowledge in the industry."

"Did you leave the room at any time?"

"No."

"Did you see anyone follow him?"

"The penthouse is immense. People were moving around. Some wanted to go to each tower to see the view. People were talking in different groups. Keeping track of everyone would have been impossible."

"Where'd you go after brunch?" Fenwick asked.

"I was interviewing people for my column."

He knew nothing more.

The last person was Jolanda Bokaru. She wore the kind of outfit you thought existed only on the runways of outré fashion shows. A clutch of thin spaghetti straps held up an acetate, viscose, and organza dress crammed with pressed orchids. Her six-inch heels helped emphasize her tall, slender frame.

"Why were you at the party?" Fenwick asked.

"I am the owner and editor of *Gorgeous* magazine."

"Never heard of it," Fenwick said.

"I'm supposed to care about that?" she snapped.

She and Fenwick glared at each other.

Turner asked, "How well did you know Cullom Furyk?"

"When I permitted him to be on the cover of the magazine three years ago, we printed an extra hundred thousand copies. We sold out completely. We still get requests for that issue. Alas, there are none to be had on the planet."

"What was so special about the cover?" Turner asked.

"Cullom is a star in his own right and sells whatever he touches, mostly GUINEVERE fashions. For that issue he was in a pair of leather pants, motorcycle boots, a chain harness, and a cap pulled slightly over one eyebrow. We also had a special section featuring him wearing some of GUINEVERE's male fashions that season. That vulnerable smile and those puppy-dog eyes drove people wild. Even I was moved."

"How so?" Fenwick asked.

"He and I screwed after the photo session."

"You had an affair?" Fenwick asked.

"Please. It wasn't even a one-night stand. He was an inept lover. More of a boy. Someone needed to teach him the ways to please a woman."

"We understood he was gay."

"I did not and do not care about his sexuality. Being a lousy lover or a terrific one does not depend on your sexual orientation. He was interesting to me for a moment. Then he wasn't."

"Where did you go after brunch?"

"Where was I when the murder was committed?" She leaned her head back and laughed. "I shall dine out on this moment for many years." She laughed some more, then said, "I finished my dessert. Munsen had the most inferior food served. I then stepped out to have a cigarette on the east terrace. When I reentered I saw Cullom with his tongue down the throat of one of the caterers."

"Can you identify him?"

"Cullom? Gorgeous, really, in a mid-twenties way. Oh, of course, you mean the catering person, don't you? Well, it was a male Caucasian in those black pants and white shirts they all wore. No distinguishing moles or tattoos. Color of hair, dark, although I couldn't say if it was black or brown."

"Where was this?"

"I happened to pass an open door to one of the bedroom suites."

"Was anyone else around?"

"I didn't see anyone. I let myself give them an intrusive look. If they'd been paying attention, they might have tried to be more discreet, or maybe not. After several moments, I moved on."

"Did you know he was lovers with Sean Kindel?"

"Who?"

"The fashion reporter for the *Gay Tribune*?"

"Nobody takes that newspaper seriously."

"You didn't meet at the party today?"

"If I did, I don't remember."

Turner took out the floor plan. "In which bedroom was the make-out session?"

She examined the map for a moment then pointed to a room in the southeast corner. "There," she said.

"Did you see Furyk or the caterer after that?"

"No. Veleshki and Heyling were trying to get me to do a major spread on them. They're such nice boys, but, really, their products just are not up to standard. I believe they are going broke."

"How do you know?" Turner asked.

"Inside industry gossip. I could never tell you precisely who told me. Everyone just knows."

"Is it true?" Fenwick asked.

"I wouldn't know. Gossip is ever so much more fun than reality."

"Why would they be going broke?"

"The blindly optimistic and least self-aware claim they are too far ahead of their time. A realistic assessment might be that they made poor choices and stupid decisions. Which do you think they announce to the public?"

She left moments later, unable to give them any further information.

Turner turned to Fenwick and said, "Furyk was lying to Kindel about where he was staying. I wonder if Kindel saw or heard Furyk and the hired help being friendly." Turner told the uniform at the door to send Kindel back in.

"When you were done with them, we let them go," the uniform said. "They were getting real anxious to leave and nobody said to keep them here."

Turner nodded. "Find out where Sean Kindel lives and send somebody to pick him up."

When Turner resumed his seat Fenwick said, "I don't like these people."

"Except for an occasional snarl, you've managed to hide that pretty well."

"I'm more sensitive now, remember?"

Next they interviewed four hotel guests found by the uniforms. These were connected to the fashion industry and staying in the hotel but not part of the brunch. They gave them no useful information. After that, Turner and Fenwick hunted for Munsen. He was in the penthouse foyer.

Turner unfolded the floor plan of the penthouse. He pointed to the bedroom Bokaru had identified. "Who was staying in this room?"

"No one," Munsen answered. "We kept all the rooms, but used only about three quarters of them."

Fenwick said, "We need to talk to the catering staff."

"They left before you came up. Why did you send someone to pick up Sean Kindel? Did he push Cullom off the balcony?"

"How can the catering staff be gone?" Fenwick asked. "Didn't we tell the uniforms to keep everyone up here?"

"Is Kindel the killer?" Munsen asked.

"Thank you for your help," Fenwick said—an obvious dismissal and refusal to answer his question.

Turner and Fenwick stopped in the bedroom in question. The slightly rumpled bedspread looked as if someone might have lain on top of it but there was no other evidence of any activity, sexual or otherwise. They put up the crime scene tape.

Fenwick went to call the caterer for the addresses of the staff from the party and to hunt for the beat cops. As he walked away, Fenwick said, "I'm gonna shoot one of them."

Turner said nothing. He was as annoyed as Fenwick at the slip-up, permitting the caterers to leave. While Fenwick went to bawl out beat cops, Turner returned to the terrace from which Cullom had fallen.

Several evidence techs were dusting for fingerprints. Turner asked them to examine the bedroom. The detective looked over the edge down into the street. He wasn't sure how accurately he could pinpoint specific movements of pedestrians. Could their witness be certain he had seen someone? He claimed he'd seen a face as well.

"Find anything?" he asked the evidence techs.

"A little bit less than nothing."

"I want you to wave to me when I get down to the pavement. I want to check out what can be seen."

When he was on the street, Turner stood where Clark Nemora claimed he'd been. He watched the evidence tech waving for several moments.

"Seems a little tough to see," Turner said to himself. "We need more evidence."

SEVEN

On their way to Area Ten headquarters, Turner and Fenwick made two stops. One was at the caterer's at Belmont and Racine to pick up the addresses and the other at Aunt Millie's for a late lunch.

Aunt Millie's Bar and Grill was on Dearborn just south of Congress Parkway. The place was more than half empty. Millie herself greeted them at the door. She was a tall woman in her late fifties with a bouffant hairdo. She was wearing a pink muumuu.

"You guys are a little late, today," she said.

"Dead bodies wait for no man," Fenwick said.

She said, "If I wasn't so fed up, I'd make the kind of crack that line deserves."

"What's wrong?" Turner asked.

"They're going to construct another one of those goddamn upscale developments in the neighborhood. This used to be a part of town with character and depth. Now it's all these trendy rich people. I had somebody in here at lunch asking for a vegetarian menu. I suggested they order the french fries and mashed potatoes."

"An excellent choice of vegetables," Fenwick said.

"Not good enough for them. They wanted to know what kind of oil we cooked our fried foods in." She shook her head. "If I had the energy, I'd retire." She nodded toward the back booth where Area Ten detectives traditionally sat. "You think I'm down, better get over there and talk to Area Ten's perfect couple."

At the back booth were Ashley Devonshire and Dwayne Smythe, the two newest detectives on the Area Ten squad. They'd started as the most know-it-all, been-there-done-that pair Turner could remember.

Each was reading notes and barely looked up at Turner and Fenwick's approach.

"Problem?" Turner asked.

Ashley sighed. "I've never heard of detectives having this kind of problem."

Even their problems were bigger than anybody else's. Turner managed to look concerned.

Fenwick didn't bother to conceal his contempt. He said, "Finally found out detective work isn't a picnic?"

Smythe said, "The commander keeps giving us these gang shootings. There's no glamour in that. No headlines. No mystery. It's just more gang crap. We want real murders."

"A gang shooting is a fake murder?" Turner asked.

"You know what we mean," Ashley said. "We want the high-profile stuff like you guys get."

"Yeah," Dwayne said. "This fashion stuff would be great. I could get a few tips. Maybe they'd want me to model."

"We get as many gang shootings as anybody," Fenwick said.

"Doesn't seem that way to us."

"Talk to the commander," Turner said. "The dead bodies don't care who investigates their murders and neither do I."

"The press does," Ashley said. "We deserve some media exposure."

"I'll try to care," Fenwick said.

Their food arrived and as usual, the mounds of glop tasted delicious. Turner could almost hear his arteries clogging as he wolfed it down.

Turner and Fenwick drove back to Area Ten headquarters. The building housing Area Ten was south of the River City complex on Wells Street on the southwest rim of Chicago's Loop. The building was as old and crumbling as River City was new and gleaming. Many years ago the department purchased a four-story warehouse scheduled for demolition and decreed it would be a new Area Ten headquarters. To this day, rehabbers occasionally put in appearances. In fits and starts, the building had changed from an empty hulking wreck to a people-filled hulking wreck. The conversion from the original radiator heating to a more modern system was scheduled to begin the first warm day this spring. No one believed this.

Area Ten ran from Fullerton Avenue on the north to Lake Michigan on the east, south to Fifty-ninth Street, and west to Halsted. It included the wealth of downtown Chicago and North Michigan Avenue, some of the nastiest slums in the city, and numerous upscale developments. It incorporated four police districts. The cops in the Areas in Chicago handled homicides and any major nonlethal violent crimes. The police districts mostly took care of neighborhood patrols and initial responses to incidents.

Across the street from the station Turner spotted two photographers hefting more cameras than a herd of tourists. He pointed them out to Fenwick. "You recognize them as any of the regulars?"

Fenwick glanced at them. "Nope. Possibly paparazzi."

"Furyk was famous," Turner said. "We could have a flood of press people before this is over."

When he arrived at his desk, Turner called his friend Ian Hume at the *Gay Tribune*. He wanted to find out as much about Kindel as he could.

Turner and Hume had been cops together many years before. Back then they were lovers for a short while and had remained good friends.

After exchanging greetings Turner asked, "We're working on the Cullom Furyk murder."

"The model?"

"You know him?"

"I know of him. In the small pantheon of gaydom in this city, he has achieved the most fame of any gay person in the area."

"You ever meet him?"

"No. He was supposed to be pretty. I don't run in fashion circles. Most of those people think they are terribly important."

"And you don't?"

"Other than the overly rich, does anyone care about those people?"

"I've never been overly rich so I'm not sure. Tell you what, I'll try being overly rich awhile and get back to you on that."

"Cullom is dead. I'm trying to care. The paper will probably do an article on him, but I'm not sure why I should be concerned. I didn't know him."

"You know Sean Kindel?"

"Writes for the paper. He's a weird guy. Just a stringer here. He does the fashion, gossip, and a couple of porn columns."

"He only mentioned the fashion and gossip to us."

"He writes the porn stuff under a pseudonym. One column he calls 'Masturbating With.' In the other, he reviews one porn movie a week. It's called something absurd like 'Lust and Thrust.' "

" 'Masturbating With'?"

"Yeah, it's kind of an odd column. The new owner thinks mixing news with porn sells. The lawyer who meets with the staff once a month insisted on those kinds of columns. At one point he specifically ordered the editor to make space for it. He claimed the new owner wanted it."

"You still don't know who the new owner is?"

"No."

"It's not the lawyer?"

"I checked him out thoroughly with my best reportorial skills, which are legendary. It's not him."

"Your legendary reportorial skills weren't enough to find out who does own the paper."

Hume let that comment pass and said, "At any rate, Kindel happened to be around on that day, and he volunteered to write a couple of the columns. He'd just done the fashion and gossip stuff before. The editor didn't much care who wrote them, so he gladly accepted Kindel's offer."

"How were the columns odd?"

" 'Masturbating With' was kind of a gay man's fantasy column. The premise for one was a two-hour finale for *Melrose Place* in which it was revealed that in actual fact all the male characters have had affairs with Matt Fielding over the years, and they were putting it over on all the women all that time. Another column might be interviewing a sports star after a championship win, but with lots of personal questions mostly revolving around sex. Like asking John Stockton, 'Now that you've won the game, how long is your prick?' or 'Could you tell our listeners about the first time you beat off?' And then he'd make up answers to the questions. Sometimes the columns would be fantasies about making love to movie stars. I don't know how he got away with that kind of stuff. It had to be libelous, but it kept getting printed. At one of our meetings, the editor complained. He said this should be a newspaper, not the perpetrator of some salacious drivel. The lawyer simply said there would be no discussion and the columns would continue. Even Kindel expressed worries at some meetings about what he wrote, but the lawyer always okayed it."

"Kindel claimed he was Cullom's lover."

"You're joking."

"That's what he said."

Ian chuckled for a few moments. "Maybe in his fantasies he was, but I find that hard to believe."

"Why?"

"Kindel is a loser. The kind of guy who stays home watching porno tapes and beating off. He is a sleaze."

"Losers can't have lovers? Aren't you being a little harsh and judgmental?"

"That was the effect I was trying for," Ian said. "I suppose they could have boyfriends and lovers, but of the stature and fame of Cullom Furyk?"

"I don't know. Why not? I've never had the stature and fame of Cullom Furyk. I don't think I want to."

"Wise man."

"Is Kindel a killer?"

Turner trusted Ian's instincts almost as much as his own.

"Kindel, a killer? I can't picture it, but I've been surprised before."

"He have another job besides working for the paper?" Turner asked.

"I think he's mostly a freelance writer. A lot of the stringers try to make it on a tight budget and working their butts off. That doesn't work very often."

"Do you know someone who's up on fashion? I think I need to talk with an expert on the inner workings of the industry but who isn't connected with the case."

"I'll see who I can find for you."

After he hung up, Turner filled Fenwick in.

Fenwick said, "Beat cops said there was no one home at Kindel's address. Was he at the paper?"

"I didn't ask."

A quick call back to Ian confirmed Kindel's absence from the paper as well. Turner then called the three numbers on slips of paper in Furyk's wallet. One was an ice cream parlor on Belmont Avenue. One was a restaurant in the north suburbs. No one in either place remembered Cullom Furyk ever being there. The last number was for the penthouse at the Archange. Both Turner and Fenwick began filling in their Daily Major Incident Log.

Half an hour later Randy Carruthers bustled up to them. Randy was the curse of the Area Ten detectives. Their nickname for him was "Bratwurst" since he wore such tight clothes on his bulging frame. Of late, Turner was less inclined to be impatient with him. Carruthers had turned out to be far less homophobic than expected.

Fenwick, however, grumbled at the bejowled presence. Carruthers knew better than to try and set his butt on either of their desks.

Carruthers said, "You guys get all the best cases. All the reporters are calling. People care that Cullom Furyk is dead."

"You heard of him?" Turner asked.

"Sure. *People* magazine had a cover article on him. My girlfriend, Janice, thinks he's really cute. She buys me the clothes he modeled."

"In tent sizes?" Fenwick asked.

"I know I don't have a figure as svelte as yours," Carruthers said. This was a reference to Fenwick's ever-expanding bulk—a sensitive area to Fenwick and not one that Carruthers normally had the nerve to bring up. The young detective had been digging in his heels lately.

5 4

The new commander of Area Ten walked in. Lately, Drew Molton had been acting commander, but had just been given the top job in what Turner considered a long-overdue promotion.

At the sight of the commander, Carruthers wandered off in search of Harold Rodriguez, his partner.

"Anything good on this Furyk thing?" Molton asked. Molton felt quite comfortable plopping his butt on the edge of Fenwick's desk. The detective kept his mouth shut.

"Might have a suspect in a guy who says he was the lover," Turner said.

"I think we should shoot some of them," Fenwick said.

"You had Judge Cabestainey today, right?" Molton asked.

"Asshole judges need to be beaten with sticks after we shoot some of these fashion people."

"Problems?"

"Supercilious, snotty, self-important," Fenwick said.

"Judges or suspects?"

"Both."

"I got a call from the mayor's office on this one," Molton said. "The fashion industry in this town has grown into big business. Lots of prestige for the city along with lovely tax-paying companies. Jobs, upper-middle-class people moving into the city."

Fenwick snorted, "Bull pizzle! It's just a case."

Molton ignored him. "Plus the dead guy was involved in lots of good causes. I remember those pictures on the buses. Good-looking and a saint. Think Princess Diana. A crowd has gathered and people are already bringing flowers to the hotel to lay on the street."

"Give me a break," Fenwick said. "This gets no more attention than any other case."

"Gossip columnists from around the world and all the big-time tabloid newspapers and television shows have called. Remember what happened when Versace was killed."

"But that was connected to a high-profile spree killer," Fenwick said.

"Protest all you want, Buck, but I'm telling you, it's a big deal. I'm just giving you information. You've got an added dimension to the case."

Fenwick sighed. "I love information."

"We saw some photographers on our way in," Turner said.

"I'll check it out," Molton said. "Before today, I never knew that this was high-fashion season in Chicago, or so I have been informed by any number of overwrought gossip columnists. Every local television station has this death as their lead story."

"Always dreamed of being in a tabloid," Fenwick said.

"I can see the headline," Turner said. " 'Annoyed detective mows down snotty suspects.' "

"I like it," Fenwick said.

"I'll field calls from reporters," Molton said. "We may have to have a press conference or two."

"And my picture in the paper," Fenwick said. "If I'd known all this when I woke up, I'd have worn my good suit."

"You only have one suit," Turner said.

"And it's a good one."

With that, Molton sauntered off.

"I'll call the ME and see if she's got anything," Fenwick said.

"Not quite yet," Turner said. His gaze was fixed behind Fenwick on the entrance to the squad room.

Fenwick turned around. A woman stood at the top of the stairs surveying the room. She wore a purple floral dress, purple boots, a purple Naugahyde jacket, and carried a purple briefcase. Accompanying her was a man wearing a white cotton tank top, cotton jeans, and a deerskin jacket.

"I believe we have visitors," Turner said.

"We're looking for detectives Fenwick and Turner," the

woman announced. "I'm attorney Betty O'Dowd and this is my client, Mickey Spitzer."

Turner called them over. He didn't think he'd ever seen anyone with broader shoulders and a narrower waist than Spitzer. The face was more crags and lumps than handsome. The black eyebrows formed one continuous line. He looked to be in his late twenties or early thirties. His jacket was artfully open to show off the torso underneath.

O'Dowd continued. "My client would like to make a statement about the Cullom Furyk incident. My client may have information helpful to the case."

"Why wasn't he questioned at the hotel?" Turner asked. He wondered which beat cop had screwed up.

"Mr. Spitzer was not at the brunch. He had an important photo shoot this afternoon. There was no other time he could be there to work with the client. As soon as he was finished working, he phoned me. We hurried here immediately."

"Murder is more important than his goddamn pretty pictures," Fenwick barked.

"You want help or you want to complain?" O'Dowd asked.

"I think I'll complain for a while and see how I like it," Fenwick retorted.

Turner ushered them all into a conference room on the fourth floor. "What have you got for us?" he asked when they were all seated.

"My client has rented the penthouse on the west tower of the Archange Hotel for the week."

"The whole thing?" Fenwick asked.

"Yes, is that a problem?"

"Not yet," Fenwick murmured.

"Mr. Spitzer had them install some simple gym equipment," she said. "It is an amenity my client needs for his work. He must remain in top shape. The workout area was on the northeast side of the west tower. Because it was pleasant out today, he had them move it outside."

Both detectives were more than a bit interested.

O'Dowd said, "Mr. Furyk was walking on the top of the wall opposite. Mr. Spitzer saw Mr. Furyk pushed from the wall. He did not see clearly who did it. He believes it was a white male, but he is unable to be more precise than that."

"Definitely pushed?" Turner asked.

"Definitely," she said.

"Can't he answer?" Fenwick asked.

"He speaks very little English. Until a few years ago, he was a field worker outside his native Kiev." She spoke a few words in a foreign tongue to her client. He nodded at her. "I would be happy to have another translator work with him as long as I am present— that is, of course, unless you gentlemen speak Russian."

Neither detective accepted her challenge.

"What time was this?" Turner asked.

O'Dowd and Spitzer spoke together in Russian. "He isn't sure. He was working out for over two hours."

"The person wasn't wearing a white shirt with black pants?" Turner asked.

She spoke to Spitzer briefly. "He cannot be certain," she reported.

"He should have come to us with this information immediately," Fenwick said.

"But he didn't, and he is here now," O'Dowd said. "Perhaps he is suspicious of the police after what he grew up with in his native land. Perhaps he is still a bit of an ignorant peasant. Has the delay caused you material problems?"

Turner examined the man closely. Spitzer sat with his knees wide apart, thick hands resting easily on his knees. The model's eyes rarely left O'Dowd's face. Turner wondered if they were more than lawyer/client.

"There is a bit more, gentlemen," O'Dowd said. "Mickey saw Mr. Furyk on the balcony earlier doing the same balancing act."

"Let me get the sequence clear," Turner said. "He sees Furyk out there dancing on the parapet. Then there is a gap of what?"

"Over an hour and a half," O'Dowd said.

"And then he sees him again?"

"Yes."

"Other than the killer, did Mr. Spitzer see anyone else with Furyk at any time?" Turner asked

A brief translation.

"He wasn't paying particular attention. Before he saw him balancing the second time, Mr. Furyk kissed and hugged a man for five or ten minutes. That person left and two others came out to talk to him. He does not know who any of them were. He doubts if he'd recognize them."

None of the people they'd interviewed had admitted to going out to the balcony after dessert.

"The last two left. Furyk then proceeded to walk on top of the balcony. While there, Furyk twirled and twisted several times. Almost as if he were dancing."

"Yah," Spitzer said. "Dance." He spoke with a distinct foreign accent.

"He understands English?" Turner asked.

"Only somewhat. Then from another door a fourth person came out swiftly, rushed up from behind and shoved Cullom."

"Our witness says the person on the terrace watched Cullom fall."

More Russian.

"Quick," he said. "Very fast. Blink." His hands made a diving motion then he spoke rapidly in Russian.

O'Dowd translated. "He hardly knew where to look or what to do. He focused more on Cullom and the fall than anything else. He was horrified and shocked."

Fenwick said, "Okay, say I buy that your client sees the murder and is stunned beyond belief. Then his first thought is 'I've got a photo shoot to get to'? That sounds nuts to me. Why wouldn't his first thought be to call for help, or at least call the police?"

"We've covered that," O'Dowd said. "We are here now, and we are willing to cooperate."

"We'll want your client to look at pictures of those involved," Turner said.

"He will try his best, but it was over two hundred feet away. He was working out, not concentrating on the details of strangers. His workouts last several hours, and he exercises very vigorously. There could have been others out there who he missed. Some of his exercises require him to be lying on his workout bench."

"Wouldn't he know some of these people professionally?" Turner asked.

"The models, yes. The heads of the companies, probably. The designers, maybe. I'm sure there were others there. Press people and such. He could hardly be expected to know all of them personally. While the fashion world might be a reasonably closed society, my client doesn't run about memorizing the faces and names of every employee of every company. Not only that, this is his first trip to Chicago. You can hardly expect him to be an expert on the local scene."

"If he couldn't recognize the others, how can he be sure it was Cullom on the balcony?" Fenwick asked.

"You have another dead body in the street?" O'Dowd asked.

Turner asked, "Did your client know Cullom Furyk?"

More translation. "They have met at a few events. They were not close. Mickey is here to work the runway for Heyling and Veleshki."

"Did they ever have sex?" Turner asked.

O'Dowd didn't even translate. "No," she said.

"Ask your client, please," Turner directed.

There was a brief colloquy in Russian, then an abrupt, "No," from Spitzer.

Turner and Fenwick promised to assemble photographs of the people in the east tower penthouse for Spitzer to look over. "We'll bring them to the penthouse as soon as we can," Turner said. "Possibly late this afternoon."

"Impossible. Mickey has a full schedule for this afternoon and this evening. Right now he should be having his afternoon vegetables and his nap."

"He's a witness in a murder case," Fenwick said.

"Perhaps we can spare a little time. We might be able to find someplace quick nearby with the quality of food Mickey needs and then come back."

Fenwick reached in his desk and pulled out a copy of Millie's take-out menu. "Here," Fenwick said. "I recommend this restaurant highly."

Turner said, "It will take us a while to assemble the pictures. If he could be available to us later on, that would be very helpful."

Back at their desks Fenwick said, "He can afford the whole penthouse? This modeling crap has got to be more lucrative than I thought. Guess it isn't just scrawny women wearing silly dresses."

"I always thought it was, although some of the men are really hot."

"That part I haven't noticed," Fenwick said. "Skinny women have never been my thing."

"I hope Ian can come up with someone for us to talk to about the fashion industry. I feel a little lost. We better get somebody assembling pictures for Spitzer to look at. I'll send a uniform over to Munsen. We'll start there and maybe the newspaper to see if they have photos of these people."

Detectives Joe Roosevelt and Judy Wilson strutted in. As they swung by Turner and Fenwick, Joe thumped Fenwick on the back.

"We got a three-bagger." Joe was almost dancing in his exultation. Joe had short, brush-cut gray hair and bad teeth. Judy rolled her chair close to Turner's desk and put her feet up on his paperwork. Judy was an African-American woman with a pleasant smile. They had a well-deserved reputation as one of the most effective pairs of detectives on the force but it was more common to see them squabbling than celebrating.

"A three-bagger?" Fenwick said. "This I gotta see."

"Our little threesome is downstairs even as we speak, being processed," Joe said. "We shall join them momentarily. We wanted you to see what successful detectives look like."

"You got confessions?" Fenwick asked.

"We got everything," Judy said. "We have witnesses. We have weapons. We have fingerprints. We have two out of three of our suspects babbling merrily away. Hell, we may even solve the disappearance of Amelia Earhart."

"How?" Fenwick asked.

Roosevelt said, "We're the cutest and most competent couple on the block."

"If Turner dumped you," Wilson said to Fenwick, "he and anybody else could come in second in the cute couple race. We hear Ashley and Dwayne are jealous of you two."

"They're jealous," Fenwick said, "because we're cuter than they are."

Wilson appraised Fenwick's bulk. "I wouldn't go that far. Those two want all the headlines, glamour, and glory of being a detective in the city of Chicago."

They all burst out laughing.

"They can have all my headlines," Turner said. "Past and future."

"I want to keep mine," Fenwick said. "They can get their own damn press."

"They could hire a press agent," Wilson said. "I'm sure the superintendent would love to hear that."

"I'll suggest it to them," Fenwick said. "I don't think they're that stupid, but we could hope."

Roosevelt said, "Somebody said you got a victim who had an argument with the pavement."

"Flat and squishy," Fenwick said.

"I hear it was some fashion model who was drop-dead gorgeous," Wilson said.

"Don't start," Fenwick warned.

"Those jumper cases are such a downer," Wilson said.

"Doesn't anybody have any fresh humor?" Fenwick asked.

"Don't let it get you down," Roosevelt said.

Wilson added, "It's the kind of case that can drive a detective over the edge."

Fenwick growled, "The commander thinks it's a big deal."

"He's probably getting edgy," Wilson said.

"Up yours," Fenwick snapped. "Don't you have paperwork to do, criminals to harass?"

"We're trying to come up with a concrete solution," Turner said.

"You too?" Fenwick asked.

Roosevelt and Wilson sauntered off.

Fenwick said, "The first person who says anything about jumping to conclusions gets shot."

Turner pulled out the maps of the penthouse the uniforms had used to record the movements of each person. At the top of each page was the name of the suspect, the rooms he or she was in, and the approximate times he or she was in them. He said, "The only one who admits to being on the terrace at any time is Daniel Egremont."

"Maybe if we threw one of them off the balcony, the rest would confess."

"I thought you were into shooting people today."

"Whatever it takes."

Turner said, "We're going to need to set up a chart so that we can be sure who can back up each person's story and who has no one to provide an alibi."

"And who can lie for whom," Fenwick said.

"Grammatically correct and sensitive," Turner said. Before Fenwick could reply, he added, "We should try finding these catering people."

"Let's stop at the ME's office first," Fenwick said. "A few dead bodies might cheer me up. We can set the chart up afterward."

EIGHT

The mid-afternoon temperature was close to fifty and a gentle breeze eased through the canyons of the south Loop. Fenwick's usual wild driving, however, could cause them to arrive at Cook County Morgue in a hearse rather than their unmarked car.

As they drove, Turner asked, "How much of Spitzer's story did you buy?"

"About as much as I believe any of these people, which means none of it, yet. I want observations confirmed. I want identifications made."

"We need to talk to all those people again."

They arrived at the stainless-steel examination room. Pieces of Cullom Furyk filled several tables.

"Don't say it," Turner said.

"You're stifling my creativity," Fenwick said.

The ME grumbled, "Get your stifled ass over here."

An assistant ME Turner had never seen before said, "Don't say what?"

Turner and the ME groaned. Fenwick grinned, swept his hand indicating all that was left of Cullom Furyk, and said, "That's him all over. The guy had a lot of guts."

Turner said, "It's not the fall, it's the landing."

"*Et tu,* Turner," the ME said. She turned to her assistant and said, "It is never a good idea to encourage a Chicago police detective, but absolutely never, ever encourage Detective Fenwick. He thinks he's funny." She turned to Fenwick. "If you were Rose Nylund, I'd hit you with a newspaper."

Turner muttered, "Do it anyway. Maybe he'll stop."

The assistant asked, "Who's Rose Nylund?"

"Can we get on with the autopsy?" the ME asked.

Turner said, "We've got witnesses who say he was pushed. Any way to confirm it wasn't suicide?"

"I can confirm that he was not dead when he fell. I can't tell what made him fall. Pushed or jumped? I have no idea. Nor can I rule out him simply being a moronic twit who slipped while he was being silly."

"Heck of a price to pay for goofing around," Turner said.

Fenwick said, "I can think of several million safer ways of taking nutty chances."

The ME continued, "As far as I can see, this was not drug related, but I'll need to get lab results before I can say for sure."

"Didn't I read a lot about the fashion industry and heroin?" Fenwick said.

"The heroin look," the young assistant said.

They all gazed at her expectantly. She explained, "Thin, scrawny, as if they were addicts."

"I thought they were always thin and scrawny," Fenwick said.

"I guess this was thinner and scrawnier."

"Or maybe somebody was making a claim about drug abuse to

get headlines," Turner said. "Wouldn't be the first time that happened."

"We'll check for heroin," the ME said. She examined several body parts. "No track marks on the left arm. I'll try to piece together the other one."

"Anything else?"

"The collision with the pole on his way down killed him. A detailed report is going to take us a little while with this mess. I'll get you a set of complete findings by tomorrow morning at the latest."

The first address they had for the catering crew was on Milwaukee Avenue just north of Grand Avenue. Ken Slatter was a short man who opened the door of his second-floor flat as far as the security chain allowed and never opened it another inch. His story was simple. He worked hard. He seldom talked with anyone else on the crew. He knew nothing.

Back in the car Fenwick declared, "I trust him."

"Why?"

"Because he was wearing a T-shirt with holes in it and dumpy jeans. No fashion crap."

"Wearing fashion crap is an actionable offense?"

"I'd like at least one of these people to have a zit."

"*Zitless in Chicago?*"

Fenwick grunted.

Turner said, "I'm sure these fashion people are kind to their parents, pet cute puppies, and rescue babies."

"I'll have to be convinced of that."

The second address at Willow and Howe didn't answer. The third address was over a restaurant on the west side of Clark Street just south of Wellington Avenue.

They buzzed the intercom on the wall next to the street-level door.

"Yeah."

"Gordon Findley?"

"Yeah."

"Police. We've got a few questions."

"What about?"

"We're not having a conversation like this, Mr. Findley," Fenwick said. "We need to talk."

The buzzer buzzed.

The narrow steps creaked louder than in a horror movie. The irises and daffodils on the wallpaper had turned to a uniform dull gray with age. The carpet on the creaking risers was bare in spots. The door on the right at the top of the stairs was open. A man in his mid to late twenties looked out at them. His white shirt draped outside his black pants. He hadn't changed his clothes from the catering job. They showed him their IDs.

"You Gordon Findley?" Fenwick asked.

The man nodded. His short brown hair stuck up in several places as if he'd awakened from a nap ten minutes ago. He was about five feet five and slender with well-defined muscles. He had a bowl of cereal in his hands.

"Come on in."

The apartment continued the decorating scheme begun in the hall. Faded flowers on the wallpaper, threadbare carpet. A table with two chairs in the kitchen to the right. To the left a wood-frame couch with flattened cushions. Findley poured some more milk into his bowl. "What's this about?" he asked.

"Cullom Furyk is dead," Turner said.

Findley gaped at them a moment. His eyes searched each of their faces. "This isn't a joke?"

"No," Turner said.

The plastic milk carton slipped out of his hands and Findley flung the bowl at the wall. "No!" he screamed. He began pounding his fists against the wall.

"Hey," Turner said. He put his hand on Findley's shoulder. The man didn't seem to notice the touch. He slowly slid to the floor. He pounded his fists on the floor. He missed the cereal debris by a few inches.

Turner and Fenwick looked at each other. Turner squatted down next to Findley. He righted the now nearly empty milk carton. He placed a gentle hand on Findley's wrist and said, "I'm sorry for your loss. You must have been close to him."

After several minutes Findley's sobs abated. Eventually he wiped his nose on his sleeve and snuffled. "What happened?"

"That's what we need you to tell us."

"I saw him at the Archange Hotel this morning. He was fine."

"He fell from the terrace wall of the penthouse," Turner said.

"My God!"

Avoiding the breakfast mess, Turner sat on the floor. He crossed his legs in a lotus position. Fenwick pulled over a kitchen chair. He leaned over and placed his left elbow on his knee and his left hand under his chin.

"How well did you know Furyk?" Turner asked.

"I can't believe he's dead. I've known him for years. We went to high school together. He was, we were . . . friends."

"Boyfriends?" Turner asked.

Findley eyed them warily. "Am I going to be treated differently by the cops because I'm gay?"

"No," Turner said. "We just need your help."

"I'm a little afraid of cops."

Turner asked, "What can I say to ease your fear?"

Findley wiped his nose and looked at Turner carefully. "For a long time he and I have been very close. No one knew him as well as I did. Okay, I guess, yeah, years ago we were boyfriends."

"Were you having a relationship with him now?" Turner asked.

"No. I was infatuated with him in high school. He was so pretty and kind, but I was more of a convenience for him. If he had nobody else to go out with, he'd call me. He was my first crush. After the first year or so, our relationship wasn't physical, but he would talk to me about all his conquests. I couldn't have him, but I could live his life vicariously."

"He had a lot of conquests?" Turner asked.

"I think he started having sex with the other babies in the hospital when he was born. He just had a natural way of attracting people. I know he bragged about one of his biggest moments being when he got the star of the high school basketball team to go down on him, which was the night after he got the same guy's girlfriend to go down on him."

"Did they know about each other?" Fenwick asked.

"Cullom said they didn't. He thought it was funny."

"He had sex with women?" Turner asked.

"Mostly he told me about guys he'd been with, rarely girls. But if it was breathing and it tickled his fancy, he screwed it. While he was in high school, he had sex with at least three of his teachers. Once he told me he went back and had sex with one of his junior high teachers. Sex was like a game to him. Or at least the seduction. Like the triumph of adding another notch to his gun. He was into being able to get someone to have sex with him and then drop them before they rejected him."

"Wasn't just being another conquest demeaning to you?"

"At the time I didn't think in those terms. I was young, horny, lonely, and in love. I remember clearly the second or third time after we had sex, I told him I loved him. He patted my head and said he'd been with six other guys that week. I was very depressed. I thought about suicide."

"You didn't break up with him?" Turner asked.

"People wanted to hang around Cullom. Be close to him. He could be very coaxing, and he was always playful. He never took things seriously. He never planned things. Like in *Casablanca* early in the movie when Rick rejects Yvonne. That was Cullom. He fell into that fashion contest which got him the contract with GUINEVERE. He just happened to be with some friends downtown."

"Have you known him well in the past few years?" Turner asked.

"When he'd come back to town, we'd get together. He'd talk about all the famous people he knew and who he'd been to bed with. I liked hearing him talk about them. He had lovers all over the world, and sex in all kinds of exotic locations. It was my connection with celebrity. Probably the closest I'm ever going to get to being famous. He claimed to have had sex with all the young male actors on one of those hip shows that got canceled."

"Did he talk about his causes?"

"Once in a while. He laughed about them sometimes. I never thought he was serious about them."

"Someone said they saw Furyk with his tongue down the throat of one of the caterers today. Was that you?"

"No . . . I . . . Wait a minute." Findley sat up straighter. He snuffled. Turner took a hand towel off the table and handed it to him. Findley used it to clean his face. "This is for sure? He was seen kissing? He wasn't very versatile in his sex. With him it wasn't a question of unsafe as much as it was that he thought it was boring. I only tried to kiss him once, but he turned his head away."

Turner said, "Maybe his repertoire expanded some since you had sex with him."

"It had to be that slut Larry Bitner."

Turner looked at his list. The name was next.

"Did Bitner know Cullom prior to this?"

"I doubt it. Bitner was born on some farm in Wisconsin. Just two months ago he moved to Chicago to be gay. I met him at a volunteer meeting for an AIDS hospice. I liked Larry and I helped him get a job with the caterer. He was awed to be at the fashion party today. He thought it was a big deal because he wanted to be a model too."

"You didn't see them together?" Turner asked.

"No."

"Did you notice when Furyk left the table?"

"No."

"Did you go out on the balcony after dessert?"

"Nope. I did my work, cleaned up, and got out of there."

"Do you work for the caterer full-time?" Turner asked.

"Part-time. Mostly I go to auditions, and I'm trying to write a screenplay, and I do a little modeling."

Fenwick asked, "Was it a coincidence that you were there today?"

"I asked to work all the fashion events that the company was catering this week. Any little in helps, I think."

"When was the last time you saw Furyk before today?" Turner asked.

"We had lunch just before he left for his vacation in Greece."

"Do you know where he was staying?"

"He wasn't staying at the penthouse?"

"Not according to the people at GUINEVERE."

"I just assumed he was."

"Did you talk to him today?"

"We just said hello."

"That's all?"

"I was working. He was busy."

"Did you know he and Sean Kindel were lovers?"

"Who?"

"A guy who writes for the *Gay Tribune*."

"Never heard of him. Cullom never mentioned him."

"He would have told you about a lover?"

"Definitely. He told me everything."

Turner took out a sketch of the penthouse. He'd run off extra copies so that when they questioned people, he could quickly fill in any new details. He added the times and places of Findley's movements.

In the car Fenwick said, "Sluts to the right of me, sluts to the left of me, sluts in front of me nymphed and fanarked all through the park."

"The rhyme scheme sort of works," Turner said, "but the last part makes no sense."

"It's poetry. It's sensitive."

"That's okay, then," Turner said. "I wonder if all those sexual exploits were true. Maybe he exaggerated his conquests to impress people."

"We'll have to ask," Fenwick said.

"Let's find Larry the slut."

At the address on Waveland Avenue just west of Wrigley Field, they got no answer.

Outside of Area Ten three blue-uniformed officers stood in front of fifteen or twenty reporters and photographers. Turner could hear an argument going on about First Amendment rights. The officer responding kept his voice low and calm.

At his desk, Turner had a message from Ian to call. Fenwick went in search of a large piece of paper to make a chart of the movements of all the people in the penthouse.

Turner called Ian at the *Gay Tribune*.

Ian said, "I found somebody. He knows everything. He's one of the fashion columnists for *Gorgeous* magazine."

"We met the owner and editor."

"This guy hates her. The traditionally disgruntled employee. He's ready to blab anything about her, the magazine, or the fashion industry to you. He knows dirt and gossip that he can't wait to spill."

"How well do you know this guy?"

"I've helped him on a few juicy stories in the past."

"I realize what a fine, upstanding journalist you are. However, my suspicious-cop nature tells me you might really be helping so you can get an exclusive story out of this."

"I'm not sure how interested I am in this murder. It does have a gay angle, but it's the fashion industry."

"Guy's just as dead no matter what his job was."

"Lots of dead people I don't care about. For now this is another one on that list. I care enough to help you because you're a friend. Yeah, if I get an exclusive, I'll run with it, just maybe not very far."

"When do I talk to your source?"

"That's the thing. The whole fashion industry in this town is nuts this week with the showing of the summer and fall lines. Lots of big events all over town every day. There's a fancy ball tonight doubling as an AIDS fund-raiser. This guy is willing to talk to you there. He could also point out people and explain relationships and connections to you."

"Excellent." Turner thought a moment. "I have nothing to wear to any kind of fashion extravaganza, nor am I going out to purchase anything. In fact, I'm not sure I can go tonight. I was planning to spend time with Jeff. I won't break a promise to him."

"Bring him along."

"Are you serious?"

"Sure. This is the fashion industry. Everybody will dress outrageously although I hear it's a construction worker theme. No one will know who you are, so what do you care what they think of you? And it's a fund-raiser. It won't look odd to have the kids there. Both of your kids might get a kick out of it."

"Maybe. I hope Ben can go. It might be kind of fun for him, but he's been staying late at work every night lately. They just switched the whole operation over to computers. They've had a lot of glitches. So," he continued, "this guy can get us that many extra tickets on such short notice?"

"Tonight's soiree is at that new Midwest Trade Center."

"I thought that wasn't finished yet."

"Even in the state it's in, you could fit half the town in there. I gave him yours and Fenwick's description. He'll find you. If you want Brian to go, just mention the name Sibilla Manetti and tell him that she'll be there."

"Who?"

"Trust me. Mention her. He'll want to go."

Turner hung up and told Fenwick the news.

"Madge will want to go," Fenwick said.

"On such short notice?"

"It's just as short for you and Ben."

"Yeah."

"I better call her. Ian's buddy can get all of us in?"

"He didn't seem to think it mattered how many of us wanted to show up. Who's Sibilla Manetti?"

"Who?"

"That's what I said. Ian told me to mention her to Brian, and he would want to go."

"Never heard of her."

Commander Molton approached them and asked for an update. After Turner filled him in, Molton said, "Be sure not to jump to conclusions."

Fenwick gaped at him. Commanders could say what they wished without fear of being shot.

Molton gave them a half smile. "I've been hanging around you too long, Buck. I'll get you overtime for tonight. You shouldn't have to go without getting paid."

Fenwick called Madge while Turner called Ben. Turner explained the circumstances to Ben, then said, "Can you or do you want to leave your computer for this kind of thing?"

"You're suggesting an evening in a mob of overdressed people smiling hypocritically at each other instead of pounding on this goddamn keyboard? Tempting as that is, I can't. This computer is driving me nuts. I had angry customers in here all day over mistakes. We almost replaced somebody's head gasket, and he only came in for an oil change. Remember, you promised Jeff the evening with just the two of you."

"I know. I hope he thinks this will be fun. It's tough to find him a sitter on short notice. I don't want to ask Brian and Mrs. Talucci isn't due back yet."

Rose Talucci was Turner and Ben's ninety–something next-door neighbor who had been a surrogate mother to Paul's children. She was used to Paul's erratic schedule and often stepped in if Paul had to work. She'd been diagnosed with cancer several months before. She hated the gatherings of over-emotional relatives and had begun taking numerous overseas trips to give herself some relief. At the moment she was in the Outback of Australia with one of her nieces.

"Do you and the boys have the right clothes to wear?" Ben asked.

"Ian says it doesn't matter."

"Yeah, as if he were a judge of what is fashionable." The relationship between Ian and Ben was cool at best. "No chance anybody will get shot at or involved in any police activity?"

"Only if they're lucky."

"What time do you think you'll be home?"

"It's a school night so it can't be that late."

He told Ben he loved him and hung up. Turner found Fenwick examining the large sheet of paper onto which they would chart the suspects' movements.

"Madge coming?" Turner asked.

"She's in the shower as we speak."

Fenwick rattled the paper and tried putting it down on the top of his desk. He began moving debris out from underneath and stacking it on the floor.

"Shouldn't we be able to make this chart on a spreadsheet on a computer?" Turner asked.

"Yeah," Fenwick said, "I'll put it on a spreadsheet the day after Judge Cabestainey apologizes for being a moronic twit."

Turner wasn't confident enough of his computer skills to give it a try either. For an hour they worked on the chart. Down the left side of the paper they placed everyone's name they had so far. Then they put the time in five-minute intervals along the top. They started from when Munsen claimed Cullom showed up to the moment the detectives arrived in the suite. They worked from their own notes, and the maps the beat cops had compiled. They were only half finished when they needed to pick up their respective family members for the fund-raiser.

N I N E

Paul Turner drove up to his house just off Taylor Street. Jeff was playing a game of chess with the computer in the living room. Paul gave his eleven-year-old a hug.

"Brian's looking for you, Dad," Jeff said. "He wants to go camping again."

Brian sauntered in. "You blabbed." He thumped his middle finger against his younger brother's head.

Jeff swatted at his brother. "Hey, stop that." He swung his wheelchair around. "I'll delete your homework from the computer if you don't quit it."

"Both of you stop," Paul ordered. "Do you guys want to go with me to a fund-raiser at the Midwest Trade Center tonight? I need to go as part of a case I'm working on."

"Can we help investigate?" Jeff asked.

"No."

"Do I have to take another bath?" Jeff asked.

"No."

"Is it going to be one of those boring, dress-up, society things?" Brian asked.

"It might be fun for you guys to go. A lot of famous people might be there."

"Like who?" Jeff asked.

"The mayor and the governor."

"Pooh, who cares?" Jeff asked.

"Ian said you might recognize the name Sibilla Manetti," Paul said.

"Who?" Jeff asked.

"Is she really going to be there?" Brian asked. "She's the hottest model in the world today."

"You know who she is?" Paul asked.

"She was in an article I read," Brian said.

"He's looking at dirty pictures," Jeff accused.

"How would you know?" Brian asked.

Lately the two boys had been having more quarrels than usual. Paul thought it might stem from the fact that as Jeff got older, he was more irritated when he felt that he had fewer choices than his older brother. Paul sometimes wondered what form Jeff's teenage rebellion would take. Living with spina bifida was difficult. Being a teenager, he suspected, added a whole other dimension.

Before their squabble could escalate, Paul said, "Let's make this easy. Who wants to go?"

"Me," Brian said.

"Me, too," Jeff said. Jeff was still in the stage where, if his older brother wanted to do something, Jeff wanted to do it too.

"It's a school night," Paul said, "so you won't be out late."

"My homework's done," both boys chorused.

"What am I going to wear, Dad?" Jeff asked.

"I'll help you pick something out after we eat," Turner said.

★   ★   ★

An hour and a half later, they were on their way to the Midwest Trade Center. Brian wore a yellow paisley acetate-cotton suit, blue cotton dress shirt, red leather double-wrap belt, and leather high-top sneakers. The clothes looked excellent on his athletic frame. Jeff wore his dark gray dress suit. Paul wore his work clothes— dark blue blazer, light blue shirt, stripped gray and blue tie, gray pants, black shoes, and a tan overcoat.

Brian drove their van. At the stoplight at Harrison and Halsted he looked at Paul critically. "You know, Dad, I would have lent you some of my clothes to wear tonight. You don't always have to look like a detective."

"I like the way Dad looks," Jeff said from the backseat.

"I feel comfortable in this," Paul said.

"You always dress so boring," Brian said.

"That's what I like," Paul said, "boring. It fits my lifestyle."

Brian gave a muted teenaged martyr sigh. Moments later they arrived at the edifice along the west bank of the north branch of the Chicago River at Kinzie Street.

Immediately inside the door was a reception area where they found tickets and the head of security waiting for them.

"Thanks for calling ahead," the security guard said. "You're not expecting any trouble?"

"No. Just part of an investigation. We'll be talking to a few people."

"Heck of a crowd," the security guard said. "These rich folks are pretty quiet, although you have to watch the silverware. Lot of weird outfits, though. Your partner is waiting for you over there."

Turner spotted Fenwick and Madge about thirty feet away. Madge hugged all three of them. Buck was wearing a tuxedo.

"Cool, Mr. Fenwick," Brian said. "Where'd you get the out-fit?"

Fenwick blushed. The cut of the formal wear enveloped his ample form perfectly. The bow tie was knotted precisely.

"I thought you only had one good suit," Turner said.

"He's too embarrassed to tell you," Madge said. "He owns the tux. He always dresses nice for formal events. He has a closet so full of chic clothes that he keeps a tailor in the neighborhood busy letting them out." She wore a long dark-blue evening gown with a simple star brooch close to her left shoulder.

Fenwick grumbled, "Gruff-hick act exposed by nattering wife."

Madge whapped him on the shoulder with her beaded clutch. "I'll natter this up your butt if you make any more cracks like that."

"I didn't like it the first time," Fenwick said.

"Hush, there are children present, Buck." But she smiled and put her hand through his arm and together moved forward with the others.

With Paul pushing Jeff's wheelchair, they entered a vast concourse that stretched forward for longer than a football field and up ten stories. The owners had wanted a building to rival both the Merchandise Mart and the Apparel Center. There were immense skylights overhead and each floor had a balcony around its perimeter. The floors and walls were all gray marble. The interior had been converted to a tropical setting with real palm trees in large buckets, tiki torches, and an ocean of sand. A multitude was crammed into this ground-floor space and Turner could see people lining the balconies for at least four stories. At the entrance they were offered hard hats. Jeff and Madge accepted them.

As they walked in, Demi Moore and her bodyguards swept by. All the caterers were wearing hard hats, tight jeans, work belts with tools in them, and flannel shirts with the sleeves ripped off. A stage had been set up in the middle of the concourse.

"Where is our contact?" Fenwick asked.

"Is that Sibilla Manetti?" Madge asked.

"Where?" Brian asked.

Madge pointed.

"I think it is," Brian said. "Wow."

A man over six feet tall with a huge belly walked over to them. He was wearing a white tuxedo, a black shirt, and a pink bow tie. He might have been in his early fifties. With him was a slender man in his mid-twenties who was wearing a navy wool-silk suit, a cotton honeycomb-weave French-cuffed shirt, a paisley silk tie, and Hush Puppies. "Mr. Turner?" the older man inquired. "I'm Arthur Oldinport, Ian's friend. This is my assistant, Battle."

Turner introduced them all. "Where can we talk?" Turner asked.

"I've secured a place. My assistant will see to it that your guests are comfortable."

They left Madge and the two boys to the party and the assistant, Battle. Turner, Fenwick, and Oldinport took an elevator up to the partially finished seventh floor. Scattered about were two-by-fours, sawdust, and construction tools. Exposed electrical wires hung from undone outlets. They stood at the balcony railing.

"Ian asked if I would give you some background information on the fashion industry," Oldinport said.

"Yeah," Fenwick said. "The whole thing is foreign to me."

"I know," Oldinport said. He glanced at their outfits. He did everything but sniff.

"You know all these folks?" Fenwick asked.

"If not all, most."

"They all as snotty as you?"

"If not all, most."

Fenwick laughed. "I don't think I like you."

Oldinport gave him a thin smile. "How lucky for me. If you'd like a good overview of the industry, why don't you pick up the latest issues of the major fashion magazines? That might give you a start."

"We'll give that a try," Turner said. "We need to know as much background as you can tell us on these two companies and on Cullom Furyk in particular. Any insights you can give into the people who were at the brunch today at the Archange would be helpful."

"The rumor is rife throughout the crowd that somebody pushed the young man, and that it had to be one of the people at the party. All the gossip papers are going to be printing it. If your identities as detectives became known to the crowd here, you could be swamped by some of the lowest and most aggressive journalists in the country. More likely they'd try and get you off by yourselves to get an exclusive. These are the kind of people who sneak in to take pictures of the corpse at funerals of famous people."

"Maybe that's what I could do when I retire," Fenwick said. "Find the people taking pictures at funerals. They could be used as traffic-safety bumps near busy expressway exits."

"Did you know Furyk?" Turner asked.

"Everyone among the elite of the fashion world knows everyone else to some degree. I had met the young man. He was very attractive and very shallow, two helpful commodities in a model."

"I understand why it helps to be good-looking," Turner said, "but why shallow?"

"You don't want them asking too many questions. The models are there to wear your clothes and make you and your product look good. A lot of brains can easily lead to a lot of attitude."

"We heard he was a sexual athlete."

"Hardly a secret. You've got to understand that all those gossip columns, magazines, and cable television shows depicting models partying the days and nights away are somewhat true."

"Haven't caught the shows," Fenwick said. "Don't read the columns or the magazines. Didn't care before now. Don't know how much I care now. Unless it has something to do with catching a murderer."

"Perhaps it will. Let me give you some background on a model's lifestyle. The men might be perceived to be gay, but their persona, especially on the runway, has to be hyper-masculine. Same in the print ads. They have to look butch. Swish and drag are totally out. Also, the men tend to look hot on or off the runway. While the women are usually gorgeous on stage, they're kind of ratty-looking off. In this world there's a lot to turn a naive boy's or girl's head. The model's life is the epitome of the fast lane. Yet, much of the time they are struggling to just get by. Mostly they are young and foolish."

"Which is the best time for that combination," Fenwick said.

"Cullom was as sensible and as foolish as any other model. He didn't stand out as outrageous or not outrageous. As for his sexual contacts, which everyone focuses on, yes, he had lots. I know he went to bed with all the male stars of the three top-grossing movies several years ago."

"You know?" Fenwick asked.

"Yes."

"How do you know?"

"I've been to bed with people who've been to bed with people who know people who know."

"Just as good as being there," Fenwick said.

Turner forbore asking for specifics. If it turned out to be important, he could ask later.

Oldinport continued, "At the Academy Awards one year, Cullom was smitten with one of the dancers in one of those interminable show numbers. By dawn Cullom was in bed with him. Perhaps more relevant to your investigation, he also had an affair with Gerald Veleshki."

"We thought that was a big secret," Fenwick said.

"Not in this town. He also had sex with women. Sibilla Manetti for sure. Jolanda Bokaru had a brief fling with him."

"But he was gay?"

"As far as I know."

"That didn't hold him back?"

"The fashion industry itself is not terribly homophobic," Old-inport said, "but it's the old story. The advertisers. A model can pick up millions in endorsements, but many advertisers still have huge problems with any kind of identification with something or someone gay."

Fenwick said, "Furyk was supposed to be rich and had lots of endorsements. How would anyone know he was gay?"

"Tabloid journalism, of course."

"I knew that," Fenwick said.

"So everyone knew he was gay?" Turner asked.

"Yes and no. Cullom was lucky that he had an exclusive deal with GUINEVERE. Franklin Munsen didn't particularly care about Cullom's sexuality. Cullom was a household name and image long before anything came out about who he went to bed with. All that was required was a well-publicized public appearance with Sibilla and rumors were quashed."

Turner asked, "He would willingly agree to public deception about his sexual orientation?"

"Perhaps it is more accurate to say that he was complicitly silent. You let the public assume what it wishes without comment."

"How about him and Mickey Spitzer?"

"I don't care for the Russian peasant very much. He and Ms. O'Dowd are an item. In spite of Mr. Spitzer being caught in a compromising position with Mr. Furyk, Ms. O'Dowd was quite forgiving."

"Spitzer is gay?"

"I have no idea. That Spitzer and Furyk had sex does not mean they liked each other or even knew each other that well. That they did not continue to have sex does not mean they disliked each other. Ms. O'Dowd was not Furyk's agent. She was and remains Spitzer's. You'd have to ask them the inner workings of their relationship to find out if hatreds existed, and if they were deep enough to cause murder."

"Neither of them was at the brunch," Turner observed.

"What kind of guy is Daniel Egremont?" Fenwick asked.

"An honest accountant. Hardly the kind of person to commit murder."

"Eliot Norwyn?" Fenwick asked.

"A severely closeted young man. He would like everyone to believe he is straight. Sometimes I believe he even convinces himself. His affair with Mr. Furyk was the talk of the modeling world for quite a while."

"Casual sex and lots of gossip," Fenwick observed. "Almost as good as hot chocolate poured over raw cookie dough. What's not to like? Although I imagine people could get sick of it pretty quick."

"All the males in the fashion industry are not whores," Oldinport said. "Nor can they snap their fingers and have sex with anyone they want."

Fenwick said, "I thought the whole point of the operation was that they were supposed to look sexy so people buy the clothes they wear."

Oldinport raised an eyebrow. "Looking sexy equals sexual promiscuity?"

"All the world thinks it does," Fenwick said.

"The world can think whatever it wishes. There is as much or as little heartache and passion in the fashion industry as there is in the rest of the world. The models are able to handle it as well or as poorly as any other celebrity."

"Was Furyk able to handle it?"

"I can't say. I didn't know him personally."

"You suggested we read fashion magazines," Turner said.

"How much accurate information will we really find there?"

Oldinport shrugged. "For all its gossip and silliness, the fashion world is basically a business world. For example, gay or straight, after a celebrity appearance in a major city, rumors abound the next day about them appearing hither and thither with or without some young lovely who they may or may not be married to. How true are the rumors? Who knows?"

"What background can you give us about the two companies?"

"Both started out in Chicago. They have been fierce competitors for years. They would do anything to cut the throat of the other. Sabotage. Bald-face lying. Stealing designs or designers. Putting out false press releases, putting out inaccurate information about each other's companies."

"We heard one of them was going broke," Turner said.

"Yes, that rumor would be about Heyling and Veleshki. The two of them started with Mr. Heyling's winnings from the Illinois lottery. He won a million a year for twenty years. He discovered that it wasn't enough to keep them going."

"They weren't earning profits?"

"Some years both companies did, some neither."

"Will Heyling and Veleshki go broke?" Turner asked.

"Heyling's due another check next week. It won't be enough unless he gets another source of funding."

"And GUINEVERE is in good shape?"

"They have to put on a good face because it is a publicly held company. My sources say their financial picture is probably not as rosy as they would like everyone to believe."

"What kind of money are we talking about here?" Turner asked.

"There are companies in the industry with revenues of over a billion dollars. Some earn over a hundred million before taxes. As with any company you can have record revenue, but if you have record expenses, you're in trouble whether you sell couture fashions or used briefs. If you invest in their stocks, some go up, some down. It can be a volatile business."

"These guys in Chicago have revenues of over a billion?" Fenwick asked.

"I certainly doubt it, but over a hundred million at least. I do not have access to their books. Do you really need that to solve the murder?"

"I hope not," Fenwick said, "math gives me a headache."

"What can you tell us about Jolanda Bokaru and *Gorgeous* magazine?" Turner asked.

"A great deal. As I am sure Ian told you, I work for her. I am not happy doing so. I love the job, but I hate the boss. Jolanda thinks she's important. In this town, she probably is. She is not anywhere else. She is generally ignored by the rest of the fashion world and this annoys her a great deal. Jolanda is excellent at self-promotion. She gets more ink for less substance than anyone I know. Where she got her money to start the magazine is kind of murky. She is rumored to have had a torrid affair with a famous drug dealer many years ago."

"What about this heroin look?" Fenwick asked. "How prevalent are drugs in this industry?"

"The hysteria of the so-called heroin look is equivalent to the set-to about the models in some of those jeans ads a few years ago. Some congressmen made a huge stink and grabbed a lot of headlines about the fashion industry using underage kids to be sexual or to encourage sexuality, or whatever puritanical balderdash they were trying to peddle. You had to look closely months later to see the tiny headlines on the articles saying that all the models were of age. That kind of hysteria makes the religious zealots and their congressional lackeys feel superior.

"You've got public pressure in being a police officer. Are there alcoholics and drug addicts in your line of work? Of course. Are there in this line of work? Of course. Is it an epidemic? No. Are the people you are concerned with involved in some kind of drug cabal? I certainly have heard of no such thing. The Chicago fashion industry is a group of terrifically hardworking wannabes. They have no time for drugs."

"No drugs?" Fenwick summed up.

"Not enough to cause murder," Oldinport said.

For a few moments they scrutinized the crowd far below.

"Who are all these people?" Fenwick asked.

"The rich, the famous, the beautiful, the desperate, the ones who have nothing better to do with their lives. There are also hardworking designers, fashion consultants, agents, choreographers, pattern cutters, pattern makers. Some have dual roles. For instance, Franklin Munsen owns the business and is also one of the principle designers."

"What about at Heyling and Veleshki?"

"Heyling does most of the designing there."

"Why is it called GUINEVERE?" Turner asked.

"Munsen had a daughter who never left the hospital after she was born. He named the company after her and put it all in caps as a memorial."

Turner nodded. He well knew the fears of losing a child, Jeff fortunately surviving his birth defect.

"He's straight?" Turner asked.

"Munsen has been married to the same woman for many years. There are no rumors of philandering, straight or gay. He is also one of the most hated men in the fashion industry."

"Why is that?"

"He comes from new money, which offends some of the haughtier European houses. He is a conniving, sniveling creep, which offends nearly everyone."

Fenwick observed, "Would hatred for him cause someone to kill his signature model?"

"Munsen is the kind who would think of doing murder to

enhance his own publicity. The eyes of the world are on Chicago because of this murder. Munsen benefits the most from the publicity."

"You really think he's capable of that?" Turner asked.

"That's for you to decide, isn't it?" Oldinport asked.

"Does he really keep spies and saboteurs on his payroll?" Fenwick asked.

"That is the rumor. I would tend to discount it although it is certainly possible. Dinah McBride is often named in the rumors as his 'enforcer.' Who knows what that really means? She is tough, immensely loyal, and just as ruthless as her boss."

"Anything interesting in the groupings down below?" Turner asked.

Oldinport eyed the assemblage. "Not that I can see."

"Thanks for your help," Turner said. "We'll call you if we have more questions." Oldinport nodded to both of them and took the elevator down.

Fenwick turned to his partner and said, "You know we were followed to the elevator?"

"Yes. Twice I just missed seeing who it was."

"A male?" Fenwick asked.

"The person wasn't in a dress. With some of the outfits around here, who knows?"

"A reporter, an asshole, a spy, a suspect, the killer?" Fenwick asked.

"Or our overactive imaginations?"

"I've got no imagination. Ask Madge. What I really want to know," Fenwick said, "is the story on Oldinport's assistant, Battle. Is he a paid paramour, a lover, or a real assistant?"

"Yes," Turner answered.

As they approached the elevator, Fenwick kicked a two-by-four out of the way. The wood made a double *thunk* against the wall.

"You kick two pieces of wood," Turner asked, "or is someone else up here?"

"I kicked once."

"Hush," Turner whispered. He motioned with his left hand for Fenwick to explore to the left of the elevators. Turner moved to the right. After twenty feet he found a corridor leading deeper into the building. Bare bulbs lit the passageway every forty feet. He waited at its entrance in silence. The noise from the party below drifted up to him.

Turner was aware of Fenwick's return. Together they peered down the same hallway. Fenwick whispered, "This is the first exit in this area except the elevator. I found escalators, but they aren't complete up this far."

With Turner leading the way, the two detectives strolled carefully forward. Unfinished doorways provided gaps in the walls. The interiors of the rooms were unlit.

"Half the party could be hiding up here," Fenwick said.

A flutter of movement at the end of the hall caught Turner's eye. "There's no breeze up here," he said.

Ahead they could see that another hallway intersected the one they were in. The lights winked out. They held still and let their eyes adjust to the lack of light. The glow from the party prevented total darkness, but the shadows had deepened. They split up and took separate corridors. Turner had gone about forty feet when he heard Fenwick shout. He turned around and saw the mass of his partner disappear around a corner. He rushed to follow.

Where his partner had turned, he found stairs leading down. He stepped slowly. At the bottom of the stairs he crouched behind a tall stack of lumber. This floor looked far more complete than the one above. He saw a large shadow detach itself from the wall on the left about twenty feet down the hall. He assumed it was Fenwick.

"Gotcha, you son of a bitch," Fenwick bellowed. This was immediately followed by a loud squawk and a string of curses from Fenwick. Turner rushed forward. He saw Fenwick chasing a vague figure. Fenwick rounded a corner. Seconds later there was a loud yelp and a startled bellow. Turner stopped at the juncture and peered around. Neither Fenwick nor the one he was pursuing was in evidence. Five feet in front of him was an unfinished ramp. The light from the party was more evident here. He peered over the edge down the incline. He saw Fenwick grasping his ankle. Mixed with louder sounds from the party, he heard retreating footsteps. There was a camera flash and a second set of running footsteps. Turner carefully strode down the ramp. Fenwick tottered to his feet. He gingerly placed his right foot on the ground. Fenwick gritted his teeth.

"Is it broken?" Turner asked.

"I doubt it. I didn't recognize the creep I was chasing. If I see someone with a camera, I'm going to strangle them."

"Half the reporters down below have cameras."

"Gonna be a lot of dead people."

Fenwick tried walking on his foot. After several minutes he could do so without limping. When they found the elevator on this floor, there was a small crowd clustered at the doors. When the well-dressed group spotted them they stopped chatting. Two of them had cameras.

Turner asked, "Have all of you been standing here together?"

"Who wants to know?" one of them asked.

Turner held out his identification. "Have you seen anyone go by in the past few minutes?" Turner asked.

They all shook their heads. The detectives gave it up and took the elevator down.

"Was that the killer or a paparazzi?" Turner asked.

"I don't care which it was, but when I find them, they will experience more pain than I will."

Turner and Fenwick found Jeff and Brian eating food in the middle of the ground-floor concourse. They were two feet from a mound of sand next to the buffet tables surrounding the stage.

"Where's Battle?" Fenwick asked.

Brian said, "He took Mrs. Fenwick off to meet some people. We decided to get some food."

"You just ate dinner," Paul said. He still marveled at the ability of his sons to put away immense quantities of comestibles.

"Any problems?" Fenwick asked.

"Mrs. Fenwick got offered a job," Jeff said, "and some old guy propositioned Brian."

"Some guy offered me a modeling job," Brian said, "in the nude for a hundred bucks an hour."

"Isn't that illegal?" Jeff asked.

"What'd you tell him?" Turner asked.

"Brian said the 'f' word," Jeff said.

Paul leaned down to his son's wheelchair. He ignored the thousands of people around them. He placed his hands on the arms of the chair and looked into his son's brown eyes. "Are you supposed to be tattling on your brother?"

"He thumped me on the head again," Jeff protested. "He's not supposed to do that either."

"Is this a contest?" Paul asked. "Do we keep score in our house on who misbehaves most? You're supposed to behave as best you can. So is he. Have I asked you for help in disciplining Brian before?"

"No."

"Nor will I be asking in the future." Paul put his hand on the boy's shoulder. "I need your help with lots of things. You're very important to me, and I'm glad I brought you along. I want you to stop tattling."

"Okay."

Paul hugged the boy and turned to his older son. "You refused vigorously. I've got that part. Anything else?"

"He didn't believe my no, so I told him I had to ask permission from my dad, who was a Chicago police detective doing an investigation here. For some reason he left in a big hurry."

"You see him again, point him out to me," Paul said. "I'd like to talk with him detective to photographer."

"Are you going to hit him, Dad?" Jeff asked.

"If he won't, I will," Fenwick said, then inquired, "Was Madge asked to pose in the nude? If she was, I'm afraid she'd say yes."

"No," Brian said. "The woman who talked to her sounded real sincere, but I think Mrs. Fenwick thought it was funny. She had this big grin on her face, but she was real nice to the woman who asked her."

Battle and Madge walked up to them with a third person in tow. She wore a gold lamé evening dress draped in purple chiffon. Madge said, "This is Sibilla Manetti." She introduced the group. Brian's mouth gaped.

Jeff said to the famed model, "My brother thinks you're real pretty."

Her voice was surprisingly low and husky as she asked, "And what about you?"

"I'm still a kid in a wheelchair."

She leaned over, kissed him on the forehead, and ruffled his hair. "If you're still available in ten years, I'll marry you."

A clutch of photographers hurried over. They took a number of pictures of Sibilla with her hand on Jeff's shoulder. Moments after that she and Battle were whisked away.

"Cool," Jeff said.

"How'd you do that?" Brian asked Jeff.

"Being in a wheelchair doesn't mean I'm handicapped. You look funny with your mouth open."

Brian shook his head.

"Did you really get offered a modeling job?" Paul asked Madge.

She laughed. "Yes, but I told them I only worked as a husband-and-wife team. For some reason they didn't want Buck."

"Too handsome," Fenwick said. "They'd get jealous, and I'd break the camera."

Madge laughed some more. "And, Paul, two people asked if you were available for modeling."

"With or without clothes?" Fenwick asked.

"What difference does it make?" Brian asked.

"Without clothes I razz him more," Fenwick replied.

"I am not available clad or unclad," Turner said.

Brian asked, "Mrs. Fenwick, how'd you get Sibilla Manetti to come over here?"

"I was being introduced to her with a lot of other people. I pointed out Jeff, and she came over immediately."

"Did you guys learn anything?" Brian asked.

"Yeah," Turner said, "never go to a fashion fund-raiser on a school night."

Just before they left, the loudspeaker system came on. The voice of Franklin Munsen welcomed everyone. He then spoke briefly about the death of Cullom Furyk and asked for a moment of silence. Turner watched the mass of exquisitely coiffed, expensively dressed, glittering people bow their heads.

In the car Brian said, "Can we go over again the reasons why I can't go camping?"

"Sure. The middle of January is too cold and the possibility of bad storms too great. No parent is going with you. It's too far. It's coed."

"I have good arguments against those reasons."

"You asked for reasons; I, however, did not offer a debate."

"Dad!"

"Son?"

"You could be a chaperone."

"You really want me around on an event with all your buddies from school, including possible girlfriends?"

"I wouldn't mind, not too much, I guess."

"I think I would mind. I would feel awkward."

"Is there anything I can say that will convince you to change your mind?"

"Brian, I really think this is a bad idea. I'd love it if we could drop the topic. Is this really so important that we need to argue about it?"

"Could I at least whine for a while? That way my teenage ego could be salved, yet my struggle with my parental unit would continue so that I develop my independent personality unfettered."

Paul was reasonably happy that Brian had switched from lobbying for a tattoo, as he had last month, but he was still opposed to this new scheme. "Whine, no. Unfetter as much as you like, just not this late on a school night."

At home Ben was still not in. Brian agreed to help his brother get ready for bed so Paul could walk over to see how late Ben would be. He could have called but it was only a short stroll, and he wanted to see his lover, not just talk to him.

Paul used his key to unlock the back door of the service station. Ben Vargas's father had started the business. They serviced mostly expensive imported cars. The light was on in Ben's office in the back. "It's me," Paul called so as not to startle him. Paul found Ben staring at the computer screen. His lover had one hand under his chin, another idly tapping the mouse. Ben shifted his eyes in Paul's direction for only a second then returned his concentration to the screen.

Paul walked up behind him and put his arms around Ben's shoulders.

"Still going at it?"

"Five minutes ago I erased half of my data."

Paul gazed at the nearly empty screen. "Try the undo function," he suggested.

"Of course." Ben pressed two buttons. The screen shifted and columns of data appeared. "Save. Gotta save it."

"Don't forget a back-up disc."

"I hate computers." Ben performed all the save functions then leaned back in his chair. Paul leaned down and kissed Ben then sat on the desk. He touched the five-o'-clock shadow on his lover's face. "Some of the guys tonight used makeup to get that effect on their chins."

Ben rubbed his stubble. "Did you find out what you needed to know?"

"It was mildly helpful and kind of interesting. I wish you could have gone. If nothing else, so we could talk about all the different people and what they wore."

"Weird?"

"Some. It was people trying to look their most impressive, which was pretty outrageous sometimes."

Ben rubbed his hands over his eyes.

"You okay?" Paul asked.

"Tired. I want this computer to go away."

"If you're done, let's go home."

"I certainly won't get finished tonight."

The temperature was above thirty and the wind was completely calm as they eased themselves home. Paul found Brian in Jeff's room. The lamp next to Jeff's bed was on. Jeff was in bed sound asleep. He was wearing his "Friends of Freddy" T-shirt, which he had worn every night since he'd gotten it for Christmas. Brian had fallen asleep while sitting up in the rocking chair. One of Jeff's books, *Freddy and the Popinjay,* was open on his lap. Paul kissed Jeff, then gently woke Brian. "Time for bed, son," he whispered. Brian nodded sleepily and padded upstairs to his own room. Paul made sure all the doors were locked then joined an exhausted Ben. They fell asleep quickly.

ELEVEN

When Turner and Fenwick walked into the station the next morning, Jason O'Leary, the cop on duty at the downstairs desk, said, "Couple of uniforms brought somebody in for you guys about an hour ago. He's in one of the interrogation rooms."

"Thanks," Turner said. "Could you send someone to pick up all the latest fashion magazines? Make sure they charge it to the department."

"I'll get on it."

As they walked up the stairs, Fenwick said, "I have been given a very specific instruction by my daughters. I mentioned Eliot Norwyn's name at breakfast. I was told that if I see him again, I am to procure his autograph."

"Even if he's a murderer?"

"I don't think they care if he kicks cute puppies and eats live babies. If I do not have this vital document in hand, I can kiss domestic bliss and tranquillity good-bye until they leave for college and I change the locks."

"We could arrest him so you could get it over with."

"It may come to that."

Commander Molton carried a copy of a tabloid newspaper. "Why," he asked, "do I have a picture of one of my detectives in this?"

Turner and Fenwick looked at the paper. Covering half the front page was a photograph of Fenwick taken from the rear as he sprawled on the floor in the Midwest Trade Center the night before. The most prominent feature of the photograph was Fenwick's prodigious butt.

"At least they got my good side," Fenwick commented.

They explained what had happened. Molton shook his head at their description of the chase. "What the hell is going on?"

"Don't know," Fenwick said. "Can I have the photograph?"

"What are you going to do with it?" Turner asked.

"Have it framed and put on my desk."

"So it was just some reporter and nothing more sinister than that?"

"We can't be sure," Turner said. "A spy, a killer, a photographer in a fortuitous spot. I think it might have been two people."

"Working together?" Molton asked.

"No way to tell at this point," Turner said.

Larry Bitner was in the interrogation room. "We found him about six this morning," a beat cop told them. "He says he was just getting home from an all-night party."

They thanked him.

Bitner wore a black T-shirt and blue jeans faded nearly to white. His fur-lined black leather jacket lay on the table in front of him. He was in his early twenties, slender, with large shoulders, and buzz-cut hair. His skin was so flawlessly clear Turner thought for a moment he must have makeup on. Bitner gave the impression of the friendly fraternity brother who quarterbacked all the touch football games and would always know the correct corsage to bring his date.

Bitner yawned when he saw them. "Hey, when can I go home? I've been up all night."

"Where were you since the brunch yesterday?" Turner asked.

"Hey, I didn't kill this guy."

"Where were you?" Fenwick let the question include a threatening rumble underneath.

"I changed at my place then stopped at a friend's house. We hung out. Last night we went to the circuit party at the Aragon Ballroom. The tickets cost a lot so we stayed late to get our money's worth."

Fenwick did the questioning. "Who's your friend?"

"Tony Valdotti."

"You spent all day and night with him?"

"Is that odd?"

"You had sex with Cullom Furyk."

"Is that a crime?"

"Just before he died? It's suspicious."

"Why?"

Turner asked, "Did you know him before the brunch yesterday?"

"No."

"How'd you wind up having sex?" Turner asked.

"It kind of just happened. I served him his salad, and he caught my eye, and I didn't look away and neither did he. When I brought him his soup, I brushed against him. He let the contact linger. When I brought him the main course, he rubbed my leg and squeezed my ass."

"Did you know who he was?" Fenwick asked.

"Sure. Him and Eliot Norwyn. I made it with Norwyn a little later."

"You had sex with both of them?"

"Yeah. I still don't see what is criminal about all this."

"How'd you wind up having sex with Norwyn?"

"Pretty much the same way that I did with Furyk. Except Norwyn copped a feel of my crotch while I served him dessert. He found me while we were cleaning up."

"Didn't anyone notice all of this?" Turner asked.

"If they did, no one mentioned it."

"What happened with Furyk?"

"We kissed a little, and I gave him a blow job. Can I say 'blow job' to a pair of cops?"

"We've heard of it," Fenwick said.

"He came pretty quick, which is a good thing because I had to get back to work. Norwyn at least reciprocated a little, although I didn't have much time. I had to help pack up to leave."

"Furyk say anything to you?" Fenwick asked.

"I remember every syllable." Bitner shut his eyes. "Furyk said, and I quote, 'Back this way, that feels great, oooh, aaaah,' end quote. Not a lot of heavy breathing from him."

"And then you just left?" Fenwick asked.

"He came. He zipped up. He left. He didn't seem interested in me. Was I supposed to complain to the sex police?"

"That's all he said?" Fenwick asked.

"Don't need to say much."

"Where was this?"

"Southeast corner of the penthouse. There was kind of a little sitting area that was part of a bedroom. He faced toward the view of the city outside. I concentrated on the view inside."

"Did you kill him?" Turner asked.

"No. Why would I? Doing him and Eliot Norwyn on the same day could make me famous on the circuit for years. My reputation is made."

Bitner looked exactly like what he was—an extremely handsome, slightly hungover, friendly goof who'd given perfectly sensible replies. Turner didn't figure he was lying.

After he left, Turner and Fenwick returned to the chart they'd been working on yesterday.

"You ever been to one of these circuit parties?" Fenwick asked.

"I've heard of them. Never been. Never wanted to go. Don't want to go. Supposed to be the drugged-up and the bulked-up enjoying each other in kind of an endless revel."

"And that's bad?" Fenwick asked.

"Reveling with Ben is plenty for me. Chasing after my kids is enough exercise."

Fenwick asked, "Bitner was that good-looking to be able to get two superstars in bed in less than half an hour?"

"He isn't my type, but he's got that collegiate stud-puppy look down perfectly. There's no accounting for taste."

On the chart Fenwick marked in the times and movements that Bitner had just given them. "He must have been the one Jolanda Bokaru saw making out with Furyk," Fenwick commented. Turner agreed.

On their desks they found a full set of photos of everyone who'd been at the penthouse brunch, and copies of the preliminary ME's report. Fenwick leafed through the information from the ME for a few seconds then tossed it down. "He's still dead," Fenwick announced.

"Lot of that going around these days," Turner said. He flipped through several pages. "Won't get results on drug tests for a while. No evident signs of addiction. I don't see anything significant here." He picked up the pictures. "I want to show these to Spitzer as soon as possible." He called the Archange. Even though he identified himself as a detective, he was forced to go through Bert Weeland before he could be connected to Spitzer's room.

Weeland apologized for the inconvenience. "I'm sure you understand, Detective Turner. We have literally thousands of people who telephone here trying to be connected to the rooms of famous people. We are very protective. The operator did the right thing by not connecting you. We've had people claim they were calling from the White House."

Betty O'Dowd answered the phone in Spitzer's room. She told him, "Mickey is out running along the lakeshore. He should be back in an hour or so. He has to go immediately to a preshow reception. Then he has a luncheon with some designers who are in from out of town. This afternoon he is making an appearance at Water Tower Place."

Turner said, "This is a murder investigation, Ms. O'Dowd. Your client needs to make himself available to us."

"My client is one of the most highly paid models in the world."

Turner let the silence on the line build past comfortable. Fenwick would have blustered. Turner waited.

Finally O'Dowd said, "He is a busy man, but, of course, he is most willing to cooperate. Can we meet this afternoon? I promise to have him here in his room."

Turner agreed. As soon as he hung up, the phone rang. It was Oldinport. He said, "I heard a strange rumor late last night. I thought I'd best give you the information. According to what I heard, Cullom Furyk was planning to leave GUINEVERE, Incorporated and be a spokesperson for Heyling and Veleshki? They were going to steal Munsen's corporate spokesperson."

"I thought they just made peace. Wasn't that what the brunch was supposed to be about?"

"Rumors in the fashion industry can get out of hand, but it is what I heard."

"Do fashion models get stolen often?"

"No. In fact they are seldom under exclusive contracts. Most models go to most shows. Normally, they can easily be replaced. Fighting for designers is much more common. Usually it's the creative, thinking people who are important and in demand."

104

"How reliable is this information?" Turner asked. "We'll need to speak to your source."

"Sibilla Manetti is supposedly the original source although she did not speak directly to me."

"How would she know?" Turner asked.

"You'll have to ask her, Detective. I picked up a strange rumor about her and Franklin Munsen having an affair. I don't believe it, but today the gossip networks are jammed with salacious drivel about people in the fashion industry. Rumors on the Internet are out of control."

"Aren't they always," Turner observed.

"Never like this, at least with regard to the fashion industry. You should be able to contact her through the offices of either company. She's modeling for both this week."

Turner thanked him. After he hung up, he told Fenwick the information. "We'll have to talk to Munsen about Furyk possibly switching."

"We need to find Sibilla. We also need to check Kindel's place. He claimed Cullom was staying with him. We need to examine Cullom's stuff. And we need to find the guy with Bitner's alibi. Tony something."

"I wonder how Kindel is going to react to finding out his supposed lover was having sex with a stranger?"

Harold Rodriguez slumped by. "Watch out for Carruthers today."

"I watch out for him every day," Fenwick said.

"He's trying to organize a Valentine's party."

"I may start being nasty to him again," Turner said.

"I told you you'd be sorry if you were nice to him," Rodriguez said. "If you're polite to him, he thinks you're his friend. He just depresses me."

"That's what this group needs more of," Fenwick said. "We don't have enough depressed, suicidal, alcoholic cops. We need more of that burnt-out, world-weary effect that people want to see in their police detectives."

"Or more people in trouble with or fighting with superiors," Turner said. "Or somebody involved in a convoluted FBI sting that no one understands."

"I shot an FBI guy once," Rodriguez said.

"For which we are eternally grateful," Fenwick said, "even though it was accidental."

"I'm just depressed," Rodriguez said. "Who wouldn't be with the most relentlessly cheerful moron as a partner?"

"Why does he bother with these stupid parties?" Fenwick asked.

"Maybe his girlfriend doesn't put out," Rodriguez said.

"That's demeaning and sexist," Fenwick said.

"And probably true," Turner added.

Rodriguez asked Fenwick, "How come you're so politically correct all of a sudden?"

"I'm always a sensitive guy," Fenwick said.

"Your wife put out last night," Rodriguez stated.

"Can we get out of here?" Turner asked.

"Ben did or did not put out?" Rodriguez asked.

"You've been divorced too long," Fenwick said.

"You're starting to think with your prick," Turner added.

"I've been taking lessons from Carruthers," Rodriguez said. He wandered off.

Turner grabbed the photos of the denizens of the penthouse and jammed them into his notebook. They took one of the unmarked cars and drove to the address they had for Kindel. He lived on Margate Terrace, which was just off Lake Shore Drive north of Lawrence. The weather remained pleasantly warm with the temperature in the low forties.

T W E L V E

"It's gotta be the large house," Fenwick said, nodding toward a three-story Victorian that stretched over two city lots.

Turner said, "They must be paying stringers a lot more than they used to."

"Maybe it's broken up into apartments," Fenwick said.

At the entrance there was only one doorbell. Fenwick pushed the button. They heard distant chimes.

Kindel answered the door. He wore a silk bathrobe over silk pajamas and carried a large cup of steaming coffee.

"Officers?" he asked.

"We need to look over Mr. Furyk's things."

"Of course." He led them into the house.

"Nice place," Fenwick said.

"Thank you."

"You can afford this on a stringer's salary?" Fenwick asked.

"I do as best I can."

Kindel brought a small suitcase and an overnight bag to a library filled with leather-bound books. Turner and Fenwick laid out Furyk's belongings on an antique mahogany table.

"This is it?" Fenwick asked.

"Yes."

"Did he have his own room?"

"No. He slept with me."

"Did you know he had sex with one of the caterers yesterday?" Turner said.

"I don't believe you. Which one was it?"

"Belief is not the issue," Turner said.

"He promised to be faithful."

"Maybe you found out about him having sex," Fenwick said. "Maybe you got pissed off about it. Boyfriend cheating on you."

"And killed him? Don't be absurd. I had no knowledge of an indiscretion."

"Did he brag to you about past sexual activity?" Turner asked.

"I knew he'd had a checkered past, but I never asked for details. It's not as if I'm totally innocent."

"How do you afford this place?" Fenwick asked.

"I worked hard and saved money. Is the American dream a crime?"

"How come you're a stringer at the paper?" Turner asked.

"I like doing it."

"Did you know Cullom was planning to leave GUINEVERE and switch to Heyling and Veleshki?"

"That's ridiculous. He would have told me. Who told you that?"

"We have our sources."

As they'd been talking, the detectives had riffled through four pairs of underwear, two pairs of jeans, three snowy-white T-shirts, four pairs of socks. The overnight bag had toothpaste, toothbrush, deodorant, and other small personal items.

"This is it?" Fenwick asked.

"Yes. He traveled light."

Turner knew Fenwick was thinking the same thing: Furyk's personal effects had to amount to more than this. A search warrant might be in order but they didn't have enough for probable cause yet.

"Where else could he have been staying in town?" Turner asked.

Kindel slumped into a chair. "I don't know. I like to think of myself as a realist. Maybe he didn't love me." He shook his head. "I'm not sure where he would have stayed. He was from here. A lot of people he knew from the fashion industry were in town. I thought I was more than a convenient place for him to stay." He gave them a forlorn look.

Back in the car Fenwick said, "Something's not right in there."

"If he didn't have actual possession of that stuff, I'd doubt if it was Furyk's."

"How do we know it was?" Fenwick asked. "They could have been anybody's, even old clothes of his own. And we only have his word they were lovers."

"What would be the point in lying to us?" Turner asked. "To make himself feel better? It only makes him a suspect in a murder case. Why bother? I'm more interested in where the rest of Furyk's stuff is. Who's got it? According to what we know, Furyk wasn't staying in the penthouse. Other than here, we have no other indication of where else he might have been."

"He could have been staying with half the men in the city," Fenwick said. "From what we've heard, all he had to do was snap his fingers and sexual partners would come running. I'd be jealous, but I used to be able to do that."

"In which lifetime?" Turner asked.

"I don't understand that type," Fenwick said. "The need to have all those conquests."

"That's because Madge would cut off your nuts if you tried anything."

"Well, yeah."

"Constant need for affirmation?" Turner suggested. "Stud muffins can be lacking in ego strength and positive self-image just like anybody else?"

"This your turn to be the sensitive type?"

"I'm taking lessons from you," Turner said. He shrugged. "I don't know. I've never understood it either. I had sex with a few guys before Ben, but it wasn't as if I was going nuts."

"We're being followed," Fenwick said. They were driving south on Clark Street just past Wrigley Field.

"You mean the gray Chevy Cavalier, big rust stain just behind the left headlight, three cars back? Blew the red light at Irving Park?"

Fenwick nodded.

"I haven't noticed."

Fenwick sighed. "You're the token gay person in this relationship. I'm the humor guy."

"Hard to see myself as stuck in the role of the straight man."

Fenwick winced. "Let's get a squad car to pull it over," he said.

THIRTEEN

They continued south on Clark Street as Fenwick placed the call. The blue-and-white appeared behind them just past Wellington. The Chevy made a sudden right from Clark onto Orchard going the wrong way on a one-way street. Fenwick floored the car. There was the usual jam at the intersection of Clark, Diversey, and Broadway. When they finally turned west on Diversey, they saw the blue-and-white's Mars lights rotating about a block ahead of them. They lost him when the Chevy abruptly pulled around a garbage truck just west of Sheffield. The police were a few seconds behind, but the oncoming traffic was quicker. In moments a line of cars filled the left side of the street while the garbage truck sat merrily on the right, ignoring the chaos it was causing. When another squad car appeared from the opposite direction, the car in the middle of the street next to the garbage truck simply stopped.

By the time the traffic unknotted, the Chevy was gone. They

talked to the uniformed officers from both cars. No one had seen the license number.

"I thought it was one person," Turner said.

"I couldn't tell," Fenwick said. The uniformed officers were equally uncertain.

Back in their car Fenwick said, "I wish I knew if this was simply nutty photographers or a killer chasing us around town."

"Why would a killer be chasing us?"

"I dunno," Fenwick said. "We could find out which of the suspects owns a gray Chevy, although I doubt if we're going to find one registered to these wealthy people."

"And not one with that much rust."

"I know criminals are supposed to be dumb, but I'm not ready to believe the killer is tootling around town following us. It's just a little obvious."

Tony Valdotti lived in an apartment on Diversey Avenue just west of Lincoln. He greeted them in red sweatpants and white athletic socks. They introduced themselves. Valdotti's shoulders and torso muscles were so outsized, Turner guessed he used steroids. His disheveled hair and blurry eyes spoke of just awakening. They followed him as he padded into the kitchen. Valdotti turned on the electric coffeemaker.

"What's up?"

"You were with Larry Bitner yesterday."

"Yeah. We went to a circuit party. Larry in trouble?"

"We're just checking on his whereabouts."

"Why?"

"We're investigating the murder of Cullom Furyk."

"Oh, yeah, he told me about that. He must have been the last guy to ever have sex with him."

"He told you about that?"

"Me and anybody else who would listen. Told us he made it with that television guy too."

"He didn't say anything last night about the killing?"

"Only that it was weird to have had sex with the guy just before he died." Tony flexed his shoulder muscles, rotated his neck. "I gotta get to my masseuse and then to the gym. You guys need anything else?"

"Larry seem nervous or out of sorts last night?"

"Nope. We went out and had a great time."

In the car Turner said, "I am living the wrong life."

"Oh, to be young, pretty, muscular, masculine, obsessed with yourself, and having sex whenever you want it with whoever you want."

"Got to be highly overrated," Turner said.

"Shallow."

"No real meaning."

"No commitment."

"No goals."

"No stability."

"No permanence."

Fenwick sighed. "Where do we sign up?"

"I've got the forms in my desk at the station."

Turner used his cell phone to call the offices of GUINEVERE, Incorporated. Dinah McBride told them they could find Sibilla in her suite at the Ritz Carlton.

Fenwick cruised off Lake Shore Drive onto Michigan Avenue. He parked the car at the entrance to the hotel. A uniformed doorman began walking in their direction. Fenwick held up his badge and told him, "We'll leave the car right where it is."

Their identification got them past hotel security and gave them a room number. Sibilla met them at the door. She was flanked by two muscular men who looked in excellent enough shape to win a decathlon. They neither smiled nor spoke. Each wore a blue muscle shirt and black jeans. Sibilla wore a baggy old sweatshirt without a logo, faded and torn blue jeans without any identifying patch on them, and blue deck shoes.

She held her hands awkwardly. "Excuse me," she said. "I'm just finishing having my nails done." She twirled her hands in a tight circle. "Please come in." They walked into the living room of the suite. Two women sat at a table with jars and bowls and vials filled with viscous liquids. Sibilla thanked them and they packed up and left. Turner looked at her nails. The color seemed to be a muted flesh tone. She saw the look.

Sibilla's voice had the same melodic depth of the night before. "One of the rages these days among models is having their nails made into these fabulous confections. I still think it is the clothes that should make the difference. I want my nails understated but perfect."

The room had an oyster-white couch, off-white walls, a table and chair set painted white, and a snowy-white rug. Sibilla sat back on the couch, which was strewn with fluffy white pillows. Gossamer curtains hung behind her, letting in soft winter light that heightened the tone of her blond hair and soft pink skin.

The two bodyguards discreetly walked to the foyer and took positions just inside the door. One took out a book to read. The other closed his eyes.

"You are the police officers from last night," she stated. "You were lucky your presence was undetected. I'm sure the tabloid reporters would not have been able to hold back. Even with your formidable reputation." She smiled at Fenwick.

Fenwick had the most fatuous grin on his face that Turner had ever seen.

Sibilla asked, "Did you really once handcuff a reporter to the bumper of a squad car and begin to drive away?"

Fenwick chuckled. Turner thought his bulky partner almost blushed.

She smiled. "I have several paparazzi in mind for the next time you try it." She turned to Turner. "And you are the father of the boy in the wheelchair."

"Yes, he has spina bifida. I have an older son as well."

"I try to do as much as I can to help children. It is never enough. What did you want to ask me?"

"Was Cullom Furyk leaving as spokesperson for GUINE-VERE, Incorporated to join Heyling and Veleshki?" Turner asked.

"Let me tell you about Cullom first. You must understand how I come to know this information. We met many years ago, when we were both teenagers. He made a fumbling attempt to seduce me. He was a dear boy and I was a naive girl, but I knew I did not want to have sex unless I was in love. We became friends over the years, I think because we did not have sex."

"We were told you did have sex with him," Turner stated.

"There are all kinds of rumors about who famous people have or have not slept with. It is best not to believe most of those rumors. The truth is always much less than what rumors make it out to be. He was a rich, handsome, genuinely kind and giving man. That brings out envy and jealousy. His reputation did exceed his prowess; nevertheless, he did have more partners than most. Cullom often said he'd never need Prozac as long as he had sex. He found it relaxing when he was tense."

"We were told he had lovers all over the world."

"I doubt that. He has one in Paris that I've actually met. He spoke about a man in Rome, but I thought he broke that off several years ago. He had very few real friends. I warned him several times about being so superficial." She shrugged. "He didn't listen so I stopped bringing up the subject. I think he used casual sex to feel close to people, and yet I was closer to him than anyone despite the fact that we never had sex. I know he became lonely at times. No matter where I was in the world, I would get phone calls late at night from him. Most often he'd be crying."

"Why?" Turner asked.

"He'd want to talk about how miserably unhappy he was. People have an odd idea about models. The world looks on the women as these emaciated, cold, automatons who wear ridiculous clothes. The men are supposed to look like pure sexual beings. They think we are all wealthy beyond their wildest imaginations and that our lives are filled with glamour and parties and the rich life. A few of us *are* very, very rich. Most are not. All of us work very hard to get where we are. I think Cullom was overwhelmed by the life."

"How did the causes he was involved in affect his life?" Turner asked.

"The pressure to do more is always intense. You can never do enough and once you help one, they all want you."

"We were told he made light of those causes."

"He cared very deeply. Sometimes you have to make a joke or you end up only crying."

"I understand," Turner said.

Sibilla continued, "Some people handle fame and sudden riches better than others. I started out in a tiny town in Ohio fifteen years ago in a silly little beauty contest. I was fortunate. I had sensible parents and an excellent agent. Cullom had no one."

"He has an agent," Turner said, "and I thought Franklin Munsen and the people at GUINEVERE took care of him."

"His agent is a horse's ass. Wealth unimaginable at an early age can get you all kinds of very pleasant attention. Having your emotional needs met is another thing entirely. You have pressures on your job, as do we all. Cullom had his. Are some of your colleagues better at handling the pressure of being a detective and some worse? I imagine so. It is the same in my world. It doesn't really make much difference what profession we are in or how much money we make. Some people panic at little bits of pressure and some are serene in the face of an avalanche. Cullom was very vulnerable. He was afraid his whole world would come collapsing down on him."

"Why? Did he spend all the money he earned?"

"No. I believe he was reasonably prudent. The burdens were psychological. Those who have made their way to the top often fear losing it."

"Did he fear losing out in his personal relationships?"

"Part of Cullom wanted to fall in love with a man and settle down. Another part wanted to play and play."

"Was he in love with Sean Kindel?" Turner asked.

"I have never heard Cullom mention that name."

"Had he broken up with anyone recently?"

"Not that I am aware of."

"Did he talk about anybody else he might be close to, especially here in Chicago?"

"He'd told me he was coming to Chicago to have some things settled by the time the showings were done."

"Did he mean personal or professional?"

"I thought more professional."

"So he *was* planning to switch companies?"

"We had breakfast early yesterday morning around six. We both had early photo shoots. At the time he told me he was switching companies."

"Did Cullom hate Munsen?"

"Many in the fashion world hate Munsen. Cullom didn't. I don't. Munsen's done more good for me than bad. All the same, I wouldn't want to cross him."

"But Cullom was unhappy at GUINEVERE?"

"He felt they were holding him back. He wanted to model for all the big fashion houses. Being the exclusive spokesperson for a company can be wonderful, especially when you are young. Most models cannot or would not sneer at a steady paycheck as they rise in the profession. What happened to him is a great way to start and become a star without a lot of risks. In the past couple of years he'd branched out with other kinds of companies, but GUINE-VERE, Incorporated had a firm contract with him that he would only model GUINEVERE clothes and their related products. They didn't care if he endorsed things like running shoes as long as it wasn't connected to any fashion house or anything GUIN-EVERE manufactured."

"Were the people at GUINEVERE furious with him for wanting to switch?"

"He was going to tell Munsen after his photo shoot but before the brunch."

"No one reported any animosity between the two of them at the brunch," Turner said. "Maybe he didn't tell him."

"Perhaps not."

"Did he say that Heyling and Veleshki had made him a firm offer?"

"No, just that they'd been having positive discussions."

"He referred to both of them?"

She thought a moment. "He said 'they,' I'm sure of that."

"Do you know if he told anyone besides yourself?"

"Not that I'm aware of. He may have. You might check with his agent. I presume he should know. Someone would have to be negotiating contracts or new bookings. He would be the logical person."

"About that brunch in general," Turner asked, "how could Heyling and Veleshki be having a peace meeting if they were planning to steal away the other company's major spokesperson?"

"I don't know," she said. "I know what Cullom told me, and I know he was happy about it, ecstatically happy."

"And you worked for both companies?"

118

"I've worked for each of them numerous times in the past. Depending on demand and your status in the fashion industry, you can be in numerous countries for a number of companies in less than a week."

"Do you know where he was staying?"

"No."

Turner thanked her and they left. "You didn't say a word," Turner said as they took the elevator down.

"I never expect to be in the presence of a more beautiful woman," Fenwick said.

"You met her last night."

"This was different. That was several thousand people and us. Here it was just her. She breathes beauty. She *is* beauty, and she doesn't have to paint up to be flawless. She is just naturally perfect."

"You mean you were too turned on and distracted to concentrate on your work."

"It's not as if you're some saint. I've seen you get distracted when we talk to hot guys."

"I didn't claim I was a saint. I wonder what happens when there are two people of the same sexual orientation working together on a case?"

"They keep their mouths shut?"

"We could try that," Turner said.

Fenwick sighed. "For her I would push a herd of intrusive reporters off the Sears Tower. . . . Who's next?"

"We need to talk to Munsen, and Heyling and Veleshki, and Cullom's agent."

FOURTEEN

The headquarters for GUINEVERE, Incorporated was on Mann-heim Road just south of O'Hare Airport. Fenwick solved the problem of jammed traffic by riding the shoulder of the Kennedy Expressway most of the way out.

The building housing the offices looked exactly as if someone had taken three vast old airplane hangars and merged them to-gether. The walls were corrugated tin. The floor was gray and black linoleum. The desks and chairs were all chrome and cracked leather. Giant swatches of gauzy, multihued cloth hung in great sweeps from the ceiling. Dinah McBride met them in the front reception area.

McBride said, "Mr. Munsen is in a production design meeting on one of the soundstages." She led them down several corridors and into a large, cool room. The ceiling stretched three stories above them. Flat black cloth covered all the walls. In the center was a desert scene against a blue backdrop. Two photographers were talking to three muscular men and three slender women all clad only in the briefest of bathing suits. Munsen was talking to a man with a light meter. McBride spoke in Munsen's ear for a few moments. Munsen glared at the detectives, shrugged, and walked over. McBride stood twenty feet away.

Munsen began with "I'm terribly busy."

"We're all terribly busy," Fenwick said.

Munsen swallowed the rest of his impatience. He asked, "Have you found out what happened to Cullom?"

"We heard he was leaving your company for your rival."

"That's nonsense. Where did you hear such an absurd rumor?"

"Cullom supposedly told people."

"Absolutely not true. He was happy here. Why would he want to leave? It was a lucrative and successful relationship for both sides."

"He said nothing to you about leaving?" Fenwick asked.

"Absolutely nothing. If this is all the twaddle you have to tell me this morning, I have better things to do. You shouldn't waste your time on what was undoubtedly an accident."

"Why wasn't he staying at the penthouse with the other people you had in from out of town?" Fenwick asked.

"Where he stayed was his business. I am not his parent."

"But you worked with him for over ten years," Turner said.

Munsen gazed at one of the black backdrops. His eyes misted over. He finally turned back to them. "I am well aware of how long he worked for me. Is there anything else?"

"Could we get a tour of your facility?" Turner asked.

"Ms. McBride has many duties, but I'm sure she can spare a few minutes."

McBride escorted them through the three gigantic buildings. They saw several more soundstages, one of which was in use. "That's a product line being developed," McBride said.

"They're all in their underwear," Fenwick said.

Three men wore the briefest and sheerest of cotton underwear.

"Egyptian cotton briefs and boxers," she said. "It is going to sweep the world. It is incredibly comfortable and light."

Turner nodded. What he knew of fabric was limited to cotton, denim, and whatever the clerk in the men's department at Marshall Fields said looked good on him. Ian had once commented that perhaps there was a defect in Turner's gay gene.

Another immense space seemed to be a showroom with an expanse down a center aisle that could have been used for a modeling runway. A large part of one hangar had employees cutting and sewing fabric. Much of the furniture here had ripped cushions or frayed fabric at the corners. The hangar walls were rust stained. One room, which McBride only let them glance into, had all the outfits that were going to be used this week.

"It's very secret," McBride said. "All the models have tried on everything and rehearsed. In a few hours this will be a total madhouse with last-minute preparations. This morning there is a slight lull."

One of the hangars also contained a mass of cubicles. They saw Egremont, the accountant. He lifted a hand toward them for a second, then went back to inspecting columns of numbers. Before they left they got the name, number, and address for Cullom's agent.

As they walked to the car, Turner said, "If this is a multimillion-dollar operation, I'd hate to see what the folks in the poor-rent district live like."

"Why did we go on a tour of the company?"

"I need to get a handle on who these people are. See them in their own element. I have no basis for forming judgments about them."

★　★　★

The headquarters for Heyling and Veleshki was in a brand-new office tower on Clark Street just south of Howard Street. The fifty-story edifice had been built with a great deal of bronze, masonry, and glass.

The Heyling and Veleshki offices had plush gold carpeting, sleek modern office furniture, and silver-studded star mobiles. People walked busily back and forth. From the entryway on the tenth floor they could see rows and rows of cubicles.

The receptionist whisked them back to a corner office. Through the windows, they could see the row of skyscrapers stretching south along the lakefront to the Loop. Clouds had rolled in, but the temperature remained in the forties.

Heyling and Veleshki greeted them. Heyling wore a brown-checked polyester shirt, Java satin jeans, and dark orange cowboy boots. Veleshki had on a brown suede shirt, brown plaid stretch-cotton cargo jeans, dark brown cowboy boots, and a black cowboy hat. Both wore bolo ties and large silver belt buckles emblazoned with bronze bucking broncos.

Each sat behind a desk equidistant from the door, windows, and each other. Veleshki's desk was covered with newspapers and clippings. Heyling's had numerous drawings of outfits.

Turner and Fenwick sat in unmatched deep-cushioned chairs. Veleshki and Heyling each leaned back in their leather swivel chairs.

"What can we do for you, gentlemen?" Veleshki asked.

"We have a few more questions," Turner said. "We have reason to believe that Cullom Furyk was leaving GUINEVERE, Incorporated to work for you."

The two men looked briefly at each other. A conspiratorial nod, or two lovers making eye contact at a significant moment, or what? Turner wasn't sure.

Veleshki said, "Our company has no exclusive models. You

have to understand how the fashion industry works. Models are rarely under contract to only one company. There usually isn't enough work. They travel around."

"So we heard," Fenwick said. "Even if he wasn't going to be yours exclusively, was he planning to do any modeling for your company?"

"There was no agreement," Veleshki said. "We'd had some informal talks with him, but we'd had talks with him before. My understanding is that many companies did. He was much in demand."

"Did you talk to him about it this week?"

"Neither of us met with him," Veleshki said.

Fenwick pointed at Heyling. "That true?"

Heyling nodded.

"No contact at all?" Turner asked.

"No." Veleshki continued to give the answers.

"You only saw him at the brunch."

"Yes."

"Did you talk to him there?"

"Only to say hello."

"We understand that your company is experiencing financial difficulties," Fenwick said.

"That lie has been printed in the tabloid papers numerous times. It's spread mostly by the press agents at GUINEVERE. Someone should examine *their* books. We are branching out with many new products and subsidiary lines—sheets, towels, furniture, fragrances, hundreds of things. They have only begun taking timid steps beyond couture collections and a minimal representation of ready-to-wear clothes. We are a much more secure and broad-based company."

"We heard you were desperate for next week's lottery check."

"Those rumors drive me nuts," Veleshki said. "We have shown record profits for the past two years."

"When was the last time you spoke to Cullom?" Turner asked.

"Prior to yesterday, not for months," Veleshki said.

"How about you, Mr. Heyling?" Turner asked.

"I've had no contact," Heyling said.

Turner and Fenwick looked at each other.

"Is that all you wanted to know?" Veleshki asked.

"How many floors of this building do you rent?" Turner asked.

"Ten. This one and nine above it."

Again they requested and were taken on a tour. Veleshki himself escorted them. There seemed to be many more photo studios in use than at GUINEVERE. One stage had two women in business outfits, briefcases in hand, behind them desks crowded with paperwork. Each woman looked sleekly professional. A photographer was urging each of them to act competent. On another stage male models in skimpy briefs were lounging in chairs. "Signature underwear," Veleshki said. "One of our new products. These won't be available until next week. We're having a huge ad campaign, big promotion, the whole works." Paul thought they might look sensational on Ben. "We're also shooting some ads this week for a line of fragrances." Turner noticed that the models were not padding the underwear in front nor did they have any need to.

Veleshki showed them the set where the print ad was being shot for their perfume. The setting was made to look as if it were a construction site. Sitting on the stage was a lone man in a construction hat, a flannel shirt with the sleeves torn off, cut-off jeans, and tan work boots with white socks peeking above the edges. His muscles rippled as he brought his sandwich to his mouth and took a bite out of it. Several people stood ten feet from him, discussing camera angles and background lighting. One entire floor was strewn with outfits, models, hairdressers, designers, and others chasing about.

"We have a lot of preparations still to do for our show this week," Veleshki said. "If we're through with the tour, I must join this happy throng." The detectives nodded. Veleski strode away.

Turner and Fenwick sat in the car without moving.

"They're both lying," Fenwick said.

Turner nodded. "How about Munsen?"

"He's lying."

"Anybody telling us the truth?"

"Sibilla."

"You only believe her because she sets your testosterone in motion."

"Do you believe her?"

"Yeah."

"Maybe you're hiding secret heterosexual tendencies."

"I'll stick with Ben. I just believed her. We have no basis for disbelieving her. The main thing she's got going for her is that she was not at the brunch. She couldn't have pushed him. Same with O'Dowd and Spitzer. On the other hand, there are all kinds of reasons the owners of both companies would lie."

"And I don't like them," Fenwick said. "I want to see Veleshki and Heyling not dressed as if they were on their way to a photo shoot."

"If Veleshki had an affair," Turner said, "maybe it wasn't his only one."

"Possible," Fenwick said.

"Maybe Cullom only let people see bits of himself," Turner said. "Maybe it wasn't so much that he had ghastly secrets to hide. Maybe he simply never confided completely in anyone."

"Possible, but then maybe all these people are telling the truth. That's a depressing thought—all the suspects in a murder case telling the truth."

"I also want to know more about this Kindel guy. He claims they were lovers. No one else confirms it."

Fenwick said, "Maybe Cullom told him one thing and everybody else another."

"Let's meet Ian for lunch," Turner suggested. "I'm dry of insights for the moment and the agent's office is near the paper. Maybe Ian can find out more about Kindel for us." He drummed his fingers on the dashboard. "I don't feel like I've got a good handle on Furyk. Kind of like I'm dancing on an oiled floor. I don't get a feeling for who he was."

"You know what we're missing in this case?" Fenwick asked.

"The murderer."

"Besides that."

"What?" Turner asked.

"Nobody's morally outraged by all this hopping into bed."

"We could place an ad in the paper—'Wanted: one morally outraged suspect.' "

"Or murderer."

"Or murderer. Apply to Buck Fenwick, Area Ten headquarters."

"I think I miss moral outrage," Fenwick said. "It would add flavor, a sense of narrowness, fuel to the fire, grease to the wheels."

"Boredom to the clichés. You want to be morally outraged, you could do it for both of us."

FIFTEEN

They met Ian at the Melrose Restaurant several blocks south of the newspaper offices. They sat up front in the corner booth with the best view of the passing scenery. Ian said he always loved this spot for people watching. He kept his long legs halfway into the aisle. Ian wore his customary slouch fedora along with khaki pants, a white flannel shirt, and work boots.

After they ordered lunch, Ian asked, "What's the latest?"

"Fenwick's doing moral outrage."

"Great. I hear it's a big trend these days. Maybe you could start a congregation. Nothing like contributions from the faithful to the morally outraged."

"If I'm good at it, I could get rich. I could give lessons, have my own little university. I see a whole cottage industry."

"For which I'm sure I'll be grateful," Ian said. "Are you being morally outraged about anything in particular or is this general, nonspecific outrage, because if it is, I'm here to tell you, you're way behind the religious right on this."

Fenwick said, "I was just curious. None of the people we've interviewed has expressed moral doubts about Cullom Furyk's sex life."

"Which was?"

"Active," Turner said. "Remarkably so."

"I'm outraged, too," Ian said. "I wish he'd have told me his secret."

"Be young, beautiful, and rich," Turner said. "Not much of a secret to it."

"You ever been to one of those circuit parties?" Fenwick asked.

"I don't find that set stimulating. I prefer people with a modicum of self-awareness and the ability to think critically beyond the question of where my next drug overdose is coming from."

"Furyk seems to be a mass of contradictions," Turner said. "We've got all kinds of people claiming they were close to him."

"Try this for an explanation," Ian said. "Often the truly famous deal with people in brief snippets. The hangers-on and the wannabees see the little bits of the personality they want to see. Their perceptions are clouded by gossip, their own desire for fame, their wanting to touch that which is famous."

"Moral outrage and snippets of fame," Fenwick said. "Doesn't sound like a best-seller to me."

Their sandwiches arrived. After taking an enormous bite, Ian said, "Strange things are afoot. I was thinking of calling you."

"What?" Turner asked.

"The lawyer who represents the owner called. We're to have an emergency meeting today."

"That's odd?" Fenwick asked.

"The rumor is that everybody is supposed to drop everything else and work on the Cullom Furyk murder."

"A famous gay person is murdered in Chicago," Turner said.

"I can see why some people wouldn't look at it as a nothing story."

"It's not real news. It's sad the guy is dead, sure, but I come from an activist mentality. That which is important must effect people's lives. It's got to have significance. This is police blotter stuff. Tabloid stuff. I'm interested in real news."

"And this is unreal news?" Fenwick asked.

"You know what I mean," Ian retorted.

"I'm not sure," Turner said. "Look at the news coverage when Gianni Versace died."

"He was the owner of a company, famous for many years, and it was connected to a spree killer. I know it sounds horrible to say, but I didn't much care when he died."

Turner said, "Young gay kids seeing someone open and successful? Isn't that important for them to have role models?"

"Who cares about the fashion world?" Ian retorted. "Everybody thinks all the guys are gay anyway. It's not news. It's a world of people who are steeped in useless opinions and dripping with silly accessories—a faintly sleazy, artsy-craftsy milieu that I couldn't care less about."

"I hate it when you hold back," Fenwick said. "Try and see if you can give us your real feelings."

"Tell me about this Kindel guy," Turner said. "We went to see him. He lives in this big old mansion."

"Beg pardon?"

"Big mansion up north of here. He had what he claimed were Cullom Furyk's clothes."

"Big mansion?" Ian asked. "He's a stringer for the paper. He took early retirement from teaching. That can't be a huge pension. The impression I've gotten is that he just barely gets by."

"Maybe he's barely getting by in a big mansion," Turner said. "He could have inherited it."

"You sure it was his?" Ian asked.

"It was his address," Fenwick said. "I suppose somebody else could own it, or he could be renting a room or two from some-one."

Turner added, "He also seemed a lot older and not as good-looking as the people Furyk was usually into."

"Maybe Furyk had eclectic taste," Ian said. "Or maybe it was a mercy fuck. Who knows? You better watch what you say about people's looks, Paul. You don't want to be accused of lookism in this day and age."

"What ism?" Fenwick asked.

"Lookism. Body fascism. That which is and those who are con-cerned with and value only those who are pretty."

Fenwick sighed. "More people to shoot."

"Could Kindel have been this guy's lover?" Turner asked.

"Hell, why not?" Ian said. "I didn't believe you when you first told me. I still don't. Kindel is such a total loser. I'll look a little more into his background if you want."

"Thanks," Turner said. "Furyk might have been lying to one and all. We've gotten some strange information that doesn't add up."

"The fashion industry doesn't add up," Ian said. "Silly, frivo-lous."

"They make millions," Fenwick said.

"That's not my fault," Ian said. "As far as I know, for the gay men involved, it is a I-can-have-anybody culture. Studly men. Lots of casual sex. Sounds like an unreal world to me."

"I didn't think you were opposed to casual sex," Turner said.

"I didn't say I was opposed to it," Ian said. "It just isn't real for most people. I think the majority of people are average-looking. They find somebody they love and settle down, or they have a circle of friends who care about each other. This I-can-have-everybody is an unreal fantasy."

"Real or unreal, we've got to get moving," Turner said.

★ ★ ★

Cullom's agent, Hartly Woodward, had an office in newly renovated space just south of Buckingham Avenue on Halsted Street. Redwood patio furniture filled the outer office. Even Turner noticed that the young female secretary's dress was spandex tight. Her overemphasized endowments gave her what Fenwick referred to as the 'I'm-available-right-this-minute' look.

Woodward was in his late forties. He wore a beige sweater, black slacks, and an emerald pinkie ring. His hair was receding in two sharp widow's peaks. His voice had a high-pitched whine.

His office continued the redwood-furniture/floral-print pattern of the outer office. "You're here about Cullom, of course. I was going to call the police, but I couldn't figure out why I should. He was a fine young man. I shall miss him a great deal. I was the person closest to him." He took a tissue from his desk and dabbed at his eyes. "I know everybody thinks agents are greedy slimeballs. I admit I will lose a lot of money with his death, but I honestly don't care about that. I'd give up every penny if it would bring him back. I loved him like a son. He was one of my first clients. As his star rose, so did mine, but it was more than that. He trusted me and I trusted him. He and my wife and I would go to numerous functions together. He was always a good man, a sensitive man. Never a bad word to say about anyone."

"Was he leaving GUINEVERE, Incorporated?"

"He and I talked many times about expanding his career. He had a lot of endorsements. See, lots of models rush around the planet desperate for work. Cullom was lucky. The work came to him. People would call here from every continent. They wanted him for their products."

"How did GUINEVERE, Incorporated feel about that?"

"In the very beginning, they were reluctant to let him endorse anything for anybody. Those people are far more paranoid than they need to be. It is true he was very identified with the company. Still is. After he became such a big celebrity, they didn't mind as much. I figured out a perfect and profitable way to get them to agree."

"How's that?" Fenwick asked.

"It's obvious. Make his outside endorsements work for them. Say Cullom was pitching buggy whips. The agreement with that company would be for Cullom to be wearing GUINEVERE, Incorporated products in the commercial. GUINEVERE actually got a lot of exposure that way. He had that certain look which a camera really falls in love with. Cullom was like Marilyn Monroe that way. From the very beginning he just looked perfect in print or on camera. Lately he'd begun to get some serious consideration for movie roles. The money was just about right and it would get him out from under Franklin Munsen."

"We heard a lot of people hate Mr. Munsen."

"Him and his hired Nazi, Dinah McBride. Those two are the toughest pair I ever care to deal with."

"How did Cullom get along with them?"

"Cullom never fought with anybody. He was sweet and kindly."

"One source left us with the impression he didn't care that much about the causes he was involved in."

"That is a lie. He cared very much. He dodged bullets in Sarajevo to visit orphanages. He traveled around the world at his own expense."

"We were told that he called up friends late at night crying because he was lonely."

"You talked to Sibilla. That woman was not good for him. I don't like her or trust her. She was out only for herself. I told him to stay away from her."

"Why?"

"She has her own agenda and her own needs."

"Did he have any confidants besides Sibilla?"

"As far as I know, he confided in me as much as anybody.

You've got to understand Cullom. His mother and dad were perfectly nice people, just not very affectionate. When you are as pretty as he is, and you know it early in life, things come easy for you. People want to be around you. On the other hand, a model's life can be very hard. Working your way up to the top is killing. Constant travel, long hours, a jammed schedule, the competition. Very few can handle the pressures and the demands. While Cullom was an enormous success, the success itself can be hideously draining. Few people realize how tough he had it. There were times when he was desperate for affection in any form he could find it. He was more needy in that area than most."

"We've heard he had a lover in Paris and one in Chicago. Were there others?"

"You hear all kinds of rumors about lovers in this country and around the world."

"They weren't enough to fill his loneliness needs?" Fenwick asked.

Woodward sighed. "Cullom was not perfect. Which of us is? Cullom was a taker. He kept the men in different cities to meet his needs. He didn't flaunt the fact of his lovers, but I've seen him drain men dry."

"How did he juggle having all these guys?"

"I don't think most of them knew about the others. He never brought people with him on his trips around the world. On the other hand, much as I hate to admit it, Cullom could be very hurtful. To find someone who wants to genuinely touch you and genuinely care for you and genuinely love you is not easy for a famous person. Too many people want to love, touch, and care for your fame or your money or your looks and not the real you."

"Bullshit," Fenwick stated. "If you want friends to like you for who you are, you pick out that kind of friend."

"You ever been young, pretty, and popular?" Woodward asked.

Fenwick glared at him.

"I didn't think so. You can sneer at the beautiful people and their problems. I'm simply trying to describe those that Cullom had—how his problems were not unique to his profession. Sneer if you want, but Cullom had things tough."

Fenwick asked, "Why not find a relationship among other rich and famous and pretty people? Wouldn't they understand the problem?"

"Pretty as he was, even Cullom could not snap his fingers and have a perfect lover appear. No, Cullom is dead and that is a tragedy. He had problems. You asked, I told you what I know."

"How many lovers and how many cities are we talking about?" Turner asked.

"He didn't have one in every city all the time and they changed periodically. Usually there was one in Paris, one in Italy somewhere, one in New York."

"Did he ever mention a Sean Kindel here in Chicago?"

"No."

"Who else knew about these lovers besides you?" Turner asked.

"I don't know."

"What if they didn't exist?" Turner asked. "Was he the type to make up those kinds of stories?"

"Imaginary lovers?" He leaned back in his chair and looked at the two of them. "I never thought to question it before. I saw no reason to."

"Did he give you details, facts about them, names we could check?"

"Well, no."

"He never brought someone around as a boyfriend or date to a social event?"

"He was seen in many famous places with many famous people. He tended to travel with a small herd of admirers, quite often with groups of other models." Woodward shrugged. "It was an ego thing to have hangers-on."

"Say we accept that all these lovers are real," Turner said. "If he had all of them to meet his needs, why was he on the phone to Sibilla crying?"

"I wonder if Sibilla wasn't exaggerating her closeness to him. She wasn't gay. How could she understand?"

"You're a straight man," Turner said, "but you claim to have understood him."

"That's different."

Turner thought Woodward's last statement was a crock. He asked, "Did he ever have any big blowups with these lovers? They can't have all been happy with the arrangement. At the very least the long absences must have bothered them. Some must have found out about the others."

"He never told me about any big fights. As far as I know, when he left a boyfriend, there was no big confrontation. He simply stopped calling or coming around. Of course, that can be even more hurtful than an explosion."

Woodward could add nothing beyond the lover muddle. Turner and Fenwick left.

In the car Turner said, "By my count that is the third person who claimed to be the 'closest one' to Cullom Furyk."

"Fame can be hell," Fenwick said.

Before they returned to headquarters, they stopped at the Blue Diamond Athletic Club. The immense edifice was on the west side of the Chicago River just north of Grand Avenue. Erika Douzane, the manager, wore a sweatsuit with the name of the club inside a large diamond shape in five different places on the outfit. She looked to be in her early forties.

In response to their questions she said, "Yes, Cullom was here. He showed up on time. A lot of these people don't. So many of them have an attitude. He seemed very sweet. Very unassuming. He got here, changed into his outfit and was ready for the shoot."

"Any problems?"

"We're used to celebrities being in the club. Still, the cameras and lights drew a crowd, and the photographers wound up needing a few extras for background. Instead of hiring people we just used members of the club. Any kind of celebrity connection is good for membership recruiting."

"Did he speak with anyone?"

"He signed autographs for whoever wanted one. Also several people were waiting to talk to him either when he finished or during breaks in the shooting. You know, most of a photo shoot is setting up lighting and angles and that kind of thing, so the models do a lot of sitting and waiting."

Turner raised an eyebrow. "Do you know who was waiting to talk to him?"

"No. I just assumed they were his people. Handlers, you know. Entourage. Hangers-on."

Turner took out the photos of the people in the penthouse. "You recognize any of these?"

She glanced at them carefully. She pointed to Kindel and Veleshki. "Both of those for sure. And there was one man in a baseball hat and sunglasses at the very end. You know how some celebrities use that to disguise themselves. It's quite simple but very effective. I wonder if it was . . . well . . . I'm not sure . . . it could have been this one." She held out the picture of Eliot Norwyn.

"Do you know the names of any of the people in the pictures you picked out?" Turner asked.

"No. I don't believe they were members, although we have so many that I don't know everybody by sight. Of course, if they're members and famous, I would. It's a little trick I have to give them the service they deserve and to keep the club one of the best."

"That last one you picked is a television star," Fenwick said.

She peered at the face carefully. "I prefer the Robert Redford type. This is just a kid. What kind of show is he on?"

"Some teen thing," Fenwick said.

"Then I wouldn't know him."

In the car Fenwick placed his hand over his forehead, closed his eyes, and said, "I sense the investigation focusing on Kindel, Veleshki, and Norwyn."

" 'Fenwick the psychic' doesn't have much of a ring to it. If you're so great in the foretelling business, how come the last lottery numbers you gave out were a bust?"

"You were paying attention? I was talking to Wilson and Roosevelt. I didn't know you played the lottery."

"Only when it's over twenty million."

"Is that supposed to increase your odds?"

"It increases my fantasies, which, as far as I can tell is the only point in buying lottery tickets."

"Sounds good enough to me. We're bringing these three down to the station," Fenwick said. "I don't like it when people don't give me complete information. We should add Heyling, too. It's time to start shaking up some of these people a little."

"I'll call headquarters and have them send people out to pick them up. On our way back we can stop and show our pictures to Spitzer."

Before arriving at Spitzer's, the detectives followed up on the caterers who had been out the first time they stopped. Everyone was in, but no one knew anything helpful.

They found Spitzer wearing a gold-colored terry-cloth bathrobe and white athletic socks. He carried a towel and his hair was wet from a recent shower. O'Dowd was nowhere in sight.

"Your lawyer is not here?" Fenwick asked.

"Pardon?" He looked puzzled.

Turner knew no Russian. "Ms. O'Dowd?"

Spitzer smiled. "Not here."

He gestured for them to enter the penthouse. Turner made a circling motion with his hands then pointed into the penthouse. "Tour?"

The three of them strode through the penthouse. On a balcony facing directly east they found eight different weight machines.

"I thought O'Dowd said these were a few simple amenities," Fenwick said. "He's got half a gym out here. This looks more than few and simple."

"Depends on your definition of few and simple." Turner sat on each of the machines. On five of them his view of the terrace diagonally across from him was unimpeded. Because of the distance, it would be difficult to make out a face even if you weren't vigorously exercising.

"You work?" Spitzer said. He placed a hand on Turner's left bicep. "Good muscle."

They stepped back into the penthouse. Turner took out the pictures. "Do you recognize any of these faces?" he asked.

Spitzer stared at him blankly. Turner spread out the pictures on a table and pointed to them. Spitzer looked at each one carefully. When he bent over, his robe opened. Turner noted that the fashion icon was not wearing underwear.

Spitzer picked out Egremont, the accountant's picture.

"Did he push him?" Turner asked.

Blank look. Turner pantomimed pushing someone off a balcony then pointed at the picture.

Spitzer shook his head.

"Then why'd you pick him out?" Fenwick muttered.

Spitzer said, "Earlier. Before."

"You mean he was talking to him before?"

Another blank look.

"We'll have to come back when O'Dowd is around," Fenwick said.

Turner pointed to the other photos. Again Spitzer examined them. He shook his head. They left.

"I found that unsatisfying," Fenwick said.

"In addition to sensitivity training, you'll be signing up for courses in Russian next."

"*Oui, oui.*" Fenwick pronounced it *ooowie, ooowie*. A cartoon character he'd seen once mispronounced it so. Turner knew the joke. He did not respond.

Fenwick continued, "We already knew Egremont was out there talking to him."

"At least we have our first confirmed bit of truth in this case. Everything else, we've had to take people's words for."

"If Spitzer understood you correctly. You must be great at charades."

"Better than adequate. Back to headquarters, O wise psychic."

SIXTEEN

Outside the station a mass of photographers and reporters surged toward them. Camera lights flicked on. Flashbulbs flashed.

"We could try the back way," Turner suggested.

"Nah. I haven't stomped on a photographer in weeks."

As they exited the car the uniforms were unable to hold back the tide of paparazzi. Shouted questions mingled with yelps and curses as the swirl of humanity nearly engulfed them. Fenwick never hesitated. He marched straight toward the heart of the crowd. The drove of reporters halted momentarily, thinking perhaps that he planned to address them. Fenwick, however, did not pause. He sailed through them as an ocean liner through a swimming pool. Turner followed in his massive partner's wake. As he passed, Turner felt hands grab at him. He smiled benignly and kept his mouth shut.

Commander Molton met them on the first floor. He said, "I need a cure for tabloid reporters."

"Shoot them," Fenwick said.

"People might get the right idea," Molton said.

"Open season on tabloid reporters," Fenwick mused. "I don't see anything wrong with that picture."

"Morons will be always with us," Molton said.

"Wise sayings of Commander Molton?" Turner asked.

"What's the latest on this Furyk mess?" Molton asked.

When they finished filling him in, Molton said, "Cullom Furyk is getting more ink than Cunanan ever did, and we don't have a suspect."

Fenwick said, "You know, Smythe and Devonshire were in earlier asking to be put on more high-profile cases. They can have this one."

Molton said, "You'll like this next bit. The tabloid papers are supposedly going to hit hard on a police cover-up of a suicide on this. That the murder investigation is a smoke screen for what really happened."

"I like it," Fenwick said. "It appeals to my sense of what is loony in the world."

Molton said, "Probably if we'd have reported it as a suicide, they'd have said we were covering up a murder."

"The triumph of paranoia," Turner said.

"I'm for it," Fenwick added, "as long as everybody thinks it's me who's out to get them."

"Are these reporters going to get to your witnesses?" Molton asked.

"Not through us," Turner said, "but it isn't a big secret who was at the luncheon."

"We could lock everybody up connected to the case," Fenwick suggested.

Turner said, "At least we'd have a lot of convicts with a sense of color and fabric."

Jason O'Leary appeared at the top of the stairs. He was leading Eliot Norwyn. O'Leary said, "This guy got caught lurking around the squad cars in back. He says he needs to talk to you."

Norwyn thanked the cop and nodded at the detectives. "Is there someplace not so public where we can talk?" Norwyn was wearing walnut piqué-polyester jeans, a brown stretch-jersey asymmetrical-zip polo shirt, and black running shoes. His hips seemed to have been poured into the jeans. He held a red baseball hat in his left hand.

"Did somebody contact you?" Turner asked.

"When I got back to the hotel, the concierge told me the police had been in looking for me. I thought of calling to arrange a secret meeting. I wanted to avoid any chance of being caught in public. I need to talk. Quietly. I'm a goddamn teenage idol, and if the people at the show found out about this, I would lose the show and my fans. I'm supposed to be a role model. I've been on the damn program for seven years. I'm twenty-seven and I'm supposed to be this perpetual perfect adolescent."

They took him up to a fourth-floor conference room.

After they were seated, Turner asked, "Why did you want to see us?"

"I wasn't completely honest with you yesterday. I've been feeling bad about that."

"What did you need to tell us?" Turner said.

"I was afraid you might find out I talked to him earlier."

"We did find out," Fenwick said. "That's why we sent people to bring you in."

"They probably didn't find me because I canceled my afternoon interview. I've been brooding down by the lakefront most of the afternoon."

"What did you and Furyk talk about?" Turner asked.

"I have to do some explaining. I've got to be very honest. First, those days at the beach house weren't the only time I've been to bed with Cullom. Last May we met in the market on Place des Lices on Saint-Tropez. I was on vacation after the television season. Both of us had gone there early to avoid the madness of late summer. I had no idea he'd be there. I know you think it's hypocritical or impossible, but I'm not attracted to guys. I really am not. It's just Cullom is so, was so, exactly perfect for me at that moment. Being with him was just different, special."

"How long did you two stay together that time?"

"Just for the week I was there. He had another five days, but I left. He never called me, and I had to be careful about calling him. We certainly couldn't be seen together here in the States. We were very careful in Saint-Tropez."

"But you wanted more?" Turner asked.

"Yes. I knew he was going to be in town here. I knew he was going to be at the brunch. I got an invitation to that, but I didn't know if I'd have a real chance to talk to him. I heard about his photo shoot, and I went there. We talked briefly. He agreed to meet me late that evening."

"Were you in love?" Turner asked.

"No. It was more like an addiction, a compulsion that I couldn't control. I never went with other guys. I've dated lots of women. I've had sex with lots of women. I prefer sex with women."

"Cullom had this hold over you?" Fenwick asked.

"No, it wasn't like that at all. Mostly he seemed pretty indifferent to me. He was friendly enough when we were together, kind of passive in bed, but that was okay with me. If he'd gone wild with the gay sex stuff, I might have been turned off. Look, I'm being honest with you guys. I'm trying to avoid being a suspect. I know it looks bad. I guess I'm hoping that honesty will get you on my side." He gazed at each of them in turn.

"So you were supposed to meet later," Turner said.

"But at the brunch he told me he had to cancel. He had to meet with someone else."

"Who?"

"He didn't say. I didn't ask. He said we could meet today."

"At the brunch, where did you talk?"

"On the terrace. After brunch."

Turner and Fenwick gazed at him carefully.

"See, I'm being honest. Plus, I figured somebody would tell you I was out there. I think at least one other person saw me."

"Who?"

"I couldn't tell who it was. Someone rushed from one of the bedrooms when I walked in from the terrace."

"Do you think that person was watching the two of you?"

"Maybe. Probably."

"Did Cullom get on top of the wall while you were there?"

"No, I swear. Most of the time he was staring over the side. Some of the time he'd wave or hold his hands as if he were on a balcony, like Evita. I had a hard time getting him to listen to me. He was like that a lot. He was kind of a space cadet. If information didn't interest him, it had no hold on his mind."

"But when did he tell you he couldn't meet?"

"He saw me a couple minutes after I got there. Nobody else heard us. Jolanda Bokaru walked in at that moment so I couldn't pursue the issue. I'd gone out to the balcony to arrange another meeting, the one for today."

"Did he seem bothered at all, upset?"

"No. He was his usual self. Kind of loose, kind of goofy."

"Did you want a relationship with him?" Turner asked. "Something that would last?"

Norwyn whispered. "I don't know."

"Did you push him off the edge?" Turner asked.

"No, I swear to God, I did not. He was fine when I left. A few minutes later, I didn't see who it was, but I heard him out there arguing with someone. That wasn't like Cullom at all. He always had this cool persona in public."

"How was he in private?"

"Kind of gentle but self-absorbed too, but I think most of us actors and models are like that. All the ones I've met are. It doesn't mean we're bad people. It's just the way we are. The way we have to be."

Fenwick said, "Self-absorption raised to the level of one of the cardinal virtues. Have to think about that."

"Do cops always make fun of what witnesses say?" Eliot asked.

"He didn't get up on the ledge at all while you were there?" Turner asked.

"No. I told you that."

Turner and Fenwick began going over every movement Norwyn claimed to have made. For an hour they kept at it. He didn't change his story.

They left him in the conference room. At their desks the two detectives considered.

"He was out there at the scene of the crime," Fenwick said. "I like that in a killer."

"We have no one to corroborate when he went out there or when he came back in. We have no idea whether or not Furyk was alive or dead before, during, or after Norwyn's appearance on the balcony."

Fenwick said, "I don't get that stuff about Norwyn's sexual confusion."

Turner shrugged. "Norwyn certainly sounds gay to me. He obviously doesn't want to sound gay to himself. Maybe they both just wanted to get their rocks off with another pretty guy. Was Eliot in love, and he didn't want to accept that? I dated men while I was married to my wife. I didn't want to acknowledge or accept my feelings."

"Gay or straight, did he kill him?" Fenwick asked.

"He's not a shabby suspect, but not a great one yet."

"I didn't get his autograph," Fenwick said. "You must swear on your life that you will never reveal to my daughters that this second interview took place."

"Won't they understand this is a murder investigation?"

"He's a hunk, you should understand the appeal."

"I'm not the one who gets turned on while talking to a witness."

"You mean, I'm the only one so far who's admitted to it."

"What is it worth to you for me not to tell?"

"Want me to tell your boys which Bears' quarterback's autograph you didn't get?"

"Deal."

Their next phone call was from Arthur Oldinport. "I have two tickets for tonight's GUINEVERE, Incorporated fashion show. Everyone will be there. If you want an understanding of the fashion industry, you should go."

Turner agreed then asked, "Did you know Furyk had lovers in many cities?"

"I'm not surprised."

"Do you know who they were?"

"I can try and find out."

Turner hung up and told Fenwick.

"I can't go," Fenwick said. "I have promised to attend my daughters' basketball game. I am likely to be late as it is. I will not be forgiven if I miss this one."

"You're not being forgiven for a lot lately," Turner said.

"Oh, lordy, I have sinned mightily."

"I knew that."

"Maybe Ben would like to go."

Turner phoned his lover at the shop. Ben said, "I'm going to throw the computer through the plate-glass window. I could use a diversion."

"Computer not cured yet?"

"I was going to work on the program at home tonight. This sounds better, and it might be fun. I know Brian plans to be home tonight."

The next person to be brought in was Gerald Veleshki. Immediately behind him was Roger Heyling. They were in the same outfits as earlier.

"This tag-team shit is going to come to an end right now," Fenwick said. He marched to where O'Leary was escorting them. "Put these two gentlemen in separate interrogation rooms."

"What's the meaning of this?" Veleshki demanded.

"Separate means not together. You go one way. He goes the other."

O'Leary already had Heyling by the elbow and was leading him to the fourth floor. Fenwick said to Veleshki, "You come with me."

Veleshki looked over his shoulder at Heyling. His partner walked with his head sunk nearly to his chest. Fenwick led Veleshki to the currently not in use squad room. Turner joined them. They sat in folding chairs in one of the corners of the room.

"You visited Furyk at the Blue Diamond Health Club yesterday morning," Fenwick said.

"Yes. I confess I met him. I freely admit it. You may lock me up for this horrendous crime. Is that why you dragged me down here? If that's all, I need to get back to my company. We have the most important days of the winter season tomorrow and the next." He stood up.

"Sit down," Fenwick ordered. "You're not going anywhere."

"You can't do this to me."

Fenwick laughed. "I can't ask you questions? Sure, I can. Watch. Why did you go to the Blue Diamond to talk to him?"

"That's where he was. Why would I go someplace he wasn't to try and talk to him?"

Fenwick's face turned an unpleasant shade of red. Attempting to head off a possible explosion, Turner asked, "What did you talk about?"

"Sex, drugs and rock and roll."

"When he's frustrated," Turner said, "my partner gets annoyed and yells and carries on. It takes forever to get an interrogation done that way. I'd like to do this in a simple way. I ask basic questions. You give basic answers. I don't get snotty. You don't get snotty. We all go home with less stress."

Veleshki mulled over his options. After a few moments Turner saw the man's shoulders slump. Light sweat broke out on his upper lip.

Turner said, "Earlier today you said you hadn't had contact with him in months. You lied. We need an explanation from you about what is going on."

Veleshki leaned forward in his folding chair. He stared at the floor for several minutes. Turner and Fenwick let the silence build. They knew the quiet worked in their favor.

Finally, Veleshki said, "I went to try and get him to continue his affair with me." He squirmed. The rubber-bottomed chair legs squeaked against the floor. "He turned me down. He said he'd had me and that was enough. He told me to go away. So I left."

"Why'd you lie?" Turner asked.

"You think I'm going to admit this kind of thing in front of my lover?"

"You could have picked up the phone and called us," Fenwick said.

"Volunteer information to the police? What planet are you from?"

"He just said no, and everything is calm and peaceful?" Turner asked. "We'll be checking with whoever was at the club. With the camera crew filming Furyk. We'll find anybody who saw you talking. You took this rejection awful well. Maybe someone else will have a different perspective."

"I was as passionate as I could be in trying to convince him in a semi-public place. He is a charming young man." Veleshki put his elbows on his knees and placed his hands on either side of his head. He took several deep breaths. "I threatened to break off the deal to have him come work for us."

"You did have a deal?"

"Yes. I also told him I'd try and keep him from working for the other fashion houses."

"You have that kind of power?" Turner asked.

"No. I don't guess anyone really does. Not with someone who has Furyk's reputation. Somebody breaking in, yeah. That would happen mostly by innuendo anyway. You float rumors that the person is hard to work with, a drug user. I was bluffing, but I didn't care. I was mad. I wanted to get even. I'm not good with rejection. I don't know if people heard us or not. I wasn't paying a lot of attention. I might have been a little loud. I doubt it."

"Did he know you were bluffing?"

"He laughed at me when I made my threat. I'd say he knew I was bluffing."

"What was it about this guy that was so special?" Fenwick said.

"Charisma? Vulnerability? You looked at him and you thought about hot sex, about touching the perfect man, about making the world safe for him. In reality, he was like the iceberg with legions of men as *Titanics* heading for him. What's worse is, I knew he was there, and I didn't stop. I'm not sure many people would. Funny thing, though. The sex with him wasn't that great. You had to practically turn yourself inside out to get a response out of him."

"Did your lover know about this meeting?" Turner asked.

"God, no. I told him I had to be in town early to check some last-minute preparations with a caterer for a big party we're having the night after all the shows in town."

Fenwick asked, "At the penthouse, did you go out on the balcony any time from when you arrived to when you left with or without Furyk being there?"

"No. Absolutely not."

"Tell us about the deal for him to work for your company," Fenwick said.

"I would do anything to defeat Franklin Munsen, even agree to cooperate if I thought it would gain me an advantage. Getting Cullom to model for us would be a coup."

"Did Munsen know about this?"

"You'd have to ask him."

"Were you and your lover having problems?" Turner asked.

"We're great together."

"Then why were you trying to have an affair?" Turner asked.

"I don't know. All the pressures of the new line and the expansion? Furyk himself? I'm an idiot? A combination of all of the above. I wanted him to work for us because it would give me an excuse to see him and talk to him. I thought if I could just keep him around, maybe I could convince him. Just looking at him, just being in his presence, was enough to take your breath away."

"You sound pretty infatuated," Turner said.

"I was a fool. After my explosion, I don't know if he presumed he was or wasn't modeling for us. I walked out on him before anything like that could be settled."

"You didn't get angry at the rejection and kill him?" Turner asked.

"If he was dead, I would never have him. Alive, there was a chance. Look, I didn't go out on the balcony. Not for an instant. I was in Roger's presence every minute. He'll vouch for me."

They left him in the room and trudged up to the fourth floor to meet with Heyling in an interrogation room. The walls, the wooden table, the linoleum, the wire mesh on the screen, and the chairs were all different shades of gray. When they opened the door, Heyling had his elbows on the table, his head in his hands, his shoulders hunched, his legs tight together. He looked at the detectives warily.

Fenwick took a folding chair, turned it around, and straddled it backward. He put his arms on the top edge and smiled at Heyling. The other man gave him a mystified look.

Fenwick said, "Your lover met with Cullom Furyk yesterday morning to ask him to renew their affair."

Heyling dropped his head until his chin almost rested on the table. "I know," he muttered.

"He told you?" Turner asked.

"I'm not stupid. Gerald has strayed before. I can sense when he is getting restless. I don't know what to do when that happens. I try to get him to talk, but he won't. I'm not very good at talking."

"How did you know they met?"

"I knew there was no meeting with the caterer. I asked Furyk at the brunch if he'd met with Gerald. He told me he had."

"What did you do?"

"What could I do? I love Gerald. I'm sorry, but I do. Sometimes I wish I didn't. Sure, I won all that lottery money, but it's Gerald who's given me a life. He showed me how to spend it wisely. He showed me how to invest it."

"He manages the money?" Fenwick asked.

"I see what you're trying to say. That he duped me and now I'm broke. That's not true. From the very beginning, it was my idea to start the company. He didn't twist my arm."

"But it was all your money," Fenwick said.

"I loved him before I won the money. I loved him when I won it. I love him now."

"Even though he's a cheater?" Turner asked.

"Why would I kill Furyk? What would be the point? Gerald

152

was the cheater. Furyk was just another in a long line. If I was going to kill anyone, it would have been Gerald. Not that I would have. I know he'll come back to me. He always has."

"Why do you take him back? What kind of dignity is that?" Turner asked.

"Love is much more powerful than dignity, isn't' it? I think it is. We may not have been legally married, but we promised each other our lives together."

"He didn't keep his promises," Turner said.

"But I do."

"Did you go out on the balcony at any time from when you arrived at the brunch until it was over?" Turner asked.

"No."

"Did Gerald?"

"No."

"Did you see anyone else?"

"No."

"Was Gerald in your presence the whole time?"

The slightest hesitation, but the detectives noticed it. "After the dessert was served, I went to the bathroom. When I left, he was in the dining room. When I came back, he was there. I was only gone a minute or so. He was sitting exactly where I left him. He certainly did not have time to hunt for Furyk and kill him."

"You left the room, though," Turner said. "Yesterday you told us you weren't outside of each other's presence. You lied to us."

"No, I didn't. You asked the question and Gerald answered. I kept my mouth shut."

Fenwick said, "That's a hell of a fine distinction for someone on their way to being a murder suspect. He lied by commission. You lied by omission. That works out to the same thing."

Turner asked, "Did anyone see you go into the bathroom and come out?"

"One of the caterers saw me go in. I don't know which one.

It wasn't a memorable moment. We just passed each other in the corridor."

"You could have found him and killed him."

"I didn't. There wasn't time for that, either. People must have seen me enter and leave."

Turner doubted if anyone could remember the times and movements of any of the others at the party with the degree of precision the detectives would need to accuse someone of murder.

Turner simply accepted Heyling's statement as something to be checked and verified as best as possible. He had listened to people lie—from vicious serial killers to spur-of-the-moment murderers, husbands and wives who couldn't take it anymore. Some were obvious liars. Some were brilliant at it. And whether they told the truth or not, it was better to get hard, physical evidence.

"If Furyk was going to be modeling for your company," Turner asked, "weren't you afraid he would try and steal your lover?"

"Cullom Furyk was not the problem. How many times do I have to tell you that? Gerald was."

"Whose idea was it to get Furyk to model for you?"

"Gerald's. He said we needed him for a boost in sales. It is true that Furyk's presence in an ad campaign has made significant differences in a company's profits. Huge differences."

"You needed him more than he needed you?" Fenwick asked.

"Yes."

"I thought your company was doing well."

"Better than ever, but this time of the year is difficult. Cash flow can be rough about now."

Turner figured they'd have to get some accounting experts to talk to in the near future.

"Would the company have failed without him?" Fenwick asked.

"I don't know! I'm a designer. I create. Gerald handles the financial aspects. I trust him."

"Why?" Turner asked. "If he was cheating on your relationship, why wouldn't he cheat with the company?"

Heyling looked as if this was a new thought. He tried rallying. "He wouldn't." He ran his hands over his face. "I want to go now," he said.

"Wait here," Fenwick ordered.

They stopped in Veleshki's room. He sneered at them. "Now what?" he demanded.

"You and Heyling were not in each other's presence the whole time."

"Yes, we were."

"He went to the bathroom during dessert."

Veleshki gazed at them. "I don't remember him leaving. If I remember correctly, during dessert I was discussing an upcoming article about the company with Jolanda Bokaru. It was very important coverage. I did not have time to monitor my lover's movements. Are you saying he was out of the room? He most certainly is not the killer. That's absurd."

"How do you know?" Fenwick asked.

"I've been his lover for fifteen years. I know him."

"How has he put up with your cheating?" Fenwick asked.

"I believe that is between him and me."

They left. At their desks, Fenwick said, "I want chocolate. There may not be enough in the entire city to satisfy me."

"You frustrated by our witnesses?" Turner asked.

"No, just hungry." He tapped his fist on the chart on top of his desk. "You realize," Fenwick said, "that this entire exercise has been futile. There's all kinds of gaps when any one of these people could have slipped out and pushed Furyk."

"Yeah. Works out that way sometimes."

"But it's such a pretty chart."

Not having a clever response to this crack, Turner said, "We need to talk to Kindel before we decide what to do next." He paused, then asked, "Did Heyling or Veleshki kill Furyk?"

Fenwick considered. "We have no physical evidence. No witnesses. Did either of them have the time? Only if they knew precisely where Furyk was. Only if they had a very quick argument with him. Remember, Norwyn said he heard an argument."

"Maybe Furyk wasn't arguing with the killer."

Fenwick considered some more. "I got no instinct either way. I know we don't have enough to arrest them."

Turner agreed. "Let's let them stew for a while and see if the uniforms can get Kindel in here."

They'd been working on the day's paperwork for fifteen minutes when the phone intercom buzzed. O'Leary said, "We just got a call on that Kindel guy you're looking for. He's in the hospital. They're not sure he's going to live."

A phone call to the emergency room doctor got them only the data that Kindel was unconscious, and he didn't know when or if his patient would awaken.

Turner arranged for there to be a police guard on Kindel's room. They were to be called immediately if he came around. Then Turner called the Twenty-first district. The beat cop who made the initial report wasn't in. The sergeant at the desk looked up the paperwork and gave Turner the basics. Found unconscious in an alley off Broadway. That's all he knew.

They had little choice but to let their suspects go. Turner was reluctant to free Heyling and Veleshki, but they had no hard evidence and certainly nothing a prosecutor could go with.

SEVENTEEN

When Paul got home, Ben was at the computer, and Jeff was watching him carefully. Paul hugged them both. "Any luck?" he asked.

Ben said, "I have not bashed it to smithereens with a baseball bat yet."

"I wish I understood the program better," Jeff said. "I wish I could help."

Ben saved what he was working on and stood up. Jeff called up a game on the computer. Paul and Ben strolled into the kitchen. Ben checked the lasagna in the oven.

"Brian home?" Paul asked.

"Yeah, I think he's given up on the camping deal, but I also think he's got a new project. I don't know what it is, but he's been whispering on the phone since he got home."

They both listened to the thudding of the older boy as he

pounded down the steps. Moments later he was in the kitchen.

"Hi, Dad. When's dinner? I'm starved. Can I borrow the car to drive to Iowa City this weekend?"

"Hi, son. Soon. No. What's in Iowa City?"

"People, houses."

"You want to talk car use or do an inept imitation of Buck Fenwick?"

"The university is having an open house for people considering going there."

"Amount of supervision?"

"I think one of the parents of one of the kids is going."

"Not a ringing endorsement designed to win over a doubting father."

"Whining do any good?"

"You used up this week's quota on the camping trip."

The phone rang once. Seconds later Jeff's voice called from the living room, "Brian, phone."

Brian picked up the extension and took it as far as the cord would allow down the basement stairs. Paul heard, "No, he won't let me go."

Ben turned to Paul. "We weren't like that when we were teenagers, were we?"

"I was," Paul answered. "So were you."

"I don't know if that's frightening or comforting." Ben sighed. "We better get them fed."

Over dinner Jeff asked, "What is this fashion show you guys are going to? Is it going to be like last night?"

Paul said, "I think this is one of those deals like you see on television with the models strolling down the runway showing off a line of couture clothes."

"What's couture?" Jeff asked.

Paul explained. "Each model wears a one-of-a-kind outfit that is very, very expensive."

"You should dress up tonight," Brian said.

"What do you suggest?" Paul asked.

"I've got some stuff I might lend both of you. You've got to make an impression."

"Ben wouldn't fit into any of your clothes," Paul said. His lover was slightly taller and more muscular.

"Maybe I can find something a little different," Ben conceded.

To the fashion show Ben wore a pair of black leather pants snug enough on his hips not to need a belt; a crisp white T-shirt that showed off his broad shoulder muscles; black boots; and a fur-lined leather jacket. At Brian's insistence Paul wore his son's iridescent plum shirt and silver pants with suspenders. He wore his own dress shoes and a dark blue overcoat. Paul went along with Brian's suggestions partly to make up for his refusal to let him go on the camping trip and partly because he figured he wouldn't meet anybody who would razz him about his outfit later. And he had to admit to himself, he did wear boring clothes.

As they were getting ready to walk out the door, Paul looked at himself in the full-length mirror in the living room. "I look ridiculous," he said. "These aren't clothes for somebody my age."

"You look perfect," Brian said. "You'll be the studliest-looking guys there."

"I like it," Jeff said. The eleven-year-old looked critically at Ben. "Ben looks like a movie star."

"We clash," Ben said. "What could be better? We'll be making our own fashion statement. You look very sexy." He kissed Paul on the lips.

When the kiss began to be prolonged, Jeff said, "Kissing's mushy."

"You'll understand when you get older," Brian said.

Paul knew if there were an emergency with Jeff, Brian would have sense enough to call the paramedics and then call him. It had been a number of years since a crisis with Jeff's spina bifida had arisen.

At they walked out the door Brian patted each of them on the shoulder and said, "You guys have a good time."

After the door closed, Paul said, "Sometimes I can't tell if he's seven, seventeen, or seventy."

Ben said, "I believe the proper medical term for that is rampant teenage hormones. With luck, we'll survive."

The fashion show that night was in the domed auditorium at the east end of Navy Pier. As they pulled off Lake Shore Drive they could see a bank of klieg lights. Their pale blue beams swirled and eddied against the winter sky. Paul and Ben were forced to park several blocks away from their destination.

Before they even got to the pier, they could see rotating Mars lights in great sweeping curves on top of the auditorium's dome. Paul and Ben walked along the south side of the pier, past the moored sightseeing boats. In the last few years, the newly renovated pier had attracted thousands of visitors. The huge Ferris wheel was one of the more prominent new sights along the lakefront skyline. They strolled with their shoulders nearly touching. The wind was down and the night was extremely fine for January. The temperature was supposed to stay above freezing all night.

They found their tickets waiting for them in a booth outside the door. A valet in a pink polyester jumpsuit took their coats and gave them redemption tickets.

Absolutely no one noticed their entrance. The crowd probably would not have noticed a herd of man-eating tigers if they loped through the doors. There was an excitement in the air not evident at last night's event. To Paul it looked like people were mostly trying to promenade in their outfits, catch sight of the famous or create their own sensation to become famous or at least noticed.

He imagined there couldn't be an ounce of shame in the room. For the sake of the denizens he hoped there wasn't, because if there was, the Embarrassment Police would have to arrest at least half the crowd.

Mounds of food covered a large buffet at the far east end of the room. People crammed around these tables. Loud, annoying rock music blasted over the throng. People shouted in order to converse over the din. Paul nudged Ben and nodded toward a group of men in the sheer underwear he'd seen earlier at GUINEVERE. "I want to get you a pair of those."

"Thank you, I have underwear."

"Not like that."

"Nobody has underwear like that. It's only for show."

"The ones I saw at Heyling and Veleshki were even sexier."

A woman walked by with more fruit on her head than Carmen Miranda wore in all of her movies combined.

"How does that stay up?" Ben asked.

"Pulleys? Wires? Magic?"

The uniquely clad mixed with those in tuxedoes or traditional gowns and exquisite furs. Immediately in front of them, three women and a drag queen strutted by in black wedding dresses. To their left one woman wore a white gown with one padded shoulder, a second a leather strapless dress, a third a fringed skirt and necklace, and another a gold-embroidered red vest and a tiered skirt in black and pink.

Arthur Oldinport and Battle joined Paul and Ben. Paul introduced Ben. Watching them gaze at the crowd, Oldinport said, "They aren't nearly as amusing as they wish they were. And not half as fashionable as I know they are not." He wore a black velvet tux with a white ruffled shirt. Battle wore a yellow-leather tux, lemon-yellow T-shirt, and mirrored sunglasses.

A woman in an orange bra and panties tapped Oldinport on the shoulder. He leaned toward her. Battle placed a fingertip on the middle button on Paul's shirt. "You look much more interesting this evening, Detective Turner."

Paul looked down at himself in the mirrors of the sunglasses. He remained silent and unmoving as the crowd swirled around them. Oldinport glanced in their direction and quickly averted his eyes. Battle began to move his finger down.

Paul didn't move. He stated flatly, "I wouldn't."

The finger stopped.

Battle smiled good-naturedly. "You could be in my runway show anytime you wanted."

Paul laughed. "I'm as much of a star as I ever want to be."

Battle moved back into Oldinport's orbit.

Moment's later Battle said, "There's one of the Kennedys."

Many in the crowd were craning their necks toward the dais.

"Which one is a Kennedy?" Ben asked.

Battle pointed to the runway, but Paul wasn't sure whom he was pointing to.

"Donald is here," Battle announced. "I think I saw Donna earlier."

"Donald who?" Ben asked.

They couldn't see Battle's eyes, but his mouth twisted in a sneer. "Trump."

"Oh." Neither Paul nor Ben asked "Donna who?"

"Look, Cindy Crawford." Battle waved.

No one that Paul could see waved back. Oldinport put an arm around Battle and said, "Why don't you get us something to drink?" After taking their order Battle scuttled off. "I have front-row seats for you," Oldinport said.

"Thanks," Paul said. "You heard Sean Kindel is in the hospital?"

"A friend called and told me. He was supposed to be here tonight. What happened?"

"We don't know. He's not awake yet."

"Poor thing."

"Did you know he and Cullom Furyk were lovers?"

"I've heard that rumor today, but never before."

"Could it be true?"

"I don't know."

"Have you found out anything about his overseas lovers?"

"Not yet."

"Where else could Furyk have been staying besides the penthouse or with Kindel?"

"I don't know." A group of men in tuxedoes approached Oldinport. They discussed outfits and personalities for several minutes. The crowd continued to swell and there was no further chance to question Oldinport.

A few minutes later Battle returned with drinks for both of them. Since he couldn't find a place to set it down, Paul held it in his hand. Moments later Battle sidled up to Ben. The young man whispered in Ben's ear. When Battle started the finger approach, Ben grabbed his hand before it touched his T-shirt.

Paul heard Battle say, "You're so rugged."

Ben said, "Good-bye."

Paul saw Gordon Findley standing near the runway. Findley was talking and laughing with a group of young men and women whom Paul thought good-looking enough to be models. Findley seemed to be hiding his grief remarkably well.

Paul listened to Oldinport and the others. He heard snatches of conversation. "No more padded shoulders" and "So liberating, so breathless" and "So boring" and "So eighties" and "The nineties look is nothing" and "Look, isn't that . . . ?" and "In these provincial towns . . ." and "Very Brad Pitt" and "Inspired by Klimt" and "It was so fabulous, after the show half the audience needed to be revived" and "I guess they have to let that Eurotrash in" and "Out here in the back forty . . ." and "Can you imagine, you can't even see over Lake Michigan" and "I've never been in a town that didn't have a real coastline." Several times Paul found himself chuckling at the absurdity and excess. He placed his untasted drink on a passing waiter's tray.

Fifteen minutes later the lights in the room dimmed while those for the runway brightened. As they moved to their seats, Ben leaned close to Paul and said quietly, "I wonder how much Oldinport pays Battle a year."

"Kept boys can't be cheap," Paul said.

"Hell of a life to live, being a slave to some Twinkie."

"I think Oldinport's the master."

Ben shook his head. "You don't make a play for someone within five feet of your sugar daddy if you don't have a lot of confidence in your own powers."

"Or you took a stupid pill just before you left for the show." Paul saw Oldinport and Battle talking to a woman in a bikini made of daisies. "I'm sure he's a three-dimensional person," Paul said. "I'm sure all these people are."

"Some people hide their talents," Ben said; "it's just that most of these people seem to have hidden them so ostentatiously."

Paul put his arm around Ben. "I'm glad you're here tonight. It's fun talking about these people in a non-police-detective mode."

Ben squeezed Paul's shoulder. They took their seats. Battle was next to Ben, and Oldinport was next to Paul.

Across the way Paul saw Eliot Norwyn in the front row talking to Matt Lauer from NBC.

"You're in for a treat," Oldinport said. "I've heard GUINE-VERE's new line is going to be fantastic." He pointed to the people across the aisle. "Munsen's got a lineup of international celebrities over there that Heyling and Veleshki will be hard put to beat." Turner thought he recognized Mel Gibson.

A trumpet fanfare was a cue for all the lights to go out. The crowd murmured. When the lights came on again moments later, Sibilla Manetti stood at the entrance to the runway.

"She's naked," Ben whispered.

Indeed, to Paul she did not look as if she had a stitch on. He couldn't wait to tell Fenwick what he'd missed. Cameras flashed brightly as Sibilla strutted forward in what Paul would call a bump and grind. She held her head rigidly above the audience as she passed them all. She stopped at the end of the runway, gazed left and right then strutted back the way she came. As she moved, it became apparent that she was covered from neck to ankle in a see-through silk body stocking, which was too sheer to conceal anything.

Paul heard Ben chuckling. Paul leaned close to him. "What?"

"The empress has no clothes. I hope this is supposed to be funny. I don't know if I'm going to be able to contain myself."

Oldinport raised an eyebrow at them. Several people glared.

As Sibilla disappeared the next woman entered. To Turner it looked as if someone had cut a hole in the middle of a bedsheet and then draped it over the woman. The woman's hair was cut short and plastered down.

"It's a bedsheet." Ben guffawed.

Paul nodded. "Got to be."

Ben pulled out his hanky and put it in front of his mouth. Fortunately, Ben's laugh was never loud, but there was no doubt to anyone nearby that he was convulsed with mirth.

When the next woman appeared, in what looked for all the world to be an old army blanket with a slit cut in the middle, Paul saw tears rolling down Ben's face. His lover bent over, attempting to control and conceal his mirth.

Oldinport leaned over. "Perhaps your friend had best take himself outside and come back when he can better appreciate what he's seeing." Oldinport's lips formed a severe, thin line and his voice cut sharper than a pair of shears.

Ben had heard. "I can't help it," he said.

Oldinport said, "Would you be so kind? For most of us this is serious business."

Ben nodded and slipped away. Paul glanced around. Few seemed to be taking real notice of them. The next woman wore what Paul thought might have been an old chenille bedspread. She was followed by a woman wearing what Paul swore was a transparent vinyl shower curtain. He saw people around him taking notes furiously or marking their programs with the numbers they planned to buy. All gave the show rapt attention. Toward the back he thought he saw a section of people who seemed ready to applaud and cheer, and ooh and aah as if on cue. He wondered if hiring cheering sections at your own fashion show was good form. The music varied between wild polkas and snatches of famous symphonies—all set to a rock-and-roll beat. Watching the women and their outfits very quickly became boring to Paul. He lasted as long as he could, observing the famous, the near famous, and those wishing to be famous take the entire affair very seriously. After half an hour he went in search of Ben but couldn't find him. He retrieved his coat and stepped outside.

At the northeast corner at the farthest end of the pier, he found Daniel Egremont smoking a cigarette. The accountant was wearing a black leather jacket, dark gray dress pants, and a white dress shirt open at the collar. The wind was calm and the night was clear with a full moon lighting the star-speckled water.

"Being here tonight part of your investigation?" Egremont asked.

"I'm not sure tonight has been very helpful."

"All this nonsense should give you some insight into how superficial and shallow these people's lives are."

"I hate to sound like I'm defending them, but I can imagine the planning and work that must go into what I've just seen. If you don't like it, why do you still work for them?"

"I want out."

"You're not happy in your work?"

"I love accounting. I used to enjoy the beautiful people merry-go-round. I don't so much anymore. Just for a while I'd like to take a break."

"I don't understand enough about the financial health of the two companies. Can you help me with that?"

Egremont was instantly wary. "Maybe."

"We may have to subpoena the books from both companies."

"In a murder investigation?"

"If Cullom Furyk was such a draw and he was switching companies, maybe it would have hurt GUINEVERE, Incorporated a great deal. Maybe people were really angry that Veleshki and Heyling would reap the benefits."

"Cullom was leaving GUINEVERE?"

"You didn't know?"

"No. Of course, Heyling and Veleshki would not have confided in me." He tossed his cigarette into the lake water ten feet below. "As for my boss, Franklin Munsen confides in no one. If he was in danger of losing Furyk, he might or might not tell anyone. He thinks he is the smartest person in the company and among the smartest in the fashion industry."

"And you don't agree?"

"Smartest? He is pretty bright."

"We were told he is the most hated man in the fashion industry."

"The most hated is a little strong, but not by much. He can be vicious all out of proportion to need."

"Would it have been devastating to GUINEVERE if Furyk left the company?"

Egremont considered. "Some, but spokespeople are a dime a

dozen. Well, considerably more than that, but you drop Furyk, so you find a sports superstar or a hot actor. There's always another pretty face."

"How much did Furyk earn a year?"

"With all his endorsements, at least several million."

"Where is all his money?" Turner asked.

"I beg your pardon."

"If he was rich, where is all his stuff? We got a small mound of clothes and that's it. Did he own homes here or overseas?"

"Not that I know of, but I wouldn't know details about his financial status. I know we paid him slightly more than nine hundred thousand dollars last year."

"And who inherits all of it?"

"I have no idea."

"Did you know he had lovers in cities in different parts of the world?"

"I'm not surprised."

"Why not?"

"He was young, rich and gorgeous. He could have anything he wanted."

"Yes, but there must be young, rich and gorgeous people who are monogamous."

"I would presume you are right. I don't make moral judgments."

"I'm not sure I want to make a moral judgment," Turner said. "I'm just baffled. That kind of money is worth playing deadly games for. There are emotional attachments of others to him, but he didn't seem attached to anybody. And then, the fashion world is foreign to me. I don't understand most of it." Turner pointed inside. "Do people seriously think someone is going to buy those clothes?"

"The idea is to make a splash. To be so hot that people want to be associated with your name. Couture is about people wanting you to be their designer. It's the name and the fame as much as the actual fabric, cut and color.''

Paul heard a shout. He looked left then right. The pier at this far eastern end was several hundred feet across. He and Egremont were about ten feet from the northeast corner. He saw two figures grappling on the southeast corner. He began to move toward them. He heard another shout. He thought it was Ben's voice. He began to run. His trench coat flapped behind him. As he neared them, one of the fighters teetered for a moment and then plunged into the water.

The person still on the pier turned toward him for a second, then fled toward the west. Paul could tell he was white, short, skinny and wearing dark clothes.

"**H**ey, help!" the person in the water called. Paul recognized Ben's voice for sure this time. He didn't waste time on the fleeing figure. He ran to the edge of the pier and looked over the ten-foot drop.

"Hey!" Ben yelled.

"Ben, it's Paul." He could barely see his lover's face in the water.

"I can't get a purchase on the damn pier," Ben shouted.

Paul knew the greatest danger at the moment came from hypothermia. He knew Ben could swim, but he didn't know where the closest place was to yank someone ashore. With the water this cold, he knew his lover could last less than four minutes.

Paul took off his coat. Quickly he twisted one sleeve around his hand and wrist. He dangled it down. He saw Ben reach for the coat and miss. Paul felt the presence of other people. Ben treaded water then lunged upward, grasping for Paul's coat. Paul felt the tug of Ben's weight on his arm. He heaved upward. Several hands reached on either side of him and grabbed at the coat.

Moments later Ben was on the pier. His teeth chattered, and he shivered violently. "Christ, I'm cold," he said.

Paul said, "We've got to get you inside and warm and out of these cold clothes."

As they ushered Ben into the ballroom, Paul glanced down the length of the pier. Whoever had pushed him had long since vanished. When a security guard appeared, Paul showed him his identification.

"What happened?" the guard asked.

"Get on your radio," Paul commanded, "and call the guards and stop anyone from leaving the pier. Do it now."

"We can't just . . ." began the guard.

Paul yanked the radio from the guard's belt. He pressed the on button.

"Hey . . ." The guard reached to grab back the radio.

Paul turned his back. He gave the person on the other end a description of the attacker. He took out his cell phone and dialed 999 to hook up directly to the local police zone. He identified himself and asked for backup and an ambulance.

Ben sat on a chair in the last row of the ballroom. A small crowd stood around him. The commotion had caused many to turn and stare momentarily, but the show had continued. Paul recognized the strains of the last movement of Beethoven's Ninth Symphony. He saw a huddle of sopping clothes a few feet to Ben's left. His lover was wrapped in layers of tuxedo jackets and elegant wraps. A mink muff held in place by three silk scarves encircled his feet.

Ben shivered. "I have never been this cold."

Paul leaned down and held his lover. A woman covered in furs and diamonds handed Ben a glass filled with liquid.

"What's this?" Paul asked.

"Brandy. It'll help warm him up."

Paul looked at the woman. "We need something warm. Liquor isn't good for hypothermia."

"Oh," she said. Her diamonds glittered and sparkled. "I'll find something." Moments later, as a squad car pulled up, she appeared with a steaming cup of coffee. Ben gulped down the scalding liquid. Paul identified himself to the uniforms. They placed Ben in the front seat of the squad car and turned the heat on full blast.

"Does he need to go to a hospitals?" a uniform asked.

Mars lights rotated on an ambulance hurrying down the pier. Paul hovered nearby as the paramedics examined Ben. In minutes they assured him Ben would probably be okay, but he should be looked at by a doctor. The woman in the furs reappeared a few moments later with a man in a tuxedo.

"Theresa says you need a doctor?" He examined Ben for several minutes, talked to the paramedics, then confirmed that he would be okay. Paul thanked him, and the doctor returned to the party. Paul looked for the elegantly attired woman to thank her, but she had gone.

Paul joined Ben in the squad car. He sat behind the wheel. The heat was stifling.

Ben gazed at him. "I look more ridiculous than you do."

The pile of elegant clothes rose and fell with Ben's breathing.

"You okay?" Paul asked.

"Starting to get a little warm. You know I'm naked under all this crap."

"We'll get you some real clothes as soon as possible, although that is probably the priciest outfit you will ever wear." He put his arm around Ben's shoulder and held him awkwardly.

"Maybe I'll start a new fashion trend," Ben said.

"Where'd you go? What happened?"

"For quite a while, I stood in the back of the hall out of the lights. I was pretty much under control, but I wasn't about to crawl over all those people to get back to my seat. I'm surprised the rich and famous don't mind being packed in like sardines. Unfortunately, I lost it again with the woman in the rainbow-colored ostrich plumes. She reminded me of a bad drag act I saw in New Orleans years ago. I couldn't stop laughing, so I got my coat and went outside. I walked down to the other end of the pier. When I got back to this end, I was thinking of going inside, but the January warmth was so pleasant, and the water was so pretty with the moon and stars reflecting off it. I kind of lost track of anything else.

"Suddenly, somebody tried to push me. I tried to grab whoever it was, but I couldn't get a good hold. I was too close to the edge. When I tried to push back, my feet slipped into nothing. The next thing I knew I was in the freezing water."

"You remember anything else at all."

Ben thought. "He kind of smelled like he hadn't had a bath in a while."

Paul asked, "Did you get any kind of look at the attacker?"

"Nothing. It all happened so fast."

A uniformed cop knocked on the car window.

Paul said, "I've got to check things out."

Ben nodded.

Outside the car several officers clustered around Paul. One of them said, "We're going to have a thousand people trying to leave in a few minutes. We don't have the personnel to stop and inspect everyone. Who are we looking for anyway?"

Paul gave them the limited he description he had.

He saw one of the uniforms gazing at his outfit.

"What?" Paul demanded.

"I never thought I'd see a detective wearing an outfit like that."

Paul had discarded his coat when it had gotten soaked in the rescue. He'd been acting too quickly to notice the cold. "You guys got here pretty quick," Paul said. "Maybe whoever it was didn't get a chance to get off the pier. Let's see if we can't organize a search party. Station a couple of people at the other end of the pier.''

Paul stood at the main exit and eyed the crowd. He saw Munsen surrounded by reporters and a large entourage. Findley hung on to the fringe of this group. He saw Sibilla Manetti in a full-length fur coat. She sported a muscular bodyguard at each elbow. They wore tuxedos under their open Burberry overcoats. The guards made no visible move, but the photographers avoided getting too close. Flashbulbs popped near her as she strode toward him. When she was close enough, she spoke softly, ''I hear there was a problem.''

''Word travels quickly.''

''Doesn't it always? May I help?''

''We need a set of clothes. My lover was pushed into the lake.''

She bent over and glanced into the car at Ben. She stood up straight. She murmured to one of her guards, ''Marco, hurry to the limousine and get a change of clothes and bring something to keep Detective Turner warm as well.''

The man at her left hurried off.

''Thank you,'' Paul said.

''A gay detective,'' she said.

''Yes.''

''Why would someone want to push your lover into Lake Michigan?''

''I don't know.''

Oldinport and Battle joined them. ''Sibilla, I haven't had the pleasure this trip.'' Oldinport sounded like a bereaved father. He leaned over to kiss the air next to Sibilla's cheek.

She stepped back. ''Go away.'' Her remaining muscular companion immediately stepped between them.

Oldinport looked as if he'd been slapped. Battle sneered. Photographers rushed toward the group. Sibilla put her arm through

Paul's and walked with him down the pier a few feet. Their backs were to the entire rest of the crowd.

"You don't get along with Oldinport," Turner observed.

"He has been vicious in his column to me for years."

Paul wasn't sure what to say to this. He muttered, "I'm sorry."

"I fear I was not completely honest with you," Sibilla said.

Paul smelled her perfume. It made him think of chalk dust in grade school. He wondered if it was supposed to be alluring. "What haven't you told me?"

"Cullom wasn't planning to leave GUINEVERE voluntarily. Franklin Munsen was throwing him out."

"Why didn't you tell me this before?"

"I have strong ambiguous feelings about Munsen. I do owe him a great deal. At one time he and I were close."

Turner hesitated about asking how close. Unless it bore directly on the murder, he was not interested in the details of another assignation among the fashion glitterati.

"In many ways he helped make me what I am today. Tonight, it was almost as if he were crazed. He was rude, abrupt and cruel to me and all the other models. It wasn't the first time he turned his vicious side on me, but always before I've let it roll off my back. Maybe tonight it was loyalty to Cullom or maybe I'm sick to death of his malevolent spite. At any rate, I wouldn't mind casting a few aspersions on him."

"Why be mean to you? Were you going to tell me he killed Cullom?"

"Munsen is an example of the triumph of paranoia. He knows you talked to me, and he thinks I may be the source of some suspicions you may have."

"Or do you have some kind of hold on him? Was he cheating on his wife with you?"

She arched an eyebrow at him.

"Sorry, my lover's been attacked. I don't have the patience I probably should with all you people. You all lied."

"If it serves their purposes, doesn't anyone? And knowing you are in the presence of a detective could make a person at least a little nervous."

"Yes," Paul conceded. He knew this to be true. In a crowd of people Paul didn't know well, he avoided mentioning his profession. He was heartily sick of people asking him his opinion of prominent cases, from O. J. to Ramsey to Cunanan. If it wasn't a case he was working on, he knew as little or as much as the rest of the public could read in a newspaper or see on television.

Turner said, "Why was he getting rid of him?"

"Cullom wouldn't tell me. He was meeting with Munsen to try and reach an amicable solution."

"He stayed for brunch, so assumedly they hadn't fought, or at least there wasn't an irreparable breach."

"If Munsen had a chance to talk to him."

"Munsen said they talked. Maybe he changed his mind about dumping him, or he could have been lying to you. Who else knew about this?"

"I don't know," she said. "It couldn't have been many people or it would have been gossiped about."

Marco returned with clothes. Paul took them over to Ben.

"You okay enough to change into these?" Paul asked.

"I'm almost warm enough. Is that Sibilla Manetti?"

"You know who she is?"

"Vaguely."

Sibilla knocked on the window. Ben rolled it down. "Are you all right?" she asked. "Do you wish me to provide you with a ride home? My limousine and my guards are at your disposal."

Ben held out his hand. "Ben Vargas. I'm pleased to meet you. I'm fine, thanks."

Sibilla held his hand for a moment.

Under the mound of clothes, Ben squirmed into the outfit Marco had provided. Paul didn't ask why Marco had an extra set of clothes in the car. He pulled on the gray sweatshirt Marco handed to him. It had a logo of the Eiffel Tower on the front. It bulked on Paul.

A squad car with lights rotating made its way slowly through the throng that was leaving the pier. Paul could see that someone was in the backseat.

If he was expecting one of the suspects from the case, he was disappointed. He saw a scruffy white youth with close-cropped hair and an earring in his left nostril.

The uniform behind the wheel of the car got out and approached Paul. "Can I talk to you?"

Paul turned to Sibilla. "Thank you for your help. I'll be with you in a couple minutes."

"We must be going," she said. "There are a number of after-show parties, and I must make an appearance. Is there anything more I can do to help? Perhaps one of my guards could return the clothes Ben has been using to keep warm."

"Thanks."

Marco distributed the clothes to those who had stayed to wait for them. Then Sibilla and her guards left.

NINETEEN

Turner gave the young cop an expectant look. The uniform nodded toward the interior of the car. "They found this guy hiding on the skyline stage. No driver's license or any other identification. He says his name is Tyler Madison. He claims he's nineteen and from Iron Mountain, Michigan. If he's nineteen, I'm the mayor. He says he was staying at the stage for the night. He's the only suspicious person we've found so far."

They were outside the southeast end of the ballroom. Toward the lake there was no one. Knots of people stood about thirty feet toward the west, slowing meandering away. Squad cars blocked the view north and south. Ben was in a car fifteen feet away. He wore an overcoat buttoned up to the neck and was rubbing his hands together.

"Let me talk to the kid," Turner said.

The uniform took the guy out of the car. As they neared, Paul felt himself trembling as if he himself had been in the water. Madison was maybe five feet seven, scrawny, and might be old enough to drive. The kid's brush-cut hair was uneven and stuck up at odd angles at random points on his head. His unzipped leather jacket was cracked and worn. His torn and baggy jeans hung low on his hips. When the uniform let go of him, he slouched forward. Up close he stank.

"What?" the kid snarled.

Paul always told himself later that if it hadn't been for the snarl, he would have been able to control himself. Paul prided himself on leaving the tradition of roughing people up to the Neanderthal days of law enforcement. Yes, he'd had to physically subdue criminals. This was different. This was personal. The uniform was on the other side of the squad car looking the other way. No one else was nearby. Paul could do whatever he wanted and there would be no witness.

Paul grabbed the kid by the coat lapels and slammed him up against the squad car.

"Hey," the kid whined. The kid tried slapping his right hand at Paul's powerful grasp.

Without a thought Paul slammed the kid up against the car again.

"That was my lover, you son of a bitch." Paul's heavy breathing came more from the emotion of the moment than the physical exertion of holding the kid in place. He slammed the kid again. "Why the hell did you shove him?"

The kid began to cry. "Please, stop."

Whether real or fake, the tears stopped Paul. He stepped back. His physical passion was spent for the moment. He waited for his breathing to come under control.

The kid had one hand on the car windshield and another clutching his side, where he'd banged into the rearview mirror.

Very quietly Paul asked, "Why'd you push him into the lake?"

"A guy offered me a hundred bucks to do it. Said he'd give me a hundred more when I was done. Why'd you hit me?"

Paul didn't say, "Because you snarled like a snot-nosed creep." Instead he asked, "Who was it?"

"I dunno."

"You took a hundred bucks to kill someone?"

"I only got half. It was just to shove him into the water."

"It's winter. You know what happens to people when they're in freezing water?" Paul's voice nearly attained the rumbling depths Fenwick's did at his most angry.

The kid cowered in front of him like a puppy who'd been hit too many times. "Please don't hit me again." He wiped his nose on his sleeve. The orangish glow of the pier lights reflected eerily on the kid's tears, snot, pimples, scabs, abrasions, and red-rimmed eyes.

Shame crept into Paul's consciousness. His training, his years of working with the pathetic and the criminal, his essential kindness reasserted themselves. His anger began to ebb. Very quietly Paul said, "They can die in moments."

"I'm sorry."

"You had no idea who the guy was who offered you money?"

"No. It was just some guy."

"Short, tall, black, white?"

"White, taller, dark glasses, talked in a whisper. That's all I remember."

"Why were you out here in the first place?"

"I knew there would be lots of rich people around. I was panhandling, and I heard that some of these old rich guys will let a kid shack up for a while. I'm not gay. I'm straight. I just need the money. I don't have a place to live."

"Would you recognize him again?"

"He had a coat on. A scarf and a baseball hat kind of hid his face."

"Could it have been a woman?"

"I guess. I just thought it was a guy."

"What kind of coat was it?"

"Dark."

"Was it fur or cloth?"

"I dunno. Dark."

"Where were you supposed to meet him to get the other half of your money?"

"At the skyline stage. He hadn't showed up yet."

"Where did you meet him the first time?"

"Maybe halfway down the pier. He was walking along and saw me. He told me there was this guy at the end of the pier that he wanted shoved into the water. He offered me money, and I didn't have to do sex for it, so I figured—great. He told me the guy was alone and wearing a leather jacket. I saw two guys at one end and this one guy by himself. I wasn't going to try two at once. I figured this must be the guy."

Paul knew Ben and Egremont were both wearing leather jackets. No one could have expected either Ben or him to be there. Was Ben simply in the wrong place at the wrong time? Had the accountant been the real object of the attack? He looked around for Egremont to ask him more questions, but the accountant was gone.

Turner motioned the uniform over. "Get this kid out of my sight. Lock him up and charge him with assault." The uniform took the kid away. Paul called a second uniform over. "I need you to find Daniel Egremont. He's an accountant with GUINEVERE, Incorporated." He gave him some more details, and the uniform hurried off.

Ben got out of the cop car. He stood close to Paul. "You hurt that kid."

"Yes."

"I've never seen you be violent."

"It's not something I'm proud of or that I'll want to tell the grandkids about."

Ben said, "Let's get the hell out of here. I want to go home."

"You okay?"

"I'm warmer. I want to be inside in my own home."

Ben was forced to wait longer in the car as Paul talked to the local watch lieutenant and made reports. Before he left, he ascertained that Egremont had not been found. His condo was under surveillance.

On the ride home Paul discovered himself holding hands with Ben. At home they sat in the kitchen. Jeff and Brian were sound asleep. Paul made Ben hot chocolate. When it was ready, he poured Ben a cup, placed a marshmallow and a cinnamon stick inside and served him. Paul drank a glass of orange juice. They sat next to each other on the same side of the table, shoulders and knees touching.

"Are you okay?" Paul asked.

"As I think about what could have happened, I get more scared. I would have died if you hadn't acted so quickly." Ben shivered. Paul put his arm around him.

They sipped their drinks for several moments in silence. Finally, Ben asked, "Are you okay?"

"Almost every day I listen to Fenwick describe various things he'd like to do to suspects. He can be pretty sarcastic, and he pressures them pretty hard. He might talk about abusing suspects and witnesses, but he's actually pretty gentle with them. He's never done something that would make a headline if it was taped and shown on the ten o'clock news. I've done even less. Hell, I've never hit Jeff or Brian. It's been enough talking, reasoning, nagging and outthinking them."

Ben took Paul's hand. He asked, "What would you do if someone attacked either of your sons?"

"I would defend them with every ounce of strength I had. I'd sacrifice myself for them."

"And if someone hurt them, physically caused them pain, and you found out about it later, what would you do?"

"I believe in justice, not revenge," Paul said.

"I'm not asking about belief. I'm talking about a father and his sons."

"I'd want to hurt them, but I hope I would stop before I would."

"Why?"

Paul sat back in his chair. He looked around at the familiar surroundings of the kitchen. The ugly plastic barometer Jeff had made and given him for his birthday last year. The pile of Brian's school books that he never seemed to be able to move from the telephone table. The pad of paper with dragons on it that they took phone messages on. The dinosaur magnets on the refrigerator that he used to display the boys' work.

"I know I'm a good cop," Paul said. "Part of that is knowing how to control my emotions. I don't beat people up."

"No, you don't," Ben agreed.

"The kid was a shit."

"Yes, and a possible killer."

"Then why do I feel lousy for roughing him up?"

"Because you're a good person who was put in circumstances none of us ever hope to be in. And you reacted as best you could at a difficult moment. I think I would react the same way you did."

"I feel guilty."

"Catholic guilt, generic guilt, or bawling-your-eyes-out guilt?"

Paul smiled. "None of the above."

They each heard the stairs creak. Moments later Brian appeared in the kitchen doorway. He wore only white athletic socks, white briefs and a baggy gray T-shirt from Banana Republic. "You guys still up?" he asked.

"Ben is," Paul said, "but I've been asleep for ten minutes."

Brian yawned. "Figures."

"What are you doing up?" Paul asked.

"Thirsty." Brian opened the refrigerator and took out a pint of bottled water. The teenager lifted the bottle to his lips and guzzled nearly a third of it. Paul didn't tell him to use a glass. Everyone else in the house preferred the Lake Michigan water from the tap. Brian's most recent health kick was bottled water.

Brian finished, muttered, " 'Night," and padded back upstairs.

Paul and Ben cleaned their cups and walked upstairs. From the closet Ben pulled out white flannel sheets. "Do you mind tonight?" he asked.

Usually the flannel was too warm for Paul. He nodded acquiescence. A few moments later and the sheets were changed. The warmth and coziness of the flannel seemed perfect. Ben hugged him fiercely under the covers and murmured, "Thanks for saving me. I never want to feel that cold again."

Paul rolled half on top of his lover and pulled him underneath. He returned the tight embrace.

"This is the best way to warm up," Ben said.

"How much warmer would you like to be?" Paul asked.

"I'd say, 'Let's see how hot it can get,' but that sounds a little too Mae West."

Their lovemaking quickly escalated to fierce passion.

T W E N T Y

Paul insisted that the family get together every morning for an unrushed breakfast. With the variety of their four schedules, it was one of the few times guaranteed to have all of them present. This was Paul's week to cook and he rose early and made French toast.

As they finished eating, Ben said, "I'm going to defeat the computer today, or it is going to die trying."

"Death to the machines," Brian said. "Power to the humans."

Ben said, "I'd give a great deal just to have a manual with a set of instructions that made sense."

"I've got a project due Monday," Jeff announced. "They're making me be in the science fair. Do I have to?"

"Yes," Paul said.

"Why?"

"Why not?" Paul said.

"I don't want to."

"Which is not yet enshrined in the list of acceptable excuses in this house," Paul said. "Isn't this kind of late to get started?"

"A little," his son conceded.

Paul asked, "What are you going to do it on, and do you want help?"

"Maybe. If I could find something I can research on the computer, that would be terrific. I'd like to do it on something gross so my teacher learns a lesson."

"How about pyin?" Brian suggested.

"What's that" Jeff asked.

"A protein in pus," Brian said.

"Cool," Jeff said.

Along with food, the boys' interest never seemed to wane in that which had to do with bodily functions and secretions—the more disgusting and gross the better.

"How do you know the word *pyin*?" Ben asked.

"The computer used it against me when I was playing Scrabble."

"Mrs. Talucci's back," Jeff announced.

"I'll try to see her tonight," Paul said.

Paul had missed the much loved next-door neighbor.

Jeff pointed out the window. "I think she's on her way over."

Paul looked. Mrs. Talucci was leading a man by the ear down the sidewalk toward their house. Behind Mrs. Talucci was her niece, Arrabella, hefting a shotgun. Next to Arrabella was another niece, Constanza, carrying several cameras.

Paul, Ben and the two boys met them at the door.

Despite her diminutive stature, Mrs. Talucci was able to yank the man inside.

"Who's your friend?" Ben asked.

"Found him snooping around between our houses a few minutes ago."

"I was just trying to—"

Mrs. Talucci cuffed him on the ear.

"Ouch! Cut that out!" He lifted his hand as if to strike back. Arrabella nudged his elbow with the shotgun, and he subsided.

"You speak when spoken to," Mrs. Talucci ordered. "I will not have the privacy of this neighborhood invaded. This is not going to become a circus playground. I heard about your case, Paul. I'll keep any reporters out of your hair around here. Elsewhere, you're on your own." Mrs. Talucci's ability to make things happen in the neighborhood was legendary. No one questioned her ability or her connections.

Mrs. Talucci rounded on the reporter. "You set foot on this street again, you will get far worse than me or this shotgun. You leave this neighborhood in peace or in pieces." She pulled a wallet out of her coat pocket and waved it in front of the man. "This is yours. I know who you are. I know where you live. Don't make me sorry for something I want to do."

"She's threatening me. She attacked me." The reporter looked at each of them and saw no sympathy. "I'll call the police."

"I am the police," Paul said.

Mrs. Talucci said, "I'll buy you some film to replace what I confiscated. You won't have pictures of this family. Give him his cameras back, Constanza. If you come back peacefully and without your cameras, I'll make you a nice dinner."

The reporter gave her an odd look.

"Leave," Mrs. Talucci ordered. He scuttled out the door.

Then Rose Talucci smiled at them.

After hugs were exchanged Paul asked, "How was your trip?"

"About average," Rose said. She patted Paul on the arm. "You've got to get to work. We can talk later. I just wanted to make an example of this creep in hopes he warns the rest of his kind to keep out. If they get the message, maybe none of them will come around. I don't hold out much hope."

After they left, Paul, Ben and the boys talked of schedules and logistics for a few minutes. Brian attempted to wheedle the car for a date on Saturday night.

Outside the wind was up and the sky was gray. A storm was approaching on a cold front. Depending on the direction the storm took, they could be in for a blizzard, heavy rain, light snow or a simple turn to much colder temperatures. The weather forecaster apologized profusely for not being able to control the weather.

Turner marched through the mass of reporters outside the station. A good cold snap might diminish the crowd. He wondered if Mrs. Talucci and her nieces hired out. Moments after Turner settled at his desk, Fenwick boomed in. "Who did what to you last night?"

"Not me. Ben."

Fenwick banged his hand down on top of his desk. He dangled the coffee cup in his other hand carefully so his emphatic slam did not cause a drop to spill. "Downstairs they said Ben was pushed into the lake. Is that true? Wish I'd have been there."

Turner filled him in on the activities of the night before.

"How come you get to have all the fun with Sibilla?" Fenwick asked.

"I'll send her over to you if I can have the bodyguards."

"Cheating on Ben?"

"Married men can have fantasies. I may conveniently forget to return his sweatshirt."

"The one who paid this guy could have been one of the people who was in the penthouse."

"We'll have to ask them. We also need to talk to Munsen about what Sibilla said about him firing Furyk."

"It makes no sense to presume you or Ben were the target," Fenwick said. "Nobody expected either of you to be out there. Egremont is the most logical person. If it was him, why? And does he know who?"

188

"If he knows why, he knows who."

Fenwick perked up considerably. "Is this the start of a comedy skit?"

"I sure as hell hope not," Turner replied.

"What's wrong?" Fenwick asked.

"Pardon?"

"You've got that distracted look you get when something's bothering you."

"I do not look distracted when something's bothering me."

"Trust me. I'm Mr. Sensitive, or at least I've known you long enough. What's up?"

Turner told him about how he'd banged around Tyler Madison.

"So?" Fenwick said.

"I don't bang people around."

"No, you don't." Fenwick eyed him carefully. "If someone attacked Madge or one of the girls, I would not be responsible for what I did."

Turner said, "Ordinarily, we're not called on to defend our loved ones. How do you know how you'd react?"

"If I was there, I'd do everything I could to save them. If I learned that they'd been attacked, I'd make every attempt to bring the attacker to justice."

"And you'd beat them up if you were questioning them?"

"Paul, what do you want from yourself? You want to feel bad about what you did? You want to analyze the situation until it comes out different? You want forgiveness?"

"I want to know I'm not going to do that again."

"I can't help you there. I can say that you're a good person, a good cop, a loving father, a man whose instincts I trust. The guy who I want backing me up. The guy who I'd want interrogating a suspect if I was ever attacked. You're not a different person from who you were yesterday. You've seen another side of yourself that makes you uncomfortable. Let yourself get used to what you did.

Analyze it more after the emotion has eased. Going around and around on it now isn't likely to help. And don't make any cracks about how sensitive what I just said was. I know I'm a wonder."

Commander Molton strode over to their desks. "I've got press conferences up the wazoo. I'm meeting with the mayor, and I've got phone calls piling up from around the world."

"Are we going to the press conferences?" Fenwick asked. "I'd rather take a bath with a school of live piranha."

"No. You will be out busily solving this case so I can get back to having normal pains in my wazoo."

Turner filled him in on the latest, then said, "We're going to Furyk's wake this morning. We need to talk to the parents. We're also hoping that several of Furyk's lovers are in from overseas."

"The mysterious boyfriends in foreign ports?" Molton asked.

"Yeah."

"Must be nice," Molton said.

"I sure as hell hope so," Fenwick said. "If it isn't, it's a hell of a lot of trouble to go through to be miserable."

"Any word on Egremont?" Turner asked.

"I haven't heard. Check with downstairs."

"We've also got paperwork up our wazoos," Turner said.

"A wazoo epidemic," Fenwick said.

"Whoever finds a cure is going to be rich," Molton said. He strolled off.

After ascertaining that Egremont had not appeared at home, Turner shuffled through the papers on his desk. O'Leary had done as he was asked. Turner now had the latest issues of all the fashion magazines. He tossed several to Fenwick. They paged through them. Turner saw lots of party pictures, scraps of gossip and snippets of information. The articles all seemed to talk in a unique fashion vocabulary that made little sense. The constant use of extreme, exotic and overblown adjectives struck him as amusing. He noted that in all the pictures of gala fashion events, there were none of two men together. He wondered if it was an oddity of the issues he happened to be looking at or a subtle homophobia. Certainly, the magazines themselves mentioned gay people.

After several minutes Fenwick said, "They must have special word-processing programs that automatically stuff their paragraphs with superlative adjectives for superfluous clothing."

Turner raised an eyebrow at him. "I may have to reevaluate my opinion of your poetic abilities."

Fenwick said, "I see lots of glitzy and pretty pictures, but I am none the wiser."

"Maybe you could pick out another tux."

"I do not wish to be teased about that."

"Fat chance," Turner said. "Fenwick in a tux. I want to put a picture on the bulletin board."

"Should I mention the rumors going around about what you wore last night?"

"That can't have gotten around this fast."

"Au contraire, mon ami."

"The French and that accent go the same place as the poetry," Turner said.

"Truce?" Fenwick offered.

Turner nodded. He pulled out a stack of Daily Major Incident Logs and handed several to Fenwick. Half an hour into the paperwork, Wilson and Roosevelt strode in.

"You should see them downstairs," Wilson said.

"Who?" Fenwick asked.

"Devonshire and Smythe," Wilson said. "They're trying to get a couple of reporters interested in a gang shooting early this morning."

"They got another one?" Turner said.

"Yep," Roosevelt said.

"Luck of the draw," Fenwick said.

"Or somebody doesn't like them," Wilson said.

"Insufferable twits, what's not to like?" Fenwick asked.

"They related to you?" Wilson asked.

"They need to take lessons from me," Fenwick stated.

The watch commander walked over and handed Wilson a piece of paper. "Address on North State Street. Somebody tried to mug a priest. Pulled a gun. Killed a little girl walking with her mother half a block away. Better hustle."

Wilson and Roosevelt hurried away.

Another fifteen minutes of paperwork and the phone rang. It was the hospital. Kindel had awakened.

Before they left, Paul phoned Ian.

His friend answered with the traditional response he gave to anyone who called before eleven in the morning; "Somebody better be dead."

"It's Paul. You find out anything on Kindel?"

Ian usually worked at the paper from early afternoon to past midnight at least six days a week. He seldom rose before noon. Paul heard a thump and a curse. He knew Ian had dropped the phone, put on his slouch fedora and was wishing he still smoked. After the usual ten or fifteen seconds, Ian said, "I've got to stop using that line to answer the phone. Every time you call, you do have a dead body. Nobody else does, just you."

"You resent the fact that I have a leg up, so to speak."

"I hope you are not taking lessons from Fenwick. The automatic coffeemaker has responded to my commands. I will be human soon. What can I do for you in the meantime?"

"You find out anything on Kindel?"

"Not until late last night. I found a guy who was his last lover. Kindel taught school for years in one of the wealthy North Shore suburban high school districts. Those places pay extremely well. All we heard at the paper was that he was a poor retired schoolteacher. This fella told me Kindel had invested his savings for years in micro-computer-soft-age-works-electronics-something stocks.

He is supposed to be worth a small fortune." Ian paused. Paul heard him slurp and gasp. Ian always gulped from the boiling hot coffee. He claimed he was used to it.

Ian continued. "He's rich. He also owns the paper."

"He what?"

"Owns the whole frigging place, building and all."

"Why keep it a secret?"

"He's an insane moron?"

"You heard he was mugged?"

"Yeah. Is that connected to the murder?"

"I don't know yet. Why is Kindel into all this deception?"

"It sure is odd."

"Fenwick and I are going to stop at the hospital on the way to the wake."

"Good luck."

As they drove to the hospital Turner said, "Thanks for what you said earlier. It helped."

First, Fenwick misjudged his speed and distance and splashed a geyser of water from the curb toward a large herd of pedestrians at Congress Parkway and Wells Street. Then he said, "You're welcome."

They found Kindel awake and watching *Oprah*. He nodded at the detectives and turned the television off. Turner stood on Kindel's left, Fenwick on the right.

"How are you feeling?" Turner asked.

"Like somebody clobbered me with a two-by-four."

"What happened?"

"I was leaving the paper. I got to the alley on Buckingham. I pay for a space halfway down the alley. I was almost to my car when I got hit from behind. I don't know anything beyond that."

"Did you see anybody as you walked to the car?"

"Nobody that I noticed or remember."

"You own the *Gay Tribune*," Turner stated.

"Who told you that?"

"Is it true?" Turner asked.

"Yes."

"How come you had to volunteer to write those columns?"

"It was a clever and fortuitous ruse. I wanted to get even with the people at the paper who were supercilious and snotty to me. By not announcing my ownership, I could spy and get even. And I wanted to find out what was really going on."

Fenwick asked, "Do you think somebody you got even with was trying to get back at you?"

"No. I haven't really fired anyone yet. I just made sure the paper took the direction I wanted."

"Have you had any fights with anyone recently?" Turner asked. "Perhaps someone not connected to the paper?"

"I've thought about that. I can't think of anyone."

"The beat cops said you weren't robbed."

"I was lucky. Maybe they were driven off before they could take anything."

"They?"

"He, she, they, whoever it was."

"Cullom Furyk was a rich man," Turner said. "Where is all his stuff?"

"I only had what I gave you."

"Didn't that strike you as odd?" Turner asked. "You knew he wasn't a poor waif off the street. Did you discuss him moving in with you?"

"Yes."

"And he said?"

"He said he'd move in. I figured that's when he'd bring more stuff."

"The two of you didn't discuss logistics."

"Of what? It's a big place."

194

"Did you know he had lovers in other cities around the world?" Turner asked.

"I'd heard rumors."

"From where?" Fenwick asked.

"I'm the fashion writer. I trade in gossip. It is one of the essentials of the profession."

"You also write the pornography column for the paper," Fenwick said. "You omitted mentioning that the first time we talked to you."

"Your point is?"

Turner said, "You didn't give us complete information about a number of things."

"None of which is connected with anything criminal."

"That we know of," Fenwick said.

"Someone tried to murder Daniel Egremont last night."

"I was here, unconscious."

"That's what they all say," Fenwick said.

Turner said, "Two people connected with a murder investigation get attacked. I don't believe in coincidences in murder cases. Maybe the same person hired somebody to hurt you."

"That would be your job to prove."

"You met with Furyk at the health club the morning of the murder," Turner said. "What was that all about?"

"I just needed to check in with him."

"According to you, he'd been at your place earlier. Why'd you need to check in with him?"

"It's a crime to talk to your lover?"

Despite questioning him for fifteen more minutes they got no useful information from him.

They drove to the funeral home in Rogers Park for Cullom Furyk's wake. Cars were double-parked all up and down Hood Street for a block in either direction. The line of mourners extended all the way to Broadway Avenue and then south for half a mile. A throng of reporters was kept behind police barricades a hundred yards away. Turner and Fenwick showed their identification and entered the funeral home.

To the left behind velvet ropes, mourners shuffled forward to view the closed casket with a picture of Furyk on top. To the right a small crowd was clustered near a silver coffee urn. Several of the mourners nodded in the detectives' direction then leaned to whisper to those next to them. Turner saw Arthur Oldinport. Battle was not in evidence. Slightly apart and nearer the viewing room was Gordon Findley. He was talking to an older couple who were clutching each other's hands.

Turner and Fenwick approached. Findley greeted them then said, "Mr. and Mrs. Furyk, these are the detectives working on Cullom's case."

Mr. Furyk said, "Are you going to be able to catch whoever did this to our son?"

They looked to be in their late forties to early fifties. Each was red-eyed.

"We're very sorry for your loss," Turner said. "We know this is a difficult time for you, but if we could ask you a few questions, it might help."

Both parents nodded. Mr. Furyk said, "We'll do anything we can to help find the person who killed our son."

Leaving Findley behind, the four of them stepped into an empty parlor and took seats.

"We can't believe all the people lining up to see him," Mrs. Furyk said, "and we're not used to dealing with those hateful reporters."

"If the Chicago police can do anything," Turner offered.

"They've been wonderful," Mrs. Furyk said. "Cullom was such a good son. You know, he called us at least once a week no matter where he was in the world. He came to Florida for all the major holidays."

"Were there any problems that he was having that he discussed with you?"

"We've been trying to imagine why this might have happened," she said. "We just can't think of anything."

"Did you know he was planning to leave or being let go from GUINEVERE?"

"He'd told us he was going to be increasing his options, doing a lot more work in the future. We didn't understand why. He was making lots of money."

"Did he have his personal things stored at your home?"

"He kept a few things in a room he always used, but he didn't store things there."

"We've only been able to recover a few items of his clothing," Fenwick said.

"Material things didn't mean a lot to him," Mrs. Furyk said. "Yes, he was famous, but all those trappings weren't important to him. People were."

"Did you know who he was close to, or if he had broken off any relationships recently?"

"He brought a few of his friends to the house," Mr. Furyk replied, "but they were never introduced to us as lovers. Certainly he never talked to us about anyone who was angry enough to kill him. Are you sure it wasn't an accident? He was always daring as a child. Perhaps he simply fell."

"We have witnesses who saw him pushed," Turner said. "They weren't near enough to see who did it."

"Did he have any enemies that you know of?" Fenwick asked.

"No," Mr. Furyk said.

"Do you know if he had a will or who inherits his estate?" Turner asked.

"As far as I know, we do," Mr. Furyk said, "but we'd give all the money and possessions to have our son back."

The parents knew nothing else helpful. A few minutes later they left.

"Who told us they weren't very affectionate?" Fenwick asked.

"Wasn't it Furyk's agent? They sure seemed like a normal mom and dad to me. Not the kind to beat their kid or abuse him psychologically. And I can't see this being a case of a closeted gay person caught in the middle of conflicting passions. His parents and his profession don't seem to be a problem."

"His love life still doesn't make sense to me," Fenwick said. "I don't see how he could hide that many lovers in that many cities. Or, if the lovers knew about each other, why they would put up with being one of many. Or why he would need that many lovers. What's the point?"

"Who knows?" Turner said. "Bragging rights, insecurity? Or maybe the number of them has been highly exaggerated."

Fenwick asked, "Why isn't at least one of them pissed enough to push him off a balcony?"

"I'm not ready to arrest the self-proclaimed lover, Sean Kindel. Veleshki, Bokaru, Egremont and Norwyn had a sexual connection, but I'm not sure any of them were passionate enough to kill him. Another lover would have had to have a hotel employee get him onto the right elevator and up to the penthouse, past McBride . . ."

"Unless she killed him or is covering for the killer."

". . . avoid all the people in the penthouse, hope Furyk was conveniently on the balcony to be pushed, and make his escape without being seen by all of the above as he reversed his route."

"Tricky," Fenwick admitted. "Although, if he wasn't on that wall, maybe there never would have been a killing."

"Yeah."

"I also doubt if it was a conspiracy of Third World orphans angry at the possible hypocrisy of one of their great benefactors."

"I didn't see a lot of orphans in the penthouse," Turner responded.

"I like McBride as a suspect," Fenwick said. "She has all the characteristics you could ask for in a fascist conspirator. She even admitted to us that she was also alone through the entire luncheon." He checked their chart. "Absolutely no one can vouch for her. Why isn't she the killer?"

"Same problem as with all the others. No witnesses. No physical evidence."

"She claimed not to know him, but if she was doing Munsen's bidding, would she have to?"

"She killed him on Munsen's orders? Possible. We need proof, which we do not have." Turner sighed. "Let's see if we can't find any of the boyfriends from overseas."

They approached Arthur Oldinport. He nodded hello. "Is your lover all right?" Oldinport asked.

"He's fine. Thanks for asking. Was last night's show a success?"

"Reviews in the local papers were generally favorable, but it is quite easy to impress those in the provinces. We'll know more when the major trade journals have their say."

"Did you like it?" Fenwick asked.

"My boss liked it a great deal. Whatever Jolanda likes, I like."

"Why don't you quit?" Turner asked.

"I find a paycheck a cheery thing. I also love the fashion world. It is exciting and alive and keeps me young."

"I thought Battle was for that," Fenwick said.

"Isn't that comment a trifle vicious and out of line for a Chicago police detective?" Oldinport asked.

"Just making an observation," Fenwick said, then asked, "How come you don't have to move with the line?"

"I'm the pool reporter. I'm the only one allowed to stay."

"How'd that come about?" Fenwick asked.

"Jolanda has connections."

"We're wondering if any of Furyk's lovers are here," Turner said.

"I have ascertained a bit of information about that for you."

"How many were there?"

"Over time? I'm not sure."

"More than a hundred?" Turner asked. "Less than ten?"

"Much closer to ten. Probably less. That does not include his casual sexual conquests. With his death I suspect that number will rise to thousands claiming to have been to bed with him. One of the rumors going around is that he had sex with a whore in Tokyo who specialized in near asphyxiation during sex. I know that one is not true. That particular whore died fifteen years ago."

"Wasn't he afraid of catching and transmitting diseases?" Turner asked.

Oldinport said, "Having sex with Cullom Furyk was almost as safe as masturbating by yourself inside a lead-lined room with the doors locked and bolted."

Fenwick asked, "Was he cautious because he was afraid of diseases, or was he inhibited because he was psychologically screwed up?"

"Or maybe that was the way he preferred to have sex," Oldinport said. "I wouldn't know. I never had sex with him."

"Why not?" Fenwick asked.

"Is that question germane to your investigation?"

"Probably not," Fenwick said.

They were talking softly while facing the line as it moved toward the casket. Battle entered, spotted them and walked over. "The line is over a mile long and growing every second. This is becoming the fashion event of the year." Battle wore a press pass outside his charcoal-gray Armani suit.

"Do you ever give it a rest?" Fenwick asked.

Battle looked genuinely confused. "What?" he asked.

"How'd you get in?" Fenwick asked.

200

"He is my assistant," Oldinport said. "We were trying to spot any of Cullom's lovers from Europe. Have you seen anyone?"

"Sure," Battle said, "as I came in, I saw Deidrich Goucher near the end of the line."

"Who's he?" Turner asked.

"Cullom's lover in Paris," Battle said. "A sweet man. I'll introduce you."

"How come you never told me this?" Oldinport asked.

Battle looked wary. "I thought I had. Sorry."

TWENTY-ONE

After introductions Turner and Fenwick ushered Goucher into the same empty viewing room where they'd talked to the Furyks.

Goucher wore a gray sweater with a black triangle pattern across the shoulders, black dress slacks and black dress shoes. Turner judged him to be in his mid-to-late twenties. He wore simple gold-rimmed glasses. He was just under six feet tall and had the build of a runner. His fingers were long and narrow. He had his blond hair in a brush cut. His palms were heavily callused.

Turner said, "We're trying to find who killed Cullom Furyk. We're hoping you can help us."

Deidrich spoke very softly. "I'll do what I can, but I know nothing."

"We were told the two of you were lovers," Turner said.

"Yes, for six years. We knew each other in Paris. I'm originally from Temecula, California. I have lived in France since I graduated from high school. I studied off and on at the Sorbonne. I don't have a lot of money. I am a sculptor, some say not a very good one. Fortunately, I speak fluent French. Occasionally I am able to do construction jobs for a company an uncle owns."

"Did you know Furyk had lovers in other cities?" Turner asked.

Deidrich entwined his fingers and twisted them together.

"He promised me he would be leaving them."

"We have a gentleman here in Chicago who says he was Cullom's lover."

"I wish that wasn't true."

"Did you know about his infidelities?"

"He had coaxing ways, charming ways. I guess I'm kind of naive. Even though I've lived in Paris, sometimes I'm pretty out of it. I just wanted to settle down to a quiet life. When he was in Paris, he was attentive and kind. We went everywhere together. He bought me things: always the most rare or out of season flowers, only imported chocolates, unique gifts. We had a place together on the Left Bank."

"Did he take you to fashion events, parties?"

"I wasn't some hidden thing, or someone to be ashamed of. I liked going out with him. He seemed to enjoy having me around."

"He had sex with at least two other people the day he was murdered."

A tear ran down Goucher's cheek. His voice became even softer. "Those weren't lovers. He told me he was going to stop both the one-night stands and having other lovers. He promised me. He knew it hurt me."

"How did you find out about the others?"

"His so-called friends in the gossip world would tell me. I stopped listening after a while. A lot of the time they were lies. Too much of the time they were the truth."

"Why did you stay with him?" Turner asked.

"I'm not sure he really let anyone in, but I loved him. He was beautiful. He made me feel wanted and needed. In many ways he was very vulnerable. The fashion industry can be very cruel. Many nights while in my arms, he forgot the pressures at least for a few moments. I treasured those times. In his way, I know he loved me."

"I'm not following something," Fenwick said. "I realize you are grieving for him, but the guy was a cheating rat."

"I can't explain it," Deidrich said. "I loved him. He made me promises, and I believed them. Perhaps I wanted to believe them." He took out a hanky and dabbed at his tears. "Cullom had a way of focusing on you. He made me feel like the most special person on the planet. His eyes were so understanding, warm, inviting, perfect. My world is mostly slabs of inert stone or sweating on the roads. His was wild and alive and fine. He took me to part of that. He knew exotic places around the world, private places. At least half a dozen times a year, we would go and have fabulous weekends. I enjoyed them a great deal, but the very best times were when the two of us spent a quiet evening in my apartment."

Fenwick asked, "Were the causes he worked for trying to use his fame, or was he trying to use them to get publicity for himself, or did he really believe in them?"

"Doesn't all of that get mixed together? Does anyone know where one starts and the other leaves off? Cullom told me he cared a great deal. He went to a lot of very unsafe places. He barely escaped with his life in Sarajevo one day, but he went back to the same neighborhood the next. If it boosted his career and helped a good cause, where was the harm? A lot of children are better off because of him."

"He have any big arguments with anyone, with you?"

"Mostly we got along great. A couple times we fought about his other partners. Once in a while we would argue about his constant travels, but he wasn't about to give up the model's life. He was immeasurably kind in public and in private. I don't think he had any enemies. He mentioned sometimes that Franklin Munsen was too overbearing, but I never got the impression that they were angry at each other. He was pretty even-tempered, mostly. He used to complain about some of the paparazzi. I think that's endemic to his profession."

"Did he ever mention leaving GUINEVERE?"

"A few times. I don't think he was serious."

"Did he say they were trying to drop him?"

"No, it was him thinking of leaving them."

"We've only been able to find a few of his things here in Chicago," Fenwick said.

"He was like a gypsy vagabond. He always said he didn't want to be tied down, and he traveled pretty light."

"Where was he staying in Chicago?"

"At the suite in the Archange that GUINEVERE rents out."

Turner shook his head.

"He wasn't?" Goucher asked.

"Where else would he have stayed?"

"I know he has old friends in Chicago. Perhaps there. He really wasn't at the Archange?"

Turner said, "I'm sorry, no."

"Where did all his money go?" Fenwick asked.

"I don't know. He didn't live an extravagant life, really. Many of his trips were for business and paid for by the companies he was working for, GUINEVERE usually. I think mostly he saved and invested his money."

"Where were you Tuesday?"

"With fifteen other construction workers doing emergency repairs on a stretch of road fifteen miles from Paris."

"How did you meet Furyk?" Turner asked.

"When I was a kid, I was the male lead's second best friend on a sitcom. The last year I was on the show, when I was sixteen, Cullom was in Los Angeles. He had sex with the ditzy but witty father and all the males on the set as well as several of the writers. He and I had a three-way with the other male secondary character."

"Where's that actor now?"

"Dead from a drug overdose. It happened the day after the final taping of the show."

"Did that have anything to do with Cullom?"

"The death was months after we had sex. I never heard him talk about Cullom. The three of us just had a good time. It wasn't anything serious. The show ended, and a year later I graduated from high school. I was sick of California and the lifestyle there. Cullom invited me to Paris. We became lovers a few years later."

He knew nothing more. After a few more questions, he left.

"Are all the people Furyk dealt with that naive?" Fenwick asked. "Not a discerning one in the bunch."

"Maybe that's who Furyk chose to hang around with," Turner said. "Maybe he didn't have relationships with discerning people."

"Sure seems to be an epidemic of naivete. This is not making sense to me."

They found no one else at the wake to interrogate. In the car they called Area Ten. "Turner's got a call from a guy named Egremont," the watch commander said. "He called about half an hour ago. Said it was urgent." He gave them the number.

Turner used his cell phone to call. The voice that answered was nearly inaudible. The background noise at the other end sounded like a wind tunnel.

"Daniel, where are you?" Turner asked.

Faint whisper. "At the Archange."

Turner put his hand over the receiver. "We need to be at the Archange Hotel. Quickly." Fenwick needed no further prodding. He jammed the accelerator to the floor. The people lining up outside the funeral home stared in their direction as they roared off.

"Daniel, what's going on?" Turner asked.

"Help me."

"We're on our way. What's wrong?"

All he heard was silence on the line for several moments, then a crackling sound and then nothing.

"What?" Fenwick asked.

"The phone went dead. All he said was that he was at the Archange and that he needed help."

Turner called to have a sector car hurry to the hotel.

TWENTY-TWO

Ten minutes later they arrived at the Archange. Turner half expected another bloody scene in the street. On the sidewalk in front of the east tower a woman and her child were standing with a beat cop. As they neared the group, Turner saw black shards at their feet.

"What's up?" Fenwick asked. He held out his identification.

Turner bent to inspect the debris on the pavement.

The woman said, "Something fell from that building and almost hit my daughter. She could have been hurt, killed."

Fenwick looked at the cop.

"My partner's inside checking it out."

Turner stood up. "It's the remnants of a portable phone."

They raced into the lobby.

"He's gotta be in the penthouse," Fenwick said.

As they entered the lobby a uniformed officer and Weeland, the manager, hurried toward them.

"Has anybody used the elevator to the penthouse?" Turner asked.

"The people from GUINEVERE still have the suite rented," the manager told him. "I don't know which of them have keys. Any one of them could have come in."

"We need to get up there," Turner said. "Something fell from the hotel."

"Are you sure it was from the penthouse?" Weeland asked.

"That's the logical place to start," Fenwick said.

They hurried to the bank of elevators. Weeland activated one for them.

The penthouse was dark as they got off the elevator. "West side first," Turner said. "That's where the phone fell from." They rushed forward. The parapet was empty.

They glanced over the side. There was no crowd gathering. The wind roared fiercely over the top of the wall and into their faces. They dashed to each of the balconies in turn. The doors leading to most of the bedrooms were locked. The rooms that they could see into were empty.

Turner and Fenwick stood at the intersection of the main halls in the middle of the penthouse. "He could be behind any of those locked doors," Fenwick said. "We better get Weeland up here to open them."

"We need to check the towers," Turner said. They quickly ascended the stairs and pushed open the door to the top of the west tower.

Lying against the wall twelve feet away was Daniel Egremont. As Turner and Fenwick rushed out the door, he leaped to his feet.

"Stay back!" Egremont shouted. He held out his hand in a halt motion. "Don't come near me!"

Turner and Fenwick stopped.

Egremont sat in one of the machicolations of the wall then swung his torso around and draped his left leg over the side. Because the opening wasn't quite large enough, the movement was awkward and took more than a few seconds.

Turner and Fenwick surged forward.

"Stop!" Egremont screamed. He put a hand on the wall and one out toward them. "If you don't stop, I'll jump!"

The two detectives halted instantly.

"Daniel," Turner said, "how can I help?"

Turner tried dredging up facts from the half-day lecture at the training academy that they'd had in handling attempted suicides. He couldn't remember a word.

Egremont stared out into space. "I'm afraid of heights, you know. They make me giddy and dizzy." He swayed back and forth then side to side. When the swaying eased a little, Turner could see he was crying. "I think I might be sick." Egremont was very pale. The wind whipped his disheveled hair. He sniffled then blinked his red-rimmed eyes.

"I'd like to come closer," Turner said.

"No. Don't. I will jump."

"Okay. I'm staying right here. We can talk at least, can't we?"

"Yeah."

"What's wrong?" Turner asked.

"Everything."

"Why did you call?"

"I need help."

"Does this have something to do with Cullom Furyk's death?"

"Yes."

"Did you kill him?" Turner asked.

"No."

"Do you know who did?"

"My boss."

"Did you see him push Cullom?"

"No."

"How do you know Munsen killed him?"

"I'm a good accountant."

"I'm sure you are."

"I never make mistakes. I'm honest. I'm too damned honest for my own good."

Turner was determined to keep Egremont talking. He vaguely remembered that as a good thing to do, and it made logical sense to him.

"Munsen tried to have me killed last night," Egremont said, "that attack was meant for me."

"Why?"

"I don't want to be accused of murder. The business is failing. I was supposed to lie to you. I have been lying to you. I can't do that anymore."

"What were you supposed to lie about?" Turner asked.

"Everything."

"What's happened to the business?"

"Poor management, poor decisions. We did make record revenues last year. We are one of the biggest fashion companies in the world. Unfortunately, we had record expenses. Millions more than we took in. Then, in the past month, one of the biggest chain stores that carried our lines went bankrupt. We may never see the money they owed us. After that happened there was no way we could be profitable for the next year."

"There's no need to kill yourself because the company is going broke," Turner said. "It isn't your money."

Egremont continued talking as if Turner hadn't said a word. "And he made stupid design decisions. The whole Egyptian cotton underwear line was a joke."

"Why?"

"Egyptian cotton is very delicate. When it is worn, it rips to

211

shreds unless it is mixed with some other fabric. He was determined to have the most sheer and revealing underwear line for men and women. He tried blending it with a variety of fabrics, but none of them worked to his satisfaction. No one could wear it for more than a few minutes before it shredded into complete tatters. He kept pouring money into a disaster, but it was more than just that. He was losing top-of-the-line clients. None of the 'right people' were wearing his designs. Not one of the royals in Europe, either pretenders to thrones or reigning royalty, had called in a year."

Egremont's swaying had lessened further. The tears continued intermittently.

"I've had to lie for the past year to everyone. I've made false reports. He made me lie. Then when the murder happened, things went crazy. He's always been an abusive boss, but it was as if he didn't have a shred of human decency. He talked about publicity from the murder causing sales to soar. He sounded as if he was glad Cullom died. I couldn't confide that kind of thing in you."

Egremont snuffled deeply. He placed his hands on either side of the wall in front of him and gripped it tightly. He continued. "The murder was a catalyst. I've been worried for myself since then. I've been trying to get reports and new accountings to make what I did not seem so bad. He found out what I was trying to do. He said he'd make it look like the company was failing because of me. That my lies would get me sent to prison. I lied to him about what I was doing, but I don't think he believed me. I've stuck by him loyally, and now he's trying to kill me."

"Because you knew about the company failing?"

"Because I know he fought with Cullom Furyk that last day."

"What did they fight about?"

"Cullom going to Heyling and Veleshki. Munsen hated the idea of Cullom leaving. They had argued about it for months. Several weeks ago, Munsen even offered him a great deal more money. I knew this was foolish."

"Why?"

"The last few ad campaigns with Cullom as spokesperson were bombs. He was losing his appeal."

"Did Heyling and Veleshki know Cullom's last campaigns failed?"

"Munsen threatened to tell them if Cullom persisted. After they talked that day, Cullom told me everything was fine."

"Did he go into details?"

"No, but I ran into Munsen a few minutes later and he was furious. He told me he was going to drop Furyk as spokesperson. He said that the 'faggot prick' wasn't going to make any more money off of him. He was going to reveal the losses the company had taken in Cullom's last campaigns. I advised against it because it would reveal our precarious finances. Munsen didn't care. I told him to wait and think it over."

"Why did Furyk stay for brunch if they'd just had a fight?"

"Aren't you listening? Cullom thought everything was fine. Munsen smiled to his face and was going to double-cross him. That was typical of his style." Egremont looked down at the ground far below. His body shuddered, and he turned even paler. He resumed, "The pressure was getting to me. After your visit to the plant, Munsen and I had a fight. I told him I was going to see a lawyer to protect myself. Munsen told me if he went down, I was going down with him."

"How could he have had the time to hire somebody to attack you last night? How did he know you'd be out on the pier?"

"We had another big fight backstage in the middle of the show. I was trying to reason with him. I know that was a stupid time, but I was desperate. I'm petrified about going to jail. There was that lull when they had that East Chicago ballet company modeling and dancing at the same time in those androgynous male-female suits."

"Did anyone else hear you fight?"

"I don't know. We were in a small dressing room to the left of the staging area. Dinah McBride is always lurking nearby, but I didn't see her or anybody else hanging around. He must have followed me outside."

Turner said, "Because you know he was involved in bad business decisions does not mean either of you is going to jail."

"We've lied to the stockholders. That's fraud. They will prosecute. I never planned to cheat anybody. It just began creeping up on me. I believed Munsen. I trusted him."

The door behind them swung slowly open. A beat cop stuck his head out. "What's going on?"

The three of them looked at the cop. Fenwick said, "We've got a situation out here. Keep everyone out. Call HBT. They'll know what to do." HBT stood for the Hostage, Barricade, and Terrorist Incident Division. Whether it was a standoff with mad bombers or a lone jumper from a building, they were the ones who were called in these situations.

The uniform ducked his head back in.

When the door was shut, Egremont began leaning his torso far out to the left. Turner began to step forward. Egremont's head quickly swiveled toward him.

"Stop!" He put his right foot up on the ledge.

Turner halted in midstride. The tableau stayed put for several moments.

"Wait," Turner said. "Please wait."

"Why?" Egremont seemed to be gazing off into space, but Turner knew he was still in the man's peripheral vision.

"I'm a working detective, not a psychologist," Turner said. "I wish I knew what words it took to get you to move back toward me and come down off there. I'm worried for you, about you. Will you look at me?"

Their eyes met for only a second.

"I'm just a guy," Paul said. "We've all had problems and doubts."

"You ever been faced with going to jail?"

"No."

"Then how do you know what I'm feeling?"

"I admit your problems are bigger than mine, okay? You win the I'm-worse-off-than-you-are contest."

The side of Egremont's lip that Turner could see twitched. Turner figured this was as close as he was going to get to a smile.

Turner said, "If you jump, he will have succeeded."

"Maybe," Egremont conceded.

"We're not here to arrest you for fraud," Turner said. "That's up to some prosecutor. You've still got a chance to get to a lawyer and take some action now. We're only interested in who killed Cullom."

"Munsen's clever. He'll destroy me. He's already killed Cullom."

"He's a crook and his business is going under, but that doesn't make him a killer," Fenwick said.

"If Cullom was deserting him, it might."

"Hold it," Turner said. "I thought you said Cullom's last campaigns were disasters, and he was planning to dump him. Why would that make him kill Cullom?"

"But Munsen hated Heyling and Veleshki. Hated them worse than if they'd been involved in a centuries-old vendetta. They've been at war so long, he would do anything to harm them. Cullom may have been a loser for Munsen, but he didn't want to risk him being a winner for them."

"Why don't you let us worry about the murder investigation?"

Turner said. He wanted to talk to Munsen again as soon as possible. "Daniel," Turner said. "Please don't jump. I care that you don't."

For the first time in a while Egremont turned full face to him. "I wish I had killed Cullom. He was so shallow and so hurtful. Last week he called me. He didn't want to stay in Munsen's suite here. I let him stay at my place for two nights. He wanted me to help him plot against Munsen. I offered to help. I should have left it at that, but I told him I loved him, begged and pleaded that we become lovers. I hated it when he rejected me. He's had millions of lovers in half the cities on the planet, but I'm not good enough for anything beyond a one-night stand. I went out on that balcony and watched him dance on the parapet. Like a fool I pleaded with him again. He barely listened to me. I dream about shoving him off the parapet and watching his body break to pieces as he hits the ground. He deserved to die."

"You don't," Turner said.

"You don't even know me."

"The first time you talked to us, why did you want us to believe it was an accident?"

"I was afraid I'd be a suspect. Now, I don't care."

Turner held out his hand. "Daniel, I'm here to help you any way I can."

Egremont began to sob. The swaying back and forth resumed more violently than ever. Turner had maybe six feet to go to catch him. When Egremont raised his right sleeve to rub his eyes, Turner lunged for him. Egremont saw him and swung his right leg over to join his left. The machicolation was just small enough that this became an awkward movement. The extra seconds gave Turner time to grab him around the waist. Turner felt more than saw Fenwick's bulk next to him. For an instant Egremont began slipping outward. Turner jammed his legs against the wall. Fenwick's heft paid off as their combined weight brought Egremont back to the terrace floor. The accountant clutched Turner, buried his head in the detective's shoulder and wept.

Half an hour later Egremont had been led away.

TWENTY-THREE

At Aunt Millie's later, Fenwick said, "Egremont makes a great suspect. I vote for him for killer."

Turner ate some glop. "We have a whole panoply of possibilities."

"You keep talking like that, Millie's going to throw you out."

"Maybe you aren't the only one with poetic aspirations." Turner put his silverware down. He ticked off the suspects on his fingers. "We've got Findley, the first, or one of the first lovers who claims to still share secrets with Cullom. We've got Kindel, the in-town lover. We've got Deidrich Groucher, the out-of-town lover, who is tough to make a suspect because of logistics."

"*One* of the out-of-town lovers. Who knows how many more might come out of the woodwork?"

"I like that—lovers in the woodwork. That has got to be a title for a teenage slasher movie."

"Nah, the sex life of termites."

Turner ticked off another finger. "We've got Egremont the disappointed lover."

"Why didn't Furyk say yes to him? Why reject Egremont? Furyk kept saying yes to half a dozen other people. What made Egremont so rejectable?"

"Furyk was picky?"

"Hardly."

Turner held up his thumb. "Fifth, we've got the stud muffin of the moment from the party, Bitner." He started on the other hand. "We've got the sexually ambiguous television star Eliot Norwyn. We have two owners of one company, Heyling and Veleshki, who were busy double-dealing. We've got Munsen, the owner of the rival company, angry and double-dealing, which makes six, seven, eight and nine."

"Throw in the fashion magazine people."

"Why?"

"For the hell of it. Bokaru is in. How about Spitzer, O'Dowd, Oldinport and Battle?"

"Same old logistics problem. They weren't at the party. Besides, I'm out of fingers."

"You forgot McBride."

"Okay, she's in without a finger."

"I like lots of suspects," Fenwick said. "Gives me lots to choose from. I like choices."

"The only thing everybody agrees on is that Cullom used his looks and charm to keep many men on lots of strings."

"Isn't it odd that so many people had different concepts of him?" Fenwick asked.

"Maybe he never opened himself up completely to anyone. We do know he was a rich, lonely sexual predator with a big smile."

Fenwick said, "Predator sounds more like someone out hunting for sex. His just came to him. What kind of problems can he really have had?"

"Enough that it got him killed."

"You know," Fenwick said, "of all these people, men and women who Furyk had sex with, not a one of them claimed Furyk said I love you. What kind of life is it to be pursued with such intensity and not reciprocate?"

"We keep trying to find out more information about him. Some depth, something beyond the surface. You might be onto something. Maybe he had a vast surface life and that's all there was. Maybe there wasn't any depth to him. For Furyk, getting to know the real inner you probably wasn't a problem. There was no real inner him. What was on the surface was who he was."

"Yeah," Fenwick said, "the book of his life would barely make a pamphlet." Fenwick finished his meal and wiped his hands on a paper napkin. "Why isn't Egremont the killer?"

"I don't know."

"We on our way to see Munsen?"

"He's the next logical person, but I want to stop at Egremont's condo first."

As they paid their bills, Fenwick said, "You handled Egremont really well out there."

"Thanks."

Egremont had been taken to the Near North Psychiatric Hospital for observation and testing. Before they'd taken him away, they'd asked Egremont for permission to examine Furyk's things at his condominium.

Egremont lived in Dearborn Park just south of the Loop and a few blocks from Aunt Millie's. The condo was airy and comfortable. It consisted of one immense room. The wall around the bathroom and closet did not extend to the ceiling. A king-sized bed was to their left. A large couch and one chair were the only furniture in the living room on their right. The kitchen had two tables and chairs of unfinished wood. They found Furyk's suitcase where Egremont said it would be. The luggage was little more than a carry-on bag. They found a paperback Barb D'Amato novel. There were two gray T-shirts, two pairs of boxer shorts, one pair of black socks, one pair of white socks, a purple knit shirt, a pair of black jeans and a small overnight bag with a razor, a toothbrush, dental floss and deodorant.

"This is it?" Fenwick asked.

"He was staying for only a week, and he must have expected to be wearing GUINEVERE fashions."

"I guess."

Turner held up the sheer, short-cut black boxers. "I'd like to see Ben in a pair of these."

"They wouldn't hide much," Fenwick said.

"Just enough to dangle a little promise."

"I thought you said Ben dangled a lot."

"When I mentioned that before, I thought it was another one of those 'more information than I want to know' moments of ours."

"You brought it up that time, too."

"Which I believe is the ultimate goal." Turner tossed the clothes back into the bag.

In a side compartment they found a return airline ticket to France and over seven hundred dollars in cash.

Turner held out the bills. "No traveler's checks. Heck of a lot of walking-around money."

Fenwick said, "Despite the cash, add this to what was at Kindel's, and this still isn't very much stuff."

Turner agreed.

They drove out to GUINEVERE, Incorporated's offices. They called ahead and were told that Munsen was rehearsing the models for a new commercial. The wind blew fiercely, buffeting some of the large semis on the highway. The temperature had begun to drop. Nothing yet fell out of the uniformly gray sky.

As he parked the car, Fenwick said, "I am not in the mood for putting up with crap from these people."

"While I agree with that apt and succinct sentiment, the problem is with the key question I asked Egremont."

"Yeah, he didn't see Munsen push Cullom."

"Precisely. We're stuck with nice until we have something definite."

"I'll go as far as sort of nice."

"Deal."

Inside the GUINEVERE complex McBride told them, "You gentlemen will have to wait until Mr. Munsen is free. We had to reshoot a scene for a major ad campaign." Her voice could have turned oceans into icebergs instantly.

"Ms. McBride," Fenwick began. His tone did not imply any kind of nice.

Turner interrupted. "Ms. McBride, we are sorry for the interruption, but we do need to speak with him. It is a murder investigation. I know you want to appear cooperative."

She put her hand out as if to lift up the phone then pulled it back. She grabbed a pencil and tapped it rapidly on top of her desk. "I'll need to call some lawyers."

"If you feel that's helpful, please do so. However, we are not here to arrest anyone. Where is he?"

"In the main hangar." She pointed toward her right then stalked out a door on their left.

As they made their way to the rehearsal stage, they got lost once and had to ask directions. In the hangar, male and female models were taking orders from a host of people. Several models strolled haughtily down a runway between sets of folding chairs. Technicians scurried amid a myriad of lights, cameras, cables and equipment. Munsen and two others stood to one side of them making comments and offering criticisms and suggestions.

As they neared Munsen, they heard him say to one model, "This is high fashion, this is couture, you are no longer a streetwalker out trying to drum up business. That was last year. This year the message is elegance."

Munsen noticed Turner and Fenwick.

"Get out," he ordered. "McBride will be fired for permitting you back here."

Turner heard Fenwick mutter, "Let's put him in the third torture chamber on the left."

Turner said, "We've had further information that we need to speak with you about. We appreciate how busy you are, but we need to talk to you. We will finish as quickly as possible."

All the people in the room had gathered around them in a circle. Turner looked at them then back to Munsen. Turner said, "We can talk here or in your office."

Munsen turned to a man in a black turtleneck and snapped his fingers. "Alfredo, keep these people practicing. I'll be back in a few minutes." He stalked away. Turner and Fenwick followed.

When they arrived in his office, Munsen stood behind his desk. "Yes?" He gave the single syllable a combination hiss and snarl second to none.

"Egremont says you guys were cooking the books," Fenwick said.

"I'm sure my legal experts will have a great deal to say about Mr. Egremont."

Fenwick said, "I expect the stockholders are going to be pissed about this whole sordid affair."

"I run a highly profitable and well-respected company. I have nothing to fear from the stockholders."

"Mr. Egremont says you tried to kill him."

"I was far too busy trying to run a fashion show last night to engage in ridiculous behavior."

"With all the models and hangers-on rushing about backstage, who would have noticed if you stepped out?"

"And just happened to run into a convenient person who I could ask to shove someone off the pier? Get real."

Turner knew what was coming. Fenwick felt his left arm with his right arm. "I feel real to me," Fenwick said.

"Your moronic humor has no place here."

"How did you find out about someone being pushed?" Fenwick asked.

"It was a secret? Half the audience knew as they were leaving. Did you think all those rotating cop-car lights wouldn't draw at least a few curious questions?"

"Maybe you were planning to push him yourself," Fenwick said, "and you happened to find an incompetent runaway to do it for you."

"I'd be willing to stand in a lineup to be identified by whoever it was that tried to kill Egremont. I wished they'd killed him before he tried to defraud the company. I didn't leave the backstage area. Interview everyone in the show, they'll vouch for me."

"You guys really going broke?" Fenwick asked.

"Hardly."

"Egremont says you are, and he's the one who does the books."

"He's going to jail. He'd say anything. Perhaps he murdered Furyk and is trying to lay the blame on me."

"Your books will be examined."

"Yes."

"I wish you sounded more worried when I said that," Fenwick said.

"I'm not. I am a great designer and a good businessman. The inferior and the inadequate hate that. I am not bothered in the least by their opinions. This business has had tough times and good times. We can certainly survive you."

"Were you or were you not going to dump Furyk?" Turner asked.

"Isn't that point moot now?"

"No. It could have been the reason for a murder."

"What difference would it make if I did drop him? I have half a dozen professional baseball players, two television and one movie star ready to take his place."

"You hated Heyling and Veleshki and were trying to double-cross them."

"I don't need to do murder to do that. I've got plans for this week that will stun them. Quite a surprise for tonight, in fact. They think we've worked out all of our problems. They will be surprised when my fashions sweep the pages of all the important magazines and theirs are ignored."

"How is that going to happen?"

"Planning on my part, naivete on their part. I'd toyed with dumping Furyk. Obviously Sibilla told you that. She's the only one I had confided that in. I must speak with her. I'd also toyed with keeping Furyk. In our last conversation he begged me to keep him. I told him I'd consider it."

"Why would he want you to keep him?" Turner asked.

"Because I could give him the better deal."

"How's that?"

"A possible movie contract. He wanted that desperately. Known to very few people is the fact that he made a film in France many years ago. As an actor he was awful. Fortunately for him it was never released in this country, and it was a bomb elsewhere around the world. Despite that, because of my contacts, I could get him a movie contract."

"With whom?" Turner asked.

"It wasn't going to be Sony Pictures, but a good small, independent company."

Turner said, "Egremont told us you were angry with Furyk the day of the murder."

"He'd say anything at this point, wouldn't he? I don't hear you saying that he had a witness to this supposed conversation."

"Seems kind of convenient to me," Fenwick said. "Furyk dies, and the eyes of the world turn to Chicago during the one week you could use the publicity. Sales will soar."

"That's disgusting," Munsen said. "You had some suspicions from an employee who was having serious troubles. I think you should take those suspicions out of here and leave."

"Did you kill Cullom Furyk?" Fenwick asked.

"No."

Turner looked at Fenwick. "I'm out of questions."

The two detectives left and drove back to the city.

"We missed something there," Fenwick said.

"Yeah, but what?"

"Dunno."

"He makes an awfully good suspect."

"Yep."

"No physical evidence. Let's go be depressed at the office."

TWENTY-FOUR

A flood of photographers surged toward their car as they pulled onto Wells Street a block from headquarters. Fenwick gunned the engine and aimed for the heart of the crowd. Cameras flashed, and the aggregation hesitated briefly before the ones in front and then the entire herd stampeded out of the way. Ten feet from where the crowd originally stood, Fenwick turned a sharp left up the alley. The car flew unmolested past the scattered mass of reporters. The detectives strode unhindered into the building.

Inside Turner stopped at the holding cells on the second floor to see Tyler Madison. When the kid saw Turner, he hurried to the bars.

"Hey, how long am I going to be in here?"

"How are you doing?"

"Man, I've been mugged and I've been arrested. All in all I'd rather be mugged."

"Why?"

"Being mugged didn't take as much time, the people were friendlier and they let me keep my shoelaces."

Turner almost smiled. "Processing takes time."

"I haven't seen a lawyer. You still pissed at me? Is that why it's taking so long?"

"I'm not as pissed. I'm sorry I roughed you up."

"You apologized. A cop apologizing. Just because you apologized doesn't mean I'm not going to sue."

Turner laughed. "I need you to look at some photos of people."

"If I recognize somebody, will I get out sooner?"

"If you recognize somebody, and you aren't making it up, and it helps our case, then maybe I'll talk to a few people for you." Turner showed him the photos of the people at the brunch. After several minutes' perusal, Madison said, "None of the guys look familiar, but this nose does." He held out the picture of Dinah McBride. "I thought whoever hired me was a guy, but I don't know . . . the cheekbones and this nose. It could be this one."

"Did this person tell you to kill Egremont?"

"No, whoever it was just said to push him into the lake. Nobody said anything about killing."

"You're lucky nobody did die."

On the third floor Turner filled in Fenwick and Molton.

"McBride ordering somebody hurt," Fenwick mused. "Munsen would have had to have given her the order. Not as far-fetched as I once might have thought. In fact, I kind of like the sound of it. I could be convinced."

"Doesn't seem to have much to do with your likes and dislikes," Molton said.

"Yeah, but I like to pretend it does," Fenwick responded.

"Absolutely had to be Munsen and his crew hiring these people to trail us. We can find out easily enough if any of them has a rusty Chevy."

"Why follow us?" Fenwick asked. "Was he petrified about being a murder suspect or worried about his company going broke?
And how does following us around help with either of those? The
hell with these questions. Let's send somebody out to get McBride
in here."

"Madison's description of her wasn't very definite," Turner
said.

"I wouldn't mind harassing her on general principles."

While they waited they sat at their desks and slogged through
paperwork.

Rodriguez slumped into the room. In a doleful voice he announced, "Carruthers is dead."

"If that was true," Turner said, "you'd be twirling noisemakers
and dancing in the streets."

"Even if he got slightly hurt, I'd be dancing in the streets.
What's worse is, I've got to ask him questions about the case we're
working on. He may have found a useful witness. It would be the
first time in all these years that he's come up with something on
his own."

Fenwick said, "I wouldn't ask Carruthers a question until some
time after eternity."

"A day with Carruthers gives meaning to the term eternity."
Rodriguez trudged away.

An hour's worth of paperwork later, Turner looked up. "We
going to be out of here before eight tonight?"

Fenwick looked at his watch and then the mound of papers on
his desk. "No."

Turner sighed. He was tired of writing. He shuffled through
the reports from the medical examiner. He found the pictures of
the crime scene and of the autopsy. He took them to the cork
board on the wall and tacked them up. He examined them carefully for the third time. One from the street in front of the Ar-

change caught his eye. He peered at it closely. The photo showed Furyk's torso in bright light.

"Come look at this," he called to his partner.

Fenwick strolled over to the rows of pictures and stood next to Turner. He peered at the picture Turner pointed to. "It's one of the brighter-lit pictures. So?"

"Look at his underwear."

"I'm not into guys' underwear. I just wear what Madge puts in the drawer. What am I looking for?"

"You don't buy your own underwear?"

"We are not going to discuss that."

"Shy?"

"What did you find?"

"Look closely. I think the type and pattern of his underwear in this picture doesn't match what we found in his luggage at Egremont's or Kindel's."

"So, he had different kinds of underwear."

"Maybe. I just want to be sure."

"You're not being kinky?"

"You don't discuss buying underwear, I don't discuss my fetishes."

Turner and Fenwick pored over all the pictures of the crime scene. Turner found another one that showed a bit more of the underwear. He held it up and inspected it minutely. "We found ordinary, slightly used white briefs at Kindel's. The underwear we found at Egremont's were boxers, one hundred percent cotton, with solid black trim around the top."

"You remember that?"

"Ben's birthday is in a couple weeks. I thought he might look good in them."

"I'll take your word for it."

"Now look carefully at the picture in the street. These are bikini-sized briefs. They're kind of tattered, probably from the fall,

230

but I'm certain of the style, and I'm sure those are thin gray stripes around the top. We saw those same kind of briefs on the tour at Heyling and Veleshki. Remember that model in the photo shoot we saw out there?"

"Not really."

"I'm sure of it. That model wore this same kind. They were very tight, and very sheer, and very revealing. Veleshki told us they were going to be unveiling a whole new line of men's underwear this week. Ad campaigns and everything. He said they aren't for sale yet."

"So how did Furyk get a pair?"

"They don't exist anywhere else. He has them because he was already modeling for Heyling and Veleshki."

Quick calls to half a dozen major department stores confirmed that they did not have any of the underwear in stock. Two of the stores expected their first shipments in about a week. One specialty store in Oak Brook was holding the underwear in reserve for the big announcement. They had been forbidden by the company to place it on the shelves until the day the ad campaign began.

"If he was already modeling for Heyling and Veleshki," Turner said, "then Furyk was double-crossing Munsen. So were Heyling and Veleshki. Or maybe he got it as a present from one of them."

"That sounds less suspicious," Fenwick said, "but either way they lied to us. I hate being lied to."

Fenwick and Turner grabbed their overcoats. They called the offices of Heyling and Veleshki and got an answering machine. They tried Oldinport, but he was not in.

"All the fashion people and the gossip people must be at an event like last night's, but where the hell is it?"

Jason O'Leary walked in leading Dinah McBride. She marched up to their desks. She stood with her hands on her hips, her legs spread wide and her fur coat open and thrust off her shoulders. "What?" she snarled.

They took her to an interrogation room.

Before either detective could ask a question she said, "My lawyer is on his way."

"Great, a party," Fenwick said.

"We understand you're Munsen's enforcer."

She smiled.

"You hire people to hurt people."

The smile became a grin.

"You hired Tyler Madison to push Daniel Egremont into the lake."

Now she laughed. "I don't see my lawyer."

Turner took a shot in the dark. "Why did you hire someone to mug Sean Kindel?"

McBride lost her smile for a second. "Don't be absurd."

"Tyler Madison picked out your photo." Turner didn't say he only recognized her cheekbones and nose.

"Quite impossible."

"What is the point of hiring thugs?" Fenwick asked.

"Where's my lawyer?"

Turner and Fenwick gave it up. They needed to find Heyling and Veleshki. They stopped at their desks, but several more calls proved useless.

"We could ask the enforcer," Fenwick said. They trooped back upstairs and asked McBride if she knew where they were.

McBride hesitated before she gave an answer, then snapped, "In McCormick Place South."

They hurried over. On the way, three drops of rain fell on their windshield.

"That's the big storm?" Fenwick asked.

"I'm sure the weather is doing its best to come up to your expectations," Turner replied.

They took Roosevelt Road to its new connection to Columbus Drive and then swooped onto Lake Shore Drive. Fenwick roared onto the ramp leading to the massive edifices on the lake that make up McCormick Place.

Traffic was light, but the foyer of the south building was jammed. The show had not started yet. Their police identification got them backstage. Models were in various stages of undress. Some were having finishing touches put on their hair or makeup.

They ran into Sean Kindel.

"Shouldn't you be in the hospital?" Turner asked.

"It's the new health care. Patch them up and get them out. I have to be at these fashion shows. There's news to be reported."

The detectives took him into a nearby seminar room on the ground floor. "We don't think your mugging was a random act," Turner said. "Why would anybody hire someone to hurt you?"

Kindel rubbed the abrasion on his forehead. His hand trembled as he did so. "I don't know what you mean."

"We have the person who was hired to harm Daniel Egremont," Turner said. "In less than twenty-four hours, two people connected with a murder get attacked. We're going on the assumption that the two incidents are connected."

"I can't imagine why Munsen would have it in for me."

"I didn't mention Munsen," Turner said.

"Who else would you be talking about?"

Fenwick snorted. "Give it a rest. You know exactly why you were attacked. Somebody went to a lot of trouble and risk to shut you up. What is it you needed to be shut up about?"

"I don't—"

"You were mugged once," Turner said. "What makes you think whoever did this is going to stop at that? Or may have stopped only because a witness suddenly appeared in the alley?"

Kindel sat in a gray metal chair. He rubbed his hands against his black sport coat.

"What do you know?" Fenwick asked.

Kindel said, "Cullom told me everything about the threats from

233

Munsen and the meetings with Heyling and Veleshki. I talked to Munsen at the brunch. I pretended I knew more than I did. I wanted to get a big scoop for the paper. I was tired of the *Gay Tribune* and me being ignored. If I got an exclusive, I could really make a name for myself."

"You got yourself mugged. It could have been worse."

"I was bluffing with Munsen. He misunderstood. I'm not sure precisely what I was on to. I suspect it had to do with his company's finances. I struck out blindly and hit the mark, I think. He got very angry. I was supposed to meet him today to talk it over. Then I was mugged." He hung his head. "I thought I could talk to him again. I thought I might be able to figure out who committed the murder. I knew I was in danger—the muggers told me to back off. But I wanted to put the paper on the map and I wanted to be a star, a real reporter. I wanted to find out who killed the kindest and gentlest person on earth and I definitely wanted it to be Munsen. Who else would warn me to back off?"

"You're lucky to be alive," Fenwick said. He called the station and asked them to send someone to pick up Munsen for questioning.

They found Veleshki on a small stage. He was talking on a cell phone. Heyling was a few feet away speaking with Jolanda Bokaru.

Turner and Fenwick hurried up to them. Veleshki bellowed into the phone, "Where the hell are those clothes? Where are the damn guards we hired? Didn't anybody check these outfits in? That was supposed to have been done this morning. Where is Louis O'Bannion? He's in charge of all this."

Veleshki flipped his phone shut and caught sight of the detectives. "I have no time for you," Veleshki snapped. "I've got a disaster on my hands."

"I told you we should have checked the outfits over ourselves," Heyling said.

"I-told-you-so is not going to help the situation," Veleshki said. "Only a third of the correct ones are here. I always suspected O'Bannion was a spy for Munsen. You're the one who wanted to hire him and trust him."

"Now who's trying to lay blame?" Heyling asked.

Veleshki ignored his comment. "If we must, we'll do the show with just what we have."

Bokaru got closer. "What's wrong?"

Turner wasn't sure whether she was asking the police or the owners.

Turner said, "We need to talk to both of you now."

"Impossible!"

Bokaru signaled to a photographer. Veleshki saw the movement.

"We truly do not have time for this," Heyling said.

"You need to take the time," Turner said. "We can do this in public or more privately, but we're going to do it now."

The four of them could see Bokaru on one side of them and a group of photographers closing in from the other direction.

They shut the door of a nearby bathroom in the faces of Jolanda Bokaru and her phalanx of reporters. After the only patron finished and left, Fenwick propped his bulk up against the door.

"What!" Veleshki barked.

"I don't think your clothes are going to arrive," Turner said.

"Why not? What have you done?"

"Unless there is a miracle, I believe the majority of your clothes have been hijacked by Franklin Munsen. He told us earlier that he had surprises in store for you and that you were naive for believing he was making peace."

"We'll sue his ass," Veleshki said. "He can't get away with this. He's gone too far."

"Would he dare to be so bold?" Heyling asked.

"Why wouldn't he?" Fenwick asked.

"I guess . . . I suppose . . . well, why would anyone do such a . . . we're business rivals . . . oh."

"You were always so naive," Veleshki said to his lover. He turned to the detectives. "If this is true, I've got to get back on the phone. They've got to be somewhere. We can start with what we've got. We can delay for a while. We've got other outfits in the offices. We'll get more clothes in here if I have to run back out to the North Side and drag them here myself." He took two steps toward the door. "You can't keep us prisoners in here."

"Why was Cullom Furyk wearing your signature underwear?" Turner asked.

"Uh?" Heyling said.

"He was what?" Veleshki asked.

"When he died," Turner said, "he was wearing underwear from your new line, underwear that was unavailable anywhere else. Our understanding is some of the time he got to keep the clothes he modeled. My guess is, either he got them from a secret photo shoot or maybe a private session with one of you two. He could not have purchased them or come by them accidentally. They would be perfect for the photo shoot he had that morning because he had to wear clinging athletic shorts cut high on the leg, which would have looked odd with his boxers hanging out. How did he get them?"

"I guess we did have a photo shoot," Veleshki said.

"You told us he was going to model for you in the future," Turner said. "You didn't tell us he'd already been modeling for you."

"I forgot."

"You son of a bitch," Heyling said. "You gave him a pair after you screwed him."

Veleshki spat, "Shut the fuck up, you stupid fool."

"When was this?" Turner asked.

"You son of a bitch," Heyling bellowed. "I know when it was.

236

Monday, when you had another one of your emergency meetings that never happened. I know. I called the contractor you were supposedly meeting with. You were already cheating with the little shit. I knew it. I knew you were. I should have pushed *you* off the balcony."

TWENTY-FIVE

This announcement was followed by a general round of silence.

Heyling clutched both hands on either side of a washbasin. His breath came in short rasps.

Turner read him his Miranda rights.

Heyling gave no indication he heard him. He spoke to Veleshki's reflection. "You don't know how much I love you, Gerald. I couldn't hurt you, but I was so angry. I went out on the balcony to plead with Furyk to leave you alone. To not bother our company and leave us alone. He just kind of laughed and was goofy. He said he didn't care. I asked him if he didn't care, then why did he want to ruin our relationship? He just teetered along the wall and kind of smiled. I was sick of it and I'm sick of you. I'm a fool for being in love with you. I didn't mean to push him off. It was an accident. He struggled and lost his grip. I didn't mean it." He let go of the washbasin, turned to them and folded his arms across his chest. "I wish I'd never won that lottery money. All this would never have happened. We should have stayed poor nobodies in southern Illinois."

"Do you understand your rights?" Turner asked.

"I heard you the first time," Heyling said.

"How'd you plan to get away with it?" Turner asked.

"I didn't plan it. What you don't know is the two of us were out on the balcony talking to Furyk earlier. He told us he was coming to our company. He wanted to sign contracts right after lunch. I went back later to appeal to him to leave my lover alone.

"So many people were in so many places, no one could possibly remember where everyone was. I guess I did kind of look around to see if anybody was watching. I was just so angry, I'm not sure how much I cared if I was caught. I needed to hit out at somebody. It just happened."

"I was not on the balcony," Veleshki said. "Don't try and draw me into this. I wasn't there at any time."

Heyling's jaw dropped. "Yes, you were," he whispered. "How can you lie?"

"It's your word against mine. In fact, I know you were out there alone with him. You were right about that, but I saw you rush toward him and push him. There was no struggle. You deliberately killed him."

"Traitor!" Heyling screamed. "Liar! You cheating whore!" Hands outstretched, Heyling rushed at his lover. The impact caused Veleshki's body to ram into the wall. His head bonked hard against the tile. They began grappling with each other until the insertion of Fenwick's bulk between them brought the fracas to a complete halt.

Finally, a couple of uniforms took Heyling away. They would get his statement in full at the station. The pop of the flash cameras greeted the opening of the door.

After Heyling was gone, and while they were still in the washroom, Veleshki said, "I didn't do anything. I'm innocent. I'm free to go. I've got to find the rest of my clothing line."

"I'm always happy to catch a murderer," Turner said, "and I find arresting Heyling based on his confession reasonable. I found your testimony repugnant. You're a shit. You had a loving man who cared for you very much yet you cheated and lied to him. Why?"

"Who are you to judge?"

"The man committed murder," Turner said. "It was misguided love, but love all the same. Someone willing to commit murder, for me, is a sick concept, but at least he cared. I can't imagine why. You aren't worth it."

"I should care what you think?"

"If you really saw him push Furyk and didn't report it, perhaps we could charge you as an accessory after the fact, maybe even a coconspirator."

"If we were allowed to marry as husband and husband, they wouldn't be able to make me testify against him."

"Gay politics or a gay agenda aren't going to save you," Turner said. "Besides, you're hardly a poster boy for any kind of marriage commitment, gay or straight. You're no sweet, innocent thing."

"I'm curious," Fenwick said, "how did Furyk get the underwear?"

"We made love the night he came to town. I ripped the pair he was wearing. I gave him a pair of the new ones. I wanted him to remember the night as special. I'm not going to apologize for my behavior. I didn't kill anyone. Now if you'll excuse me, it's late, but I may be able to salvage something."

Fenwick blocked the door.

"Let me pass," Veleshki ordered.

Turner laughed. He walked to the door and motioned Fenwick to follow. The camera flashes lit the washroom doorway. Reporters fired questions. Turner said, "Mr. Veleshki has an important statement to make about the Cullom Furyk murders." He and Fenwick stood aside and slipped through the crowd.

Veleshki found himself trapped by the herd of yammering reporters. Turner hoped the sensation and the reporters' lust for news would prevent Veleshki from solving his problem any time soon. The detectives walked away.

"Very clever," Fenwick said.

"Thank you. Let's get to the station, get this guy booked, fill in Molton, do some paperwork and go home."

"I like how you do a list like that in one breath."

"I'm thinking of giving lessons."

At the station Munsen was in a gray detention room. Fenwick walked up to the designer and business owner and clapped him on the back. "I enjoy bringing rotten news to people I truly don't like. Kindel has told all. Egremont has told enough. In just a little bit you and your business are going to be inundated by cops and lawyers and prosecutors—oh, my."

Munsen gazed sternly at Fenwick. The elderly magnate said, "You must be joking."

"Alas, this one time, I am not."

"You can't prove anything," Munsen said.

"Why'd you have us followed?" Turner asked.

"I didn't have you followed."

"You own a gray Chevy, big rust spot?"

"Where's my lawyer?" Munsen asked.

"Is your lawyer the same as McBride's?" Turner asked.

"She's here?" His confidence seemed slightly less certain.

Fenwick said, "What Egremont told us must be true, otherwise, why would you want him shoved off the pier? You order any murders prior to this?"

Munsen looked into the two-way mirror and tried to ignore the cops.

Fenwick got in his face. "I don't like being chased around town and I hate being shoved down stairs. Sometimes my likes and dislikes get in the way of my charming personality. Your whole idiotic scheme is going to unravel. I'm surprised you didn't kill Cullom Furyk to get publicity for your silly company."

"Who did kill him?" Munsen asked.

They left him wondering.

As he was settling into the chair at his desk, Turner spotted Carruthers and Rodriguez stomping into the squad room. Even though Carruthers was trying to hide his head more than the most embarrassed criminal, Turner could tell his cheeks were bright red. Rodriguez looked ready to eat nails. Then Turner caught sight of their handcuffed wrists.

When they arrived at Carruthers' desk, Rodriguez snarled, "Just find the damn keys." The younger detective rooted frantically through the drawers. Rodriguez glared around at the other detectives. He drew a deep breath and said, "There's good news and good news. First, my moronic twit of a partner solved a case on his own." He held up their shackled together wrists and continued, "The other good news is he may be dead before morning."

Fenwick had the rare grace to say nothing. Turner knew it was better to save razzing Rodriguez for a less volatile moment. He stifled a smile and reached for some paperwork and handed a sheaf of forms to Fenwick.

ER was just finishing as Paul walked in his front door. Ben had a tear in his eye. "You missed a good episode," Ben said.

"Did you tape it?"

"Yeah."

Paul found Jeff working on his science fair project in his room.

"You still doing it on pus?" Paul asked.

"I need to find some samples."

"You should get ready for bed."

"Okay. There was a news bulletin that you solved the case."

Brian bustled into his brother's room.

"No schemes tonight," Paul told his older son. "I'm not chaperoning anything."

"Just innocently looking for the dictionary." Brian pulled it out from under Jeff's bed. He thumbed through it for a moment while Paul read over what Jeff had written on the computer screen.

"You still need to do a spell check," Paul told him.

Jeff hit the requisite keys.

"Uh, Dad," Brian said.

"Uh, Son," Paul said.

"This isn't a scheme, just information for you. I've decided to shave my head, join a cult, worship Satan, and become addicted to illegal drugs."

Without looking up from the computer screen, Paul said, "Do I still have to pay for half of your car insurance?"

Brian said, "I think they have a benefits package that includes health insurance and reduced rates for teenagers on their automobile coverage."

Ben appeared in the doorway. "You get the news on the cult?"

"Just now."

"I told him I'd help him pack," Ben said.

"He is not leaving," Jeff said.

Paul glanced at his older son. "I'm not worried. No one could afford to keep him in all the food he eats." He patted Brian on the shoulder. "You know, I think this means we need to do more father-son things together, go more places together as a family."

Brian said, "I was working on the concept that you'd see my need for independence and give me more freedom."

Paul took a shrewd guess. "You want the car for a date next weekend."

"How do you know these things?" Brian asked.

"It's in the parent contract we sign when you're born."

Brian said, "I want to see this contract."

"Impossible. That's one of the secrets of the contract. No teenager has ever seen a copy. If any parent ever allows that to happen, they are automatically cursed with three more children. Why didn't you just ask for the car?"

"It was kind of more fun this way, and you said you didn't want any schemes tonight."

Paul said, "You may borrow the car if you have money for gas."

"Got it covered."

"And I need to know where you're going and with whom."

"Just hanging out with alien invaders from the planet Zardoz."

"Again?" Paul said. "And why do you need a car for that?"

For a few minutes they discussed the requisite logistics until Paul was satisfied. Reasonably pleased, Brian thumped back upstairs. Paul helped Jeff call it a night.

Later in their room, Ben and Paul got undressed for bed. Paul began loosening his tie and then unbuttoning his shirt.

Ben said, "I beat the computer today. I feel like I could lick the world."

"We'll have to celebrate."

Ben said, "I feel so good, I think I could match wits with a herd of teenagers. You're good at that."

"Just lots of practice and some trial and error. I'm sorry you had to watch the boys tonight."

"I was home with the kids, and I enjoy that."

"You're great with them," Paul said. He stopped undressing. "I'd like it if you moved in permanently."

"Do I have to share space with beings from the planet Zardoz?" Ben asked.

Paul threw his shirt in the dirty clothes pile and walked over to

244

Ben and took him in his arms. He enjoyed the warmth of their closeness, Ben's smell of machine shop mingled with aftershave, and the feeling of belonging right where he was. They'd talked about Ben moving in before.

"You're here all the time now," Paul said. "I know it'd be mostly symbolic if you got rid of your place, but I'm ready for it if you are."

Ben's arms pulled Paul close. They kissed, then rested their heads against each other. "This is perfect," Ben murmured. "I love you. Let's do it."